# HOT *and* IRRESISTIBLE

# HOT *and* IRRESISTIBLE

## DIANNE CASTELL

**BRAVA**

KENSINGTON PUBLISHING CORP.
www.kensingtonbooks.com

*Chapter One*

Paranoia is what keeps you alive . . . or maybe it's bis-cuits and gravy. Being a cop, Bebe Fitzgerald was usu-ally up to her eyeballs in paranoia, but right now she'd much rather have the biscuits.

She aimed her flashlight around the scorched hull of the old casket room in the partially rehabbed morgue. She should be concentrating on the crime scene but, sweet mother, she was starved! She hadn't eaten in how long, an hour? Was this stress eating brought on by this fire that nearly toasted her two best friends, an old murder now turned personal, missing jewelry everyone thought they had a right to, and fretting over what might happen next in the Promised Land of butter, cream, and all things fried?

The odor of damp and charred hung in the Savannah air even though the fire was three days old. A layer of grimy soot blanketed the ceiling, chandelier, and floor, ruining her new gray suede Hush Puppies. The fire marshal chalked the fire up to spontaneous combustion from cleaning rags in the corner; Bebe chalked it up to Prissy and Charlotte snooping where they shouldn't and winding up in the mid-dle of bad mojo that followed Prissy everywhere.

A door creaked. "I'm a cop. Come out. Bring food." Never do a case on an empty stomach. She tore for the opening, ran down the hall, then up two steps yelling, "Stop." Least that's what she started to say till ramming a broad chest covered in a McCabe's Tavern T-shirt with beer and burger logo. She'd kill for a beer and burger . . . and the broad chest looked pretty yummy.

He pointed toward the retreating footsteps. "I'm a cop, too. I'll take the front." He shot across the scarred marble floor, leaping paint cans and drop cloths; she headed for the half-rebuilt porch on the south side. Edging between the double doors, she rounded a pile of lumber and smashed flat-out into burger guy.

"Umph!" His eyes—brown like jumbo chocolate chips—widened. Their bodies fused like grilled cheese to bread till they stumbled and fell into a pile of sand waiting to be concrete.

"Damn." He closed his eyes and flopped back. Then the eyes opened and a slow grin tripped across cherry marmalade lips. She had a thing for cherry marmalade. Until this moment she didn't realize just how big a thing.

"Or maybe not damn at all."

And maybe not cherry marmalade at all. The smile grew.

"Sorry your intruder got away." His breathing slowed, hard leg muscles relaxing against hers, his hand at her waist, warm and strong. Sun sliced through the partially collapsed roof as she licked her bottom lip, thinking of his lips and all the rest of him snuggled nice and close.

"You're new at the station?" Dumb question. This guy she'd notice with his great abs, ripped torso, and the foody shirt.

"Got in from Atlanta last night."

"Atlanta? Atlanta's a fine place. I have to babysit some hotshot detective from Boston and did you know that fraternizing with other cops is nothing but trouble, and I'm thinking you might be trouble. Did I really just say all that? You wouldn't happen to have a package of peanut butter crackers on you by any chance?"

He shook his head, and she tried to think of something besides lips and limbs and peanut butter. "How long did you say you're here for?"

"I think I'm your baby."

That got her attention and she shoved crackers to the back burner and sat burger guy on the front because he was . . . hot. She'd heard of instant attraction, but for her this was a first. The fact that this guy was holy-crap handsome and she hadn't had a man in her life for over a year might have something to do with it.

She touched his cheek, because a year was a long time between cheek touching. Rough, stubbled, strong, male. Her negative ideas about fraternizing vanished, and she kissed him, wanting to see if he tasted as good as he looked.

And he tasted better! She must taste pretty darn good, too, or he wouldn't be kissing her back as his leg snuggled between hers looking for its own soft place to land.

"God bless Atlanta." Her mouth formed the words against his as the sky parted and angels sang "Cheeseburger In Paradise." So this is what she'd been hungry for! Bon appétit!

"More like Boston to Atlanta," he said against her mouth. "Then drove to Savannah. The precinct captain sent me here to find you, and if this is your take on babysitting, I think I'm a fan."

"Boston? You're Boston?" The angels vanished, taking the cheeseburger, and she scooted back, sand grinding against her skin and creeping down her back, into her panties and places where she'd be finding sand for a week.

"I was in Atlanta for a conference and some Georgia

congressman said you have a problem with an organized gambling ring. I wound up here, not that I'm complaining."

"But I am. It's another Northern invasion. Yankees think they got to be in charge or we'll start running around down here and lynching folks, is that it? This here is Savannah and the only things organized are church time, party time, and martini time and not necessarily in that order, and are you sure you're from Boston?"

"Does the name Ray Cleveland mean anything to you? Looks like you and I are working together investigating him."

"Mr. Cleveland owns a restaurant out on Thunderbolt Island. I ate there last week and the only ring was of the onion variety." A sweet-looking guy finally comes into her life and then he has to open his cop mouth and Ray Cleveland pops out.

"Word has it Cleveland runs a hell of a lot more then food."

"Word has it that interfering cops who don't know squat about the Low Country should damn well butt out of what doesn't concern them and go back where they came from." But he really did have a great kiss.

"Well as I live and breathe," said Prissy St. James as she sashayed around the corner of the morgue, hands on swaying hips, auburn hair flowing like she was some African goddess coming down the Nile. "What is all this ruckus about and . . . oh my goodness . . . looky what we have here, a little beach party smack dab in the middle of my rehab project. Mighty convenient for you two that the owners are away shopping in Beaufort for the day and my crew and I are late showing up."

Sister Roberta and Sister June followed Prissy. Dressed in baggy overalls and carrying a circular saw and paint buckets, they didn't look their usual Sunday degree of sisterliness, and that was good since damn and hell had just been thrown out for all the world to hear. Bebe stood, swiping sand from her skirt and blouse. "I came to check on the fire damage and see if we overlooked anything that might give us a clue as to what happened here with the fire. Then I heard someone rummaging and—"

"And then you went and found him." Looking totally put together in overalls and white blouse, Prissy shook Burger's hand. "I'm Prissy St. James of St. James and Sisters, the heavenly rehabbers. These are Sisters Roberta and June, who also run a shelter for teens, and that's our sand-pile you two are cavorting in."

"Actually it's Ray Cleveland's sandpile," Bebe said. "And this man's here with the intention of putting Cleveland in jail."

"Saints preserve us and holy mother in heaven!" Prissy yanked her hand away and the sisters gasped, made the sign of the cross, and took a step back as if the devil had landed. Prissy said, "Ray Cleveland in jail! Now that is without a doubt the very worst idea I've ever heard. What if we go and find you someone else to put in jail? There are enough scallywags here in Savannah that you could have your pick, because Mr. Cleveland's a fine man. He lent us the money to start up St. James and Sisters, donated that brand-spanking-new wing over at the senior citizens' center and the sit-a-spell reading room at the library, and—"

"And plays Santa to the kids at the orphanage," Burger said, his face still all cop. He slid his badge from his back pocket, pulling his jeans tight, and he had really great tight jeans and . . . and for the love of Pete, did he have to be from Boston?

"I'm Donovan McCabe, and that great-guy routine is how criminals cover up what they really do. Look good to the community on one side while fleecing it clean on the other. You need to take a closer look at Cleveland."

"And maybe I need to be MapQuesting you back where

you came from," Prissy muttered as Bebe cursed herself for wanting nothing more then to fleece Donovan McCabe right here and now. He was some great kisser and she was downright pathetic.

He nodded at the sisters. "Nice meeting you." He faced Bebe. "I'll see you at the station."

"Not if she sees you first," Prissy snarled as Burger made for the front of the morgue. "She'll be running the other way as fast as she can."

Sister June and Sister Roberta hoisted a ladder toward the front porch as Prissy kicked at the pile of sand and said to Bebe, "Well, wouldn't you know it? You finally get a man in your life and he winds up being some pitiful low-rent come-here intent on stirring up a boatload of trouble for no good reason except for putting away Ray Cleveland, and that simply cannot happen. So, just don't stand there like a fence-post, Bebe Fitzgerald, think of something to fix this."

"Huh? Me? Why me?"

"He's a cop, you're a cop, and maybe you shouldn't do all that running away, after all, because you're even a pretty woman cop. For once in your life you're going to have to use the pretty part to get the job done."

"I don't get it."

"I know, I know," Prissy whined. "And that's the most sorry part of all of this. How can someone who looks like they should be prancing down a runway in New York City be so clueless about their own demeanor? I'm thinking you need to flirt, strut, shake your moneymaker to distract this McCabe person from his Ray Cleveland obsession. You need to ditch the ugliest suits God has seen fit to put on this here Earth and somehow you went and found and probably paid good money for. You need to show off some of your come-to-mama cleavage and this-way-to-heaven thigh and your can't-touch-this derriere and . . ."

Bebe grabbed her jacket at the throat with one hand and

held down her skirt with the other. "I don't strut or cleav-age or heaven."

"Well you had a good start going over there in the sand-pile and you'll just have to keep it up for a while till we can think of another plan to get rid of Boston Boy. We're desperate here and you two were exchanging feels-ups and spit a minute ago. If Mr. Cleveland gets sent up the river, half of the new businesses and charities in Savannah will go begging, including me and the good sisters, and we're right in the middle of rehabbing the morgue. You don't want to be on the bad side of the sisters; that's like being on the bad side of God." She narrowed her brow. "And you definitely don't want that now, do you?" Prissy pushed Bebe's hand away and undid the top button of her new navy poly-blend suit.

Bebe rebuttoned. "Think of something else."

"Guess I need to pull out the big guns." Prissy held up her scarred pinky finger, batted her big black eyes, frowned like a ten-year-old, and added a girly sniff for good measure. "One for all and all for one. The four of us with our cut tiny ten-year-old fingers in Bonaventure Cemetery under that big full moon, pressing pinky-to-pinky, blood-to-blood, making us sister-to-sister."

"And BrieAnn fainted, Charlotte got lost, and the cops came and dragged us all back home and our parents grounded us for months."

"But we're blood sisters forever; there's no changing that." Prissy flashed the pathetic look and no one did pa-thetic better than Prissy . . . except maybe Charlotte and BrieAnn when they needed something.

"I never pull the blood-sister routine on you guys. You and Char and Brie always pull it on me."

"Honey, you're a cop with a big old gun hanging off your hip and a siren and flashing lights on your car. You don't need the pinky routine."

"I should have been an IRS agent. Bet you wouldn't be wanting me to do pinky stuff if I worked for the IRS." Bebe took a shortcut between the flaking white-painted columns on the porch. She ran under the sisters' stepladder, not worrying two cents about having bad luck since she'd gotten her quota for the day. She caught up with the man who had turned her day into . . . well . . . crap.

"Look," she said, huffing from the ten pounds she'd put on from her sudden food addiction. She pulled Burger to the side behind the three-tiered moss-covered iron fountain she remembered glistening in the sun years ago. "Why are you doing this? I mean, Cleveland hasn't been a blip on anyone's radar for thirty years. Why now all of a sudden?" And why in holy blazes did he have to smell of sunshine and sex? The sunshine part she could handle, but the sex part . . .

"This Georgia congressman says he has firsthand information on Cleveland running a gambling syndicate, and he wants it shut down. Gives his state a bad name. I'm here to poke around and see what's going on."

"You have no jurisdiction."

"That's where you come in."

"What if I can interest you in poking something else, something better?"

His eyes went to black, her breathing stopped along with her heart, because what he thought was not what she meant . . . was it? He backed her against the fountain, the rim of the lower pool at her legs, the cool metal not doing squat to get rid of the heat in her stomach even if he was the enemy. She sizzled. He smiled. Some enemy.

"You are definitely the most interesting thing to come my way in a long time. Why do you wear that suit? Those shoes?"

"The department frowns on us running around naked."

Her mouth went dry at the thought of being naked next to Burger.

"You have great hair." He unsnapped the clip at her nape like a man who unsnapped a lot. An unsnapping pro. "And you have incredible blue eyes and a dynamite body." He grabbed a handful of material at her waist, drawing her suit tight to her frame. "Better."

And before she could tell him that it wasn't better at all, his mouth took hers, making conversing impossible and . . . Lord in heaven, the man could kiss, she'd give him that. What she couldn't give him was Ray Cleveland. Remember? Wrong side of God!

"Enough." She took a step away. She held up her hand to keep McCabe at a distance, or maybe herself from falling back into his arms. "I didn't mean me as the distraction."

"That's not what the kiss said. I don't go around doing this with every girl I just meet, but you're different. Most women flaunt what they've got, you got it and keep it under a brown tent."

"What about an unsolved murder and missing jewels, how does that sound for intriguing? Makes Ray Cleveland seem like small potatoes." She pulled a pose to look confident and in control like Prissy did.

"Are you okay? You look sick."

So much for being in control. "Here's the deal. Thirty years ago gangs ran Savannah. No one lived in the city." She nodded across the street to Forsyth Park, big white fountain glistening in the sunlight, sprays of water flinging skyward, mothers strolling babies, kids playing. "Then a few gutsy men who loved this city found buyers for the big old Southern homes and saved them from being sold for taxes and the wrecking ball turning them into parking garages. Look around, there's no place like Savannah, it's the real old South all spiffy and put back together. Cleveland took care of the crime. He still does. He's one of the good guys, you got him all wrong."

"Thought you had a police force around here to handle the crime part."

"Cleveland goes places we can't get to. No one crosses him or gets on his turf. There are over a hundred islands off the coast of Savannah. Do you have any idea what kind of drug smuggling, gun smuggling, or any kind of other problems we could have?"

"That makes him a vigilante."

"That makes him a concerned citizen protecting a fine city and good folks."

"He's no saint."

"Like you are?" That brought a smile and a hint of a blush and she hadn't counted on the blush that suggested he wasn't quite the rat she thought. Except it didn't matter what she thought. Just get him off the blasted case.

"About the same time Savannah was getting cleaned up, there was a murder at this very morgue and jewels went missing. Now someone's back trying to find the jewels that might be here and out to get rid of anyone who has claim to them. It's a cold case that's suddenly hot and that's the reason I was out here looking around in the ashes." That, and Prissy and Charlotte were the ones almost toasted in that fire and Bebe wanted to find the person responsible.

She continued, "Whoever we were just chasing was probably here looking for the jewels, too. Finding a murderer who's resurfaced is more important than a few gambling tables doing no one no harm."

"You don't know that for sure. We all have reasons for doing what we do. You grew up in Savannah and know the city and everyone in it, and now we're going to do our jobs and nail Cleveland. That part's not going to change, no matter what you think of him or what you think of me or where I come from or how much you love this city and everyone in it. Or what you do to your hair."

*And,* Donovan McCabe thought to himself, *why the hell did he say that about Bebe Fitzgerald's hair?* Why'd he give a damn about anything to do with her? Then he remembered how she kissed him and staring into the bluest eyes on the earth turned his brain to sawdust. Mystery solved. It was one of those instant attractions, man to woman, except there was a police badge thrown in to make things impossible.

He'd get over it, dammit. Hell, he'd just gotten over a one-month attraction and before that a two-month attraction. He was the short-attraction king. "We'll meet up tomorrow at the station, then pay Cleveland a visit. Maybe I can convince him to cooperate."

Bebe stiffened her spine, her breasts moving under her jacket. Small breasts, about a handful, just the way he liked them. They went with her slender hips and legs that reached clear up to her damn armpits. How'd a woman get legs like that, and why hide them under one butt-ugly suit that went below her knees?

"I sincerely doubt if anyone in this city will be cooperating with you in any way, shape, or form for as long as you're here."

"Except you." And she had dynamite shape and form . . . somewhere. Before he snagged her back into his arms for a kiss he wouldn't want to end or she offered up another rant on the virtues of the local mobster, Donovan headed for his car. Damn, he hadn't planned on meeting up with someone as distracting as Bebe Fitzgerald. Then again, he didn't plan much these days except putting one foot in front of the other and somehow getting on with his life.

And that life was moving damn slow at the moment. Ten miles an hour? This place wasn't Savannah so much as Slow-vannah. And what was with these parks in the middle of the damn streets? Drive along . . . make that creep along . . . and suddenly he couldn't go any farther because there was a park and he'd have to go around the park to get to the rest of the street. What idiot planned a park in the middle of the street?

Circling Monterey Square, he stopped for a tribe of picture-taking tourists. "Crosswalks? Did you all ever hear of crosswalks? And haven't you all ever seen flowers before," he muttered and where the hell did that "you all" part come from? He was forgetting how to talk.

He powered down the window to a warm April breeze. Moss hanging from oaks-on-steroids drove home that this was definitely the Low Country. He honked at tourists and got the evil eye from their guide. In Boston he would have gotten the finger and a string of four-letter words that turned the air blue.

He rounded three more squares—Madison, Chippewa, and Wright—then pulled his Jeep to the curb in front of Magnolia House Hotel, with its glass doors, brass chandelier glowing, and wrought-iron railings. If that Colonel Sanders guy came strolling out with a bucket of chicken tucked under his arm, Donovan wouldn't have been surprised.

He considered his last gig in that crumbling shit-hole down by the Boston docks. Of course, that was ten months ago doing undercover vice when Sly was still alive, cracking jokes at McCabe's Tavern every night and Ma serving him corned beef on rye, double coleslaw, no pickle. Donovan glanced at the empty passenger seat beside him, the pain of loss so sharp it took his breath away and he closed his eyes. So much for getting on with life. Fuck.

"Afternoon, Mr. McCabe," the doorman greeted. "I'll park your car and take real good care of her now, you hear. Don't you worry about a thing."

Donovan gave him a tip and almost said, "Hey, buddy,

it's a Jeep not a Beemer, no sweat." But somehow Donovan didn't think it mattered. The car would be taken care of . . . period.

"We hope you're having a good day now, Mr. McCabe." Daemon Rutledge, first-rate hotel manager complete with lapel rose, smiled. Donovan headed toward the piano music mixed with polite bar chatter. Nothing like the neighborhood bar his family owned for fifty-something years. Donovan claimed a stool, the bartender setting down a Guinness and frosted mug, same as Donovan ordered last night after he drove in late from Atlanta. Till he got to Savannah he figured Southern hospitality was like beans in Boston, a stupid cliché.

"Next time give Moon River a try," said the guy next to him. He held out his hand. "I'm Beau, and the Moon's our beer of choice here in Savannah. Welcome to the South, Yank."

Donovan took the hand and offered his name. "How'd you know?"

Beau grinned, the kind that made women dreamy-eyed and probably got him a piece of ass anytime he felt the need. "It's Savannah, everyone knows everyone." The grin grew into more of a gotcha and he read Donovan's shirt. "McCabe's Tavern, West Broadway and H. I vacationed a year in Afghanistan with a Southie. Recited the neighborhood bars like the litany of the saints. So, what's a Southie like you doing in the land of Paula Deen?"

"Took that same Afghanistan vacation myself. Next time I'm doing Disney World." Donovan passed on the glass and drank from the bottle. "Ever have one of those jobs you thought for sure would be a slam dunk and the only thing that got dunked was you?"

"Woman problems do that to you every time." Beau lowered his voice. "Fact is, I got dunked so damn bad I'm taking kissing lessons. Well, piss," Beau added with a sheepish boy grin and took another swig of beer. "That's what happens when I drink too much, I talk too much. Now you gotta understand, I love women, I really truly do. All kinds, have since kindergarten. I was one of those early bloomers."

"Kissing lessons? Hell, man, I think you'd have it nailed down by now."

"I did. I was an ace . . . till I met this girl. *The* girl. You know, the one that gets you right in the gut and sets you on your ear." Beau lowered his voice even more, staring at the wet rings his beer made on the bar. "And now I can't . . . perform. Nothing on me works proper, lips, hands, other more crucial elements. I'm thinking it's payback for all those gals I loved and left. Not that I led them on or anything, but I didn't hang around much either."

"Women getting even?"

Beau's head popped up doing the holy-shit bob, his eyes widening with understanding. "Well, merry hell, I didn't consider that one. It's an out-and-out organized female plan. I think you're on to something, Donovan. I'm nothing but a cursed man."

Donovan offered a grin of his own. "I've been cursed at so damn many times I've lost count, but it never killed my performance."

"Not that kind of cursing. The kind that involves the hour for doing good, the hour for doing evil, settling scores if you've been wronged. I think some gals are getting even with me that way. Dang."

Donovan put his hand on Beau's beer and looked him square in the eyes. "I think you're wasted, man."

"I think I'm screwed and in this particular instance not in the good way." He ran his hand over his face, looking a little pale.

"Well, there's only one way to find out if you're right or not."

"See Minerva about a potion?"

"More like see if you're the kissing teacher's prize student. If nothing else it'll be more fun than swinging a dead cat under a full moon."

"Around here it's little rag dolls with sharp pins and maybe women have done pinned all my important spots. That's got to be the answer."

*Ouch*, Donovan thought. He squirmed, his dick shriveling. "You really believe in that stuff."

"Jeff Teller's boat sank right out from under him when his wife decided she'd done had enough of him catfishing every Sunday and she paid a visit to Minerva. Tubby Hendricks nearly got roasted in his own bed when sleeping with some hooker from Beaufort and his wife found out and made that same visit to Minerva."

Beau checked his watch and gritted his teeth. "I'm late for class." He ran his hand through his sun-bleached hair. "I'd sure appreciate you keeping all this performance stuff under your hat while you're visiting here in town."

"And with any kind of luck that should be as short as possible," Bebe Fitzgerald said from behind Donovan, making his blood flow faster and hotter and his dick unshrivel. "In fact," she said to Donovan, "why don't you pack up and go back to Boston where you came from?"

"Hey," Beau said, sliding his arm around Bebe as she kissed him on the cheek. "What brings Savannah's prettiest law enforcement officer to this neck of the woods and why are you all over Donovan's case? The man just got here, give him a break, pretty girl."

For a second Donovan thought Bebe was Beau's girl, the one who turned him into underperformance guy. But that was a friend kind of a kiss, putting a grin on Donovan. It also enrolled him in dumbass-of-the-year club, since the chances of him and Bebe-the-bombshell getting together had more strikes against it than a Sox game.

Why did he have this thing for Bebe? He usually went for the hot chicks out for a fun time. Bebe wore no makeup except for a little lip gloss, a suit that was definitely from a bargain basement somewhere and definitely no bargain at any price. And were those Hush Puppies like Grandma McCabe's?

Bebe Fitzgerald was completely oblivious to how gorgeous she was. So, that's why he liked her. To Donovan McCabe, there was nothing sexier than a sexy woman who didn't know she was sexy at all. But how the hell could she not know? She looked at herself every day in the mirror and her friends must have clued her in at some point. Beau just did.

"I want you to meet someone," Beau said to Bebe. "This here is Donovan McCabe. He's visiting Savannah all the way from Boston and he's a downright smart guy, even if he is from the wrong side of the Ohio River."

Her eyes went to half-closed and totally angry. Her hands fisted on her hips. "And he's also the last person on earth you want to be sharing a beer or conversation with. Detective Donovan McCabe, meet Beau Cleveland, as in Ray Cleveland's son, the guy you're wanting to lock up in the slammer and throw away the key."

Well, damn, he never saw that one coming. Beau put down his beer with a thud, looking like a guy who could perform just fine in tearing off Donovan's head and stuffing it where the sun didn't shine. Bebe said to Beau, "Remember last month when that fancy-dancy politician from Atlanta rented out the Cove for the weekend for himself and his cronies, then proceeded to lose his shirt?" Bebe patted Donovan's cheek. "Well, guess what, Detective McCabe here is revenge sent in by the sore-loser politician to settle up the score. Politician loses his money, Ray loses his establishment."

Everyone at the bar pulled away from Donovan like the good sisters did earlier. He was now Savannah's answer to Typhoid Mary.

Beau said, "You're here to close down the Cove because some jerk can't shoot craps?"

"You mean can't shoot *for* crap," Bebe added. "And that's shoot as in doing a little target practice, that's what we're talking about here. No one's admitting to any gambling of any sort."

Donovan downed his beer. "Good, because shooting craps is illegal in Savannah."

"And so is spitting on the sidewalk and jaywalking and double-parking on Whitaker," Bebe said. "But the police have more important things to tend to around here and I don't need to be preached to by the likes of you." Bebe pointed a stiff finger to the doorway. "Take a hike, Yankee boy. And take all your fine advice with you."

Except Donovan had no intention of leaving. Bebe Fitzgerald was his partner in this, whether she wanted to be or not. She had no idea the bad guys played by their own set of rules and situations turned deadly in a blink of an eye. He was here to stop the gambling because it was an ugly business that hurt a lot of people and he was not losing another partner to a bad situation. He'd underestimated the enemy once and it was not happening again. Cleveland was the enemy, no matter how many charities he kept afloat or how damn terrific everyone thought he was.

Donovan stood and tossed some bills on the bar. "I'm hanging around here for a while, so you all might as well get used to it." He eyed Bebe. "You're talking to one stubborn Yank."

Bebe huffed, "Well, this is the South, Bubba, and stubborn has a whole new meaning here. Fact is, I'd say we're downright ornery, especially when it comes to protecting our own from outsiders trying to kick up a ruckus for no good reason. And you, Detective McCabe, are aiming to cause one hell of a ruckus. We don't want any part of it or of you."

*Chapter Two*

Gatsby let out a string of give-me-food meows, Daisy circled Bebe's bare legs, and Carraway did the Olympic cat leap from fireplace mantel to Bebe's head as she opened her apartment door. "BrieAnn, it's six a.m., honey, have you gone and lost your ever-loving mind? You're never up this early, and neither am I if I can help it."

"I believe I have lost my mind and then some. I need to talk to you before you go off to work and did you know you have a cat perched on your head? I swear you're turning into one of those crazy cat ladies."

Brie entered the apartment as Bebe watched a black tail swish in front of her eyes. "They need a home, I have a home. It works for both of us."

"Where'd the black one come from?"

"Souvenir from the morgue. I opened my car door, he decided I was his chauffeur and you were supposed to meet me at four at Magnolia House yesterday, not six this morning. Go bother Beau. Now there's someone who'd love to be bothered by you at this hour of the morning."

Brie slid off her pink leather jacket, fluffed her hair, then searched her purse for spray, and gave her do a blast. BrieAnn Montgomery does perfect Southern belle no matter what time day or night. "I'm not bothering Beau Cleveland, because I don't know how to bother that man, okay?" She pushed open the French doors to the kitchen, then flipped the lights. Bebe blinked in the brightness while Carraway leapt to the counter. "My Beau's seeing another woman. LulaJean, and—"

"Waitaminute." The fog cleared from Bebe's muddled six a.m. brain and she took Brie's arm. "LulaJean is on the down side of forty and sings jazz at the Blue Note. The only time Beau would visit the Blue Note was if Kenny Chesney paid a visit. LulaJean is not Beau's type. You are."

Brie jutted her chin and reached for the coffeemaker; the cats stared adoringly at the can opener. "For your information, I did go to Magnolia House yesterday but left 'cause I was feeling poorly after seeing Beau . . . my Beau . . . skedaddling out the back door pretty as you please with *that* other woman. And I like LulaJean, I truly do, and now this. But why do I even care? The man kisses worse than a hound dog, so I should do myself a big favor and let him go, right?"

Brie started coffee and Bebe spooned cat food into crystal glasses. Some cats had owners, hers had staff, least that's what the pillow in her office said.

"Maybe he's so pitiful with me because he's truly into LulaJean . . . and if I can't get things going with Beau soon, Mama's going to insist I go to that medical convention with Lamont Laskin and I'd just as soon jump off the Talmadge Bridge, thank you very much."

"Doctor Lamont Laskin? As in chief of surgery Laskin? Family on the board of hospitals, libraries, theaters, and every museum in Savannah Laskin? Honey, Beau could be the king of sex, but he's the local gangster's son, your daddy's a judge and Laskin is a catch, least by your parents' standards. Do you see a teeny little problem in the making here?"

"But if I knew for sure that Beau and I were good to-gether, I would fight for him and make Mama and Daddy understand how I feel."

"I hate to tell you this, but that most unfortunate Yankee occupation of some years past would be a trifling skirmish compared to the fight you'd have on your hands with your parents over you getting together with Beau when you could have Lamont. I know your mama and your daddy does what your mama says. Beau's a lost cause and not because of LulaJean."

"But I love him," Brie wailed in a very non–Southern belle way that would cause her mama to throw a hissy. "I truly do, and I can't help it, so I have to find a way to make this work. You're the police, what can one person do to another and get away with legally?"

"Well you can't go shooting Lamont for sniffing after you; that just proves the man has good taste. And you can't shoot Beau for bad sex, though I'm sure there are women out there who have given that one a thought or two."

"Good grief! I want to fornicate with the man, Be, not render him deader than General Lee, bless his soul. So, I can do almost anything and get away with it?"

"Beau's a gentleman and whereas he might not take a liking to what you have in mind right off, if you get him in the right kind of mood I bet he's probably not going to press charges. But for heaven's sake leave me out of it. If I know what's going on, then I have to do something about it."

"Sort of like Ray Cleveland and the gambling, which gets me to the second reason I'm here. Prissy sent me, something about you seducing the new detective in town. Does that man from Boston really want to be putting Ray Cleveland in jail? What is he thinking? Men and their notions." Brie headed for the bedroom.

Bebe stomped after Brie, getting madder by the minute. "I just knew Priss wouldn't let this go. You're not going to find anything in my closet that qualifies as seduction apparel. If you and Prissy would have been around for the scene at the Magnolia House bar yesterday, you'd know Donovan McCabe wouldn't be attracted to me no matter how many buttons I undo. The sexpot ship has sailed." She caught sight of herself in the hall mirror—electrified hair, baggy eyes, cat fur in her brows. She stifled a scream. "To tell you the truth, I don't think that particular ship was ever in port."

"Only because you don't want it to be. At least wear eyeliner today to show off your big baby blues. Prissy said you were headed out to the Cove with McCabe, so you might as well make an impression along the way. It's worth a try." Brie came back sliding something in her pocket with one hand and holding an eyebrow pencil in the other. "Use this and for crying in a bucket put on a pair of heels for a change."

"I can't do liner. I always poke myself in the eye and it hurts and have you ever tried to catch a criminal in heels? Only on TV does that work."

"You're trying to catch that detective and not by running. And while you're out there at the Cove today, find out if Beau's going to be out boating. I have a plan that just might work and you do not want to know the particulars and you can just wish me luck."

"What did you take from my room? I can't believe I actually have something in the seduction category that you don't."

"I took out some luck insurance is all." Brie tossed her hair, which didn't move because of the spray, and left. Bebe got her 9mm from the locked desk drawer, then studied her shoe selection. Gym, slipper, sensible, insane. She'd bought insane when shopping with Prissy, Charlotte, and

Brie to shut them up in their never-ending Bebe-makeover project. Why couldn't Brie have taken the insane shoes instead of whatever she did take from this room?

In the name of friendship Bebe slid on the heels, wobbled, then dropped her Hush Puppies—now with black smudges thanks to the morgue fire—in her pocketbook. Catching a crook would go something like . . . *Stop, police! And could you give me a minute here to change my shoes so I don't break my neck when I'm running after you?*

Locking the door, she blessed the beautiful April morning and turned smack into Dara getting out of her car.

"Well now, if it isn't Savannah's worst excuse for a cop that ever was. You're plumping up, dearie, and your roots are showing, but then nothing's going to improve that bale of straw you call hair. And you're wearing heels? Oh my God, what a waste on the resident giraffe, though it does provide the good citizens with a laugh."

"Go to hell, Dara."

"I already did, I had you for a daughter. You weren't cute when you were a kid and you sure haven't improved any with age. Lot of wrinkles for thirty. Bet they use you for undercover as one of those bag ladies."

She glanced at her watch. "I'm showing a brownstone around the corner. Stay away, will you, dear? You'll give the street a bad name and I'll never be able to sell anything if someone spots you." Dara strutted off and Bebe sucked in a deep breath and rubbed the place in her stomach that felt as if she'd swallowed acid.

"Who the hell was that?" McCabe said from behind her.

"And this day just keeps getting better and better." Bebe turned to face Donovan. "Dara's none of your business, so forget her."

"Dara who?" He had his cop stare firmly in place. She

hated being on the receiving end of cop stares, because it meant the cop wasn't budging till he got an answer.

"Dara is my mother-of-the-year. Make that stepmother. There, now you know. Happy? And what are you doing here anyway? Thought we were meeting at the station?"

Donovan's eyes widened and he let out a soft whistle, his gaze on Dara retreating down the street. "How the hell did that happen?"

"You're not letting this go, are you?"

"What do you think?"

"I think you're a pain in the ass." But the crack wasn't as sarcastic as she intended because he wasn't all pain and he certainly had a nice ass. And right now he was all yummy with his black hair damp from a recent shower and a soft navy shirt and worn jeans hugging lean hips. "I'll give you the ten-cent version to shut you up. Best I can figure Dara was paid to take me and, no, I don't know why, and, no, I don't intend to find out because my real parents must be total scum to sell a kid. And, yes, I did change my name and don't you dare go feeling sorry for me because I sure as hell don't need a pity party and now you want to tell me what you're doing on my front stoop at this hour?"

Her gaze met his and she braced herself for the *Oh, you poor thing* look, but instead Donovan bent his head and kissed her. She started to protest, but her lips were busy and suddenly her tongue was, too, and then her arms got into the act and then her insides melted into hot goo, which had acid beat all to hell and back. This kiss was all wrong on every level except one . . . Donovan McCabe felt so darn good when she was feeling crappy as hell.

How many times had Dara struck and no one had been there? Bebe's whole damn life. But here and now on this beautiful spring morning, there was Donovan McCabe and as much as she didn't want him here . . . he was. She breathed, a sense of peace filling her up like a glass long empty and she leaned into him and took one more kiss, just a little with a tiny nibble of his bottom lip to chase away the lingering chill of Dara. Then Bebe stepped back. Every cell in her body . . . except the two rational cells still functioning in her brain . . . insisted she was the most stupid woman on planet Earth for not staying locked in Donovan's arms.

"What was that all about?" The question was as much for her as him because she didn't know what to think about the effect he had on her.

"You look like a woman who needed a hug and the kiss part just snuck in." His voice was steady, but there was an unsure spark in his eyes. But she didn't need him to be Mr. Sympathy to her and she wished like hell he hadn't seen Dara. That was part of Bebe's private life, the part she kept tucked away as best she could. It was over and done with usually, except for those times Dara happened to crawl from under a rock to harass her. "Are you playing me, McCabe? Softening me up so I'll help you nail Cleveland? Well, I won't, and I can handle Dara."

"How about I look the other way and you just shoot her?"

Bebe broke into a laugh, and today she didn't think she'd be laughing about anything. "I'll lend you my gun," he continued, looking perfectly serious. "Or at least blast the bitch verbally. I've seen you in action, Bebe. You're a hellcat when riled. Why not now?"

If he hadn't offered his gun she would have told Donovan to butt out, but he did offer and he'd kissed her when she needed it, and she wasn't in the habit of needing much. Good cop, bad cop all rolled into one cop. "To tell you the truth I think it's a conditioned response from when I was a kid. Dara's favorite game was to threaten to leave me in the marsh if I didn't do what she said. Scared the hell out of me to the point that I still freeze up when she's around and you never did say why you're here." Why the hell was she telling McCabe all this? Fallout from the dynamite kiss, of course.

"When my mother tells me to stand up straight and get a haircut I still do it." A gentle smile that comes from thinking of good stuff softened his face. "Except my mom's nothing like yours, though I do remember getting threatened with military school a few times."

He leaned against the side of the apartment building looking as if it were the building where he lived, where he belonged. He was that kind of guy, one who fit in anywhere, probably even military school. Bebe felt as if she fit in nowhere and she'd lived in Savannah all her life.

He said, "I'm here because I didn't want to air our problems in front of the whole station. We need to talk about how we're going to handle Ray Cleveland."

This was better. Arguing over work was a piece of cake, reminiscing about a screwed-up childhood was a piece of crap. "I said I'm not helping you with Cleveland and I haven't changed my mind, so there's no need for kisses that curl my toes."

Well, damn. She was on a roll till the toes part. When Donovan was around she had to learn to think before she opened her big mouth . . . which could lead to more kissing and then tongues. What in the almighty hell was she going to do with Donovan McCabe?

*Well, dang*, Donovan thought. He expected Bebe to rant a bit about the kiss he gave her to get her mind off the pink-suited witch tramping down the street as if she owned it. But the other part he didn't know was coming at all? "I . . . I really curl your toes?"

His cop side said he should let this conversation drop, but his guy side said no way. He liked Bebe. He wanted to find out more about her and not just because she was one hot babe buried under yards of ugly fabric. She had guts and stamina, was loyal to her friends, and liked animals, at least that's what the cat fur on her suit suggested. And she was a survivor . . . on the outside. On the inside he wasn't so sure.

"These darn shoes are curling my toes and I was co-erced into wearing them and I'm not telling you why." Bebe kicked off the heels and stood barefoot on the sidewalk till she fished out the god-awful Hush Puppies. She slid on one, then the other, then pointed to the PT Cruiser parked at the end of the block. "We might as well get this Cleveland visit over and done with or I'm going to hear about it all day. Climb in before I leave you standing on the sidewalk watching my tailpipe fade into the distance. This is really a waste of time," she said as she stomped to the car. "You won't find anything at the Cove. Maybe then you'll head on over that bridge that got you here in the first place and leave us alone."

The morning sun turned her hair golden and gave her skin a soft natural glow. Bebe Fitzgerald was the stuff makeup commercials were made of, yet she didn't wear any. "Do you honestly think I'm going to leave?"

"It's early; I'm hopeful. A girl can dream, can't she?" She climbed in the driver's side, forcing him to take shotgun. Sly was probably looking down from that great cop bar in the sky laughing his ass off. "Want me to drive?"

"You want to drive my car? You Yanks have some sense of humor." Bebe fired the engine and hooked a right onto Bay, weaving in and out of rush hour traffic, at least as rushed as Savannah ever got.

"Uh, that was a red light back there."

"Let me tell you about driving in the South. Green is go, yellow means *ya'll have a nice day now, ya' hear,* and red's a right friendly suggestion to sit a spell."

They turned onto I-80, the traffic thinning. "Now this is my favorite drive," she said, a little whimsy in her voice, the wind coming though the rolled-down window playing in her hair. "We have wild oats and marsh, stretching from here all the way to the sea. And we have turtle crossings. You got to love the turtle crossing signs."

"It's right up there with snakes, alligators, black flies, palmetto bugs." They took a hard left onto an unmarked sandy road, the Cruiser skidding on loose gravel, dust seeping in through the bottom of the car. "How old is this car?"

"Never ask a woman her age."

Marsh closed in tight nearly brushing the side of the car. "If you don't know where you're going around here, you'd be in the soup in no time. Think there might be something at the Cove to hide?"

"We're heading for a beach house, not Fenway Park. No need for an expressway." A rambling white clapboard with big verandas and green awnings and potted flowers flapping in the breeze came into view. Palm trees swayed against a blue sky and boats bobbed at the dock. "Let me guess. The big-ass Donzi at the end of the pier is Cleveland's ride."

"Outguns any boat around. Rumor has it Cleveland headed off a drug operation just last month. The Coast Guard crew brought him a bottle of champagne. Good party."

"And Ray Cleveland parts the Savannah River to get to the other side and hangs the moon and stars."

"Only on Sundays." She parked the car in the deserted lot and slammed the dashboard to kill the engine.

"Ever think of upgrading?"

"Ever think of going back to Boston?" Bebe nodded at the lodge. "Ray and Beau's living quarters are around back, restaurant's in the front. If your mama taught you manners, now's the time to dig them out and use them."

"This isn't a social call."

"It's the South, McCabe, everything's a social call, and the sooner you get used to it, the better off you'll be around here."

He followed Bebe past a wood sign, the simple shape of a seagull in flight. A stone path led around back, the bay lapping the shoreline not twenty feet away. Bebe knocked on the screen door and Ray Cleveland opened it. Donovan had seen pictures of Cleveland, but he hadn't been ready for the blue eyes and ready grin that said "Life's what you make it and it ain't all bad." Closing in on sixty, he looked completely at home in shorts, boat shoes with no socks, and faded red polo. Hair short, more gray than blond, and he had one of those forever tans from being outdoors every day of his life. Lucky bastard.

"Well, now, if it isn't Bebe Fitzgerald." Ray wiped his hands on a towel tied at his waist, then hugged Bebe like a daughter and kissed her on the cheek. He led the way to a country kitchen, pine table in the middle with a dozen chairs and a full breakfast that smelled like home. Cleveland nodded for them to sit down and said to Bebe, "How're Miss Charlotte, Miss Prissy, and Miss BrieAnn getting on these days? You four always were joined at the hip. I hear tell Prissy and Charlotte went and got themselves engaged. Griff Parish is a fine man, none better, and I hear good things about that Sam Pate fella, too. Even if he is from Atlanta, we'll turn him into a real Southerner soon enough."

He chuckled as he extended his hand to Donovan. "And I'm guessing you're Detective Donovan McCabe all the way here from Massachusetts to pay me a little visit. And how are your mama and daddy? Some say South Boston is a right nice place to live if you can put up with that god-awful cold and snow and all the yuppies moving in like they owned the place."

So, Donovan wasn't the only one who'd snooped around.

Ray continued, "Ya'll are just in time for some of my eggs Benedict, fresh squeezed juice, and Cynthiemae's secret buttermilk biscuits. She left me the recipe in her will, you know."

"No thanks," Donovan said trying to keep this all business, till Bebe said, "Are you kidding? I'm starved. This is the first good thing that's happened to me all day."

Hey, what about that kiss? Donovan thought. He glanced at Bebe, who said to Cleveland, "Lordy, I think you made all my favorite foods."

"Sit down, boy." Ray pointed at the chairs. "Take a load off. It's breakfast, not a bribe. You gotta eat sometime and there's plenty to go around, always is."

Ray parked himself next to Bebe, who was already slathering apple butter on a biscuit. "I love your boysenberry jam."

"How about that, those are my favorite, too. A touch of nutmeg—always add a touch of nutmeg." Ray stabbed a plump sausage done to golden brown and Donovan considered the South Beach granola bar and black coffee he had for breakfast. South Beach sucked.

"Beau would be joining us, but Skip Radel's fishing boat went and knocked out again and Beau's fetching him in before he finds himself drifting to the Azores." He nodded at Donovan. "And I suppose you're here about our friendly little poker games."

"We're here about the sizable gambling casino that you probably have in that building down the road at the dock." Donovan nodded out the window to the white beach house some distance away and right now he'd kill for a biscuit and apple butter.

"It's a boathouse, son. No need to trouble yourself about that."

"Mighty fancy digs for watercraft. Mind if we take a

look see?" *Mighty fancy? Look see?* Shit, he'd really forgotten how to talk!

"Mind if I see your warrant?" Cleveland said as if discussing the weather. He passed Bebe a plate of hash
browns, and Donovan bit his tongue to keep from salivating. "We house some fine yachts out there and can't just
have anyone poking around now, can we? Wouldn't be
right to the folks who own 'em. I'm the only one who
minds 'em, even Beau doesn't get out there to see what's
going on."

"Won't take me long to get that warrant."

Ray snagged himself a softball-size biscuit, dropped it
on a blue china plate, added a glob of the apple butter, and
handed it over to Donovan. He stared him in the eyes, his
still twinkling, a sly grin on his lips. "If you say so."

"Which is Savannah-eeze for not in this lifetime?"

"Now that just could be. You never know what can
happen in Savannah."

Donovan took a bite, his eyes rolling back in his head
out of sheer ecstasy. This was a bribe and it was working!
No wonder the good-old-boy mentality worked in the South.
It was built on great eating and beautiful women, like the
one sitting right in front of him.

"We should go," Donovan said around a mouthful as
Bebe gave him an evil look, stuffed the rest of an egg in her
mouth, and stole two biscuits for the road.

"Sorry to have bothered you, Mr. Cleveland," Bebe
mumbled around biscuit. "You do lay a wonderful spread.
Have a nice day now, you hear?"

"Come on out anytime. My door's always open, you
know that, even without a warrant." He gave a soft laugh.
"But it sure is a mystery to me how you two are going to
find time to be pestering me when you can't take your eyes
off each other." Cleveland gave a little salute to Donovan,

winked at Bebe, and opened the screen door to let them pass, the door then banging shut behind them.

When Donovan got halfway down the path, Bebe stopped mid-chew and swallowed, then turned to him. "Okay, why were you looking at me 'cause I sure wasn't looking at you. I was eating."

"I'm not looking at you. Cleveland's trying to throw us off the case." Donovan stepped around Bebe while hoping like hell his statement was true. The woman was driving him nuts. For every two thoughts he had about work there was one thought about Bebe . . . or was it the other way around? He had to quit screwing around. Except he hadn't gotten anywhere near the screwing part and something inside him was regretting it.

*Focus, McCabe, focus!* He needed to get back to Boston and the strike force he was heading up against organized crime and he had to forget about the blond strike force in Savannah that was warping his brain.

Donovan climbed back into the Cruiser and they took off down the sandy road. He needed to say something to get their minds off what they were both thinking about . . . each other. "What I don't get is why he does it?"

"Who does what," Bebe said in a rush, her hands tight on the steering wheel, her cheeks pink, eyes straight ahead. Yeah, she was thinking about what Ray said, all right. "Why the gambling? Doesn't look like Cleveland needs the money."

She took in a big breath, her breasts rising right along with his dick. "You're thinking like a Yankee. Money's important here, to be sure. Who your mama and daddy are is more important by a long shot, but holding Savannah in high esteem matters plenty, too. Think of the Cove as a public service. Gives folks a safe place to hang out and have fun and keeps out the lowlife that could spring up without Cleveland around. They'd bring in thugs and drugs and money laundering and prostitution and God knows what else. The Cove is like laying claim to an area. Marking a territory safe."

"How do you know Cleveland isn't up to his ears in illegal crap?"

"Because I know Ray Cleveland, and why are you so hot to hang him out to dry?"

"He's breaking the damn law. If the guy next door steals a car but has a good reason, why not let him off the hook, too? The law's an all-or-nothing situation. It's not law buffet style, where you pick and choose what suits you."

"Did you know in Georgia it's illegal to use profanity in front of a dead body, that donkeys may not be kept in bathtubs and—my personal favorite—you can't carry an ice cream cone in your back pocket on Sunday? They're all on the books, so don't go harping on about choosing this law or that one. Cops do it every single day."

She pulled up in front of the station. "There's more going on with you than just upholding the law because you happened to be in Atlanta for a conference and some congressman made you his go-to guy to get even with Cleveland. You have a bee up your butt, McCabe. Oh, you're all fine and dandy on the outside while something's eating you up on the inside making you pissed as hell."

"That's you with Dara, not me." He watched her sparkling eyes go flat. Shit . . . that's exactly what he was, a big fat pile of shit. Dara was poison to Bebe and he was an ass for mentioning Dara's name. But Bebe got too close to the truth, that losing Sly was tearing at him night and day and he didn't know how the hell to make things right. Throwing himself into work was his only salvation right now. "I shouldn't have said that to you."

"Forget it," her voice all cop. "We've all got baggage. I'd say we've both been pooped on from great heights for one reason or another and nothing's going to change that."

She nodded at the station. "I've got another case I'm working on, so I'll catch you later . . . if you're still hanging around."

"We're partners; I'll go with you."

"We're not partners on this. Let me know when you get that warrant." She shrugged; a little smile . . . the one he liked most, the one that gave a hint of dimple, lit her face. "Then again," she continued, "I'd already know if you got it because there'll be a foot of snow over there on Bay Street and winged piggies will be tearing a path across the Savannah sky. See you later, Boston boy."

"Boston, for sure. But boy . . ." He suddenly wanted to kiss her and prove he was no boy. Hell, who was he kidding? He wanted to kiss her because she smelled good and had great hair and had enough sass to keep him on his toes and he wanted a repeat performance of their time at the morgue. And he didn't like hurting her the way he did. She deserved better. "I'm no boy, Bebe. And I am man enough to admit when I'm wrong and made a mistake. I'm sorry about the Dara crack. I'm sorry about Dara period. No kid should have to put up with what you probably did."

"Others have it worse. You should hear some of the stories from the kids over at the runaway shelter, the shelter that Ray helps keep afloat."

"Why am I not surprised?" He slid from the car and watched Bebe drive off, then took the redbrick steps into the police station that was once an army hospital during the Spanish American War or some other war. Every building in Savannah was once something else before. Not much new in the city except for parking garages and the convention center. The locals considered both obscene.

After identifying himself at the front desk, he climbed the worn marble stairs to the second floor and usual cop/criminal chaos. Joe Earl Hunter looked up from his desk, phone clamped between shoulder and craggy cheek, his graying left wild eyebrow cocked, which said he knew what happened out at the Cove before Donovan told him. "So how come you only went and had yourself one biscuit?" Joe Earl asked as he hung up. "Least you could do was swipe one for me."

Donovan perched on the edge of the desk. "Is there anything that happens in this town that's not public knowledge in five minutes flat?"

Joe Earl chuckled. "You sure you want to pursue this case? We have others you're welcome to." He sat up and slid a picture across the desk. "Edwina and Shipley Raeburn, two snobby come-here's from up your way. They dropped this off earlier. They're staying over at Magnolia House and want Bebe to call them about it."

"A diamond necklace? Looks a little out of Bebe's price range."

"Only by a few million or so. The thing went missing thirty years ago during a murder at the morgue. The Raeburns say the necklace is theirs and if Bebe finds it, they want it back. She's the one working the case." With a twinkle in his eye, Joe Earl added, "Chasing after jewelry with Bebe ain't all bad. You should give it some thought."

Donovan picked a green poker chip stamped with a white gull from Joe Earl's desk and flipped it in the air. "And it gets me off Ray Cleveland's back."

"There's more to it than that. That murder I mentioned was over this necklace and the killer and the jewelry were never found and now—" Joe Earl rushed on before Donovan could interrupt "—the murderer's back and looking for the jewels. A few days ago there was a suspicious fire at the morgue and then somebody showed up yesterday when you and Bebe were there." Red-faced, Joe Earl pulled in a deep breath to replace all that oxygen that just spewed out of his lungs.

"I'm willing to bet that is the fastest anyone in this town's ever talked."

"Nearly killed me. I need a damn nap." Joe Earl sucked in another breath.

"How do you know the jewels were never found?"

"The morgue's haunted, or at least someone wants to give that impression. Something's been scaring the bejee-bers out of folks who bought the place for years now, making them give up restoration, sell, and move on. Then two months ago these I-talian brothers bought the place and they won't budge from it no matter how hair-raising things get. Now I don't believe in ghosts, either . . . least not this time . . . so the question is, why would someone go to the trouble of keeping folks out of the morgue all these years unless there was something mighty valuable in-side?"

"Like the missing jewels that were never found? But why would the Raeburns think the necklace belongs to them?"

"Their daughter inherited it. She and her husband were the ones murdered thirty years ago in the morgue when trying to sell it off. The murdered-daughter part doesn't bother Ship and Ed nearly so much as not having the jew-els they think belong to them."

Donovan ran his thumb over the chip. "Interesting, but not my thing. I've got bigger fish to fry."

"The person trying to buy the necklace from the daugh-ter thirty years ago was none other than Ray Cleveland. That made him a suspect in the murders, but there wasn't enough proof at the time to make it stick. Lately Ray's been seen hanging around the morgue almost as if he's looking for something."

"The missing necklace? You think he's the murderer? Why the hell are you telling me all this? I thought Cleve-land was your friend."

"Hell, we play golf every Saturday out at his country club. Tee-off time ten a.m. sharp, been doing it for the last fifteen years." Joe Earl took the chip from Donovan. "I want you to prove Ray innocent. He's got the money enough now, all right, but he's had a tough life. When he didn't get that necklace for his wife and wound up being the number-one suspect in the murder investigation, his wife left him, took his baby, and he's been living under this suspicious cloud too long. I can't do anything about the wife and kid, they just vanished, South America somewhere, but I can get you involved and try and make things right. You're a big-city hotshot detective and with a little luck, maybe you can find the real killer and Ray can put this part behind him."

"You're baiting me? That if I can't get Cleveland for gambling I get him for murder?"

"Tempting, ain't it? You get him one way or the other. The way I figure maybe there's something at that morgue that's been overlooked. A fresh eye like yours is what we need around here. Hell, you gotta do something while you're waiting for that warrant to search the Cove and that's assuming you ever get the damn thing in the first place. Getting Ray for murder doesn't require a warrant."

"Shit."

"And Ray said you and Bebe were giving each other the dreamy-eye look and as far as I know Bebe's never had the eye or anything else for any guy around here. Go after the necklace and you'll be working with her, not against her. Not a bad way to spend some time. Fact is, I'm willing to bet she's over at that morgue right now." Joe Earl grinned like a damn fool. "She's got a personal interest."

"You're taking a big gamble. What if Cleveland is the murderer and I find proof?"

"He didn't murder anyone, Donovan. I know the man better than I know myself."

"One of the good old boys?"

Joe Earl's grin grew and he slipped the chip in his shirt

pocket. "Losing his baby girl damn-near killed Ray. He fought tooth and nail for custody of Beau from his second wife, who was a mean drunk and treated the kid like crap. Ray's the best, you'll see."

"Or he's been pulling the wool over your eyes for years, involved in more than you can imagine including murder for the necklace and laughing all the way to a bank in the Grand Caymans with the money he pulls in from the gambling casino and other stuff he's probably involved in that you have no idea about. That's how it works. Gambling is never just that. It's drugs and guns and smuggling and anything else that makes a dirty buck." Donovan snagged up the necklace photo. "I know gangsters, Joe Earl. They're more than what they seem. My bet's on the Caymans."

Donovan trotted down the steps to his car. Ray Cleveland was guilty as a priest in a whorehouse, Donovan was sure of it. Just look at what was going on with the guy. There was a murder and Cleveland's name comes up; there's a missing necklace and Cleveland's name comes up; then the gambling and Cleveland is there front and center. No way was this guy pure as the driven snow like everyone thought. In Donovan's world coincidence was a word people used when they couldn't come up with the truth or didn't want to face it.

Donovan remembered to circle right around Oglethorpe Square, Lafayette, then Calhoun and yield to oblivious tourists, orange trolleys, horse-drawn carriages, and every other damn thing going less than five miles an hour and that was pretty much the whole city. He pulled into the driveway beside the morgue and parked behind Bebe's Cruiser. He made for the front door, which needed a varnish job and new hardware. Knocking, he tried the door. Locked, and no one answering.

So where the hell were St. James and Sisters? Weren't they supposed to be mixing concrete for that porch and painting? And where were the Italian brothers who owned this derelict? And why in flipping hell was Bebe here alone with a murderer running around? Sly had done the same damn thing, going into a warehouse alone, without back-up . . . without Donovan.

His insides turned to ice. There was already a suspicious fire and somebody had been in here yesterday. Donovan's palms began to sweat. Fuck!

He headed for the doors under the collapsed portico where he and Bebe had made out. That sure was a better time than this. "Bebe?" The doors were unlocked . . . double fuck . . . he ran in. "Bebe? Where the hell are you?" Red dots marred the white marble floor. Blood? Blood! His vision blurred and he saw Sly lying facedown, still and alone. Heart pounding, Donovan followed the dots to the main hall and then into the kitchen with Bebe bent over, staring into the guts of an open fridge. "What the hell are you doing?"

She spun around, eyes wide, a leg of chicken in each hand. "What are *you* doing here?" Least that's what he thought she said; hard to tell with a mouthful of chicken.

"Trying to keep you from getting yourself killed."

She swallowed. "It's cholesterol, McCabe. I'll take Lipitor. Chill."

"Why didn't you answer me when I called for you? There's blood on the floor. Shit! Fuck! Hell!" He ran his hand through his hair in frustration and basic gut-clenching fear as she gazed at him as if he'd lost his mind. He added, "We're partners, dammit. Partners."

"That blood's probably raspberry filling from a doughnut. I was hungry. It's lunchtime and I didn't get to finish my eggs or anything else at the Cove, thanks to someone right in this very room."

She pointed a chicken leg toward the fridge. "And my head was in there and I was concentrating on Anthony's cooking, which is to die for . . . not literally . . . so don't go flipping out on me, okay? And I get that we're partners, even if I don't want to be, but I'll share the food with you." She held out a chunk of chicken to him. "But you're going to have to do something terrific to get me to share the double chocolate cake with butter icing. There's only one piece left. And I ask you, why would someone who can cook like Anthony and Vincent want to open a mortuary? I don't get that at all. It makes no sense, not one bit. Got any ideas on what's going on?"

She was fresh, energetic, and genuine with a spot of cream chicken gravy on her chin and standing right in front of him looking bewitching as hell. And he could have lost her. He could have lost his partner. It could have happened all over again. He pulled her into his arms and kissed her hard, her mouth yielding easily to his. This time kissing Bebe wasn't to reassure her against a blast from Dara but to reassure himself against what could have been. She tasted warm and wonderful and alive and felt every inch a woman.

His insides caught fire against the ice. The chicken legs dropped to the floor with a soft plop and Bebe's eyes widened right in front of his own. "Okay," she said, her lips to his, her breath hot. "That's . . . that's pretty terrific all right. I think you win, you get the chocolate cake."

"Forget the cake. I want you." That surprised the hell out of him . . . the saying part, not the wanting part. "The question is do you want me?"

"Define want."

He bunched up her skirt.

"We work together. You're after Cleveland. We're in the middle of a kitchen, and anyone can come walking in on us and for the love of Pete, you're a Yankee!"

"Is that a yes or a no?" He wedged his leg between hers, inching hers apart.

"You're serious."

He slid her up onto the wood kitchen table, her bare thighs skimming his hips. Her eyes widened more as he freed his erection from his jeans.

"Well, I'd say that is, uh—" she swallowed "—seriously serious."

"I'm taking that as a yes." He pulled a condom from his wallet, covered himself, and in an instant he buried himself inside her.

"Yes!" She gasped. "Ohmygod, yes!"

## Chapter Three

The cove sparkled in the final rays of sunlight as BrieAnn stood on the dock at the Cove watching Beau steer his boat her way. It kissed the pilings with masterful grace and ease, as if making love to it, as if . . . Okay, that proved beyond a doubt that she was obviously sex deprived or she wouldn't be thinking about a boat making love to a dock. Why the heck couldn't Beaumont Cleveland kiss her that way . . . tender, meaningful, like a pro! What was wrong with him? What in blazes was wrong with her?

She looked at her tan capris and teal blouse and new strappy sandals. And she had new highlights and a tight tummy she worked out four days a week to keep even though she hated, hated, hated to the depths of her soul exercising. What did LulaJean have that she didn't? Bigger boobs! Was Beau a boob man? Was that it? She looked down at the girls. They weren't that bad. There was some cleavage there, somewhere. She undid another button.

"Well now, this sure is a pleasant surprise." Beau gave his heart-stopping, knee-weakening grin as he jumped to the dock and tied off the lines to secure the boat.

She held up a basket and forced a smile and the forcing part didn't come from not liking Beau Cleveland . . . heck, she was crazy nuts about the guy . . . but it was a little iffy the way the rest of the evening might play out. "Hi, Beau. Hope your daddy's doing well and you had a good day out there on the water. Spring sure is a lovely time of year here in Savannah, don't you think? Want to take me for a spin and we can find a nice deserted beach and . . . picnic?" Or talk about the first thing that pops up and, merciful heaven, a certain part of his anatomy had to do that sooner or later, didn't it?

He raised a brow at all her chatter. Nerves did that to a woman. He said, "You're not throwing in the towel on me?"

It wasn't for the lack of trying to put the man out of her head, but Beau was too handsome with all those outdoor military muscles that hadn't vanished because he'd been home almost two years now. And he was too sweet with bringing her little presents like the blue earrings he said were a perfect match for her perfect eyes, and just too darn nice of a guy all around. She held up the basket, making it do a little dance. "I don't give up, Beau Cleveland. I'm a hound with a bone and you might as well get used to it."

He flashed that smile that made her weak in the knees and the brain. "Sounds good to me, sugar."

"Oh I hope so, Beau. I truly do. You just need to keep that thought." Before he could question the last part, which sort of slipped out of her mouth due to a bad case of stress, she swung her leg over the boat hull. "Okay, sailor boy, I'm ready. Let's get a move on."

"Actually it's marine, and it's getting late, and why don't we just eat here on the docks? The marshes can be tricky at night and—"

She grabbed a fistful of his soft cotton polo shirt with the outline of a flying gull on the pocket and yanked her marine right off balance, his face an inch from hers, eyes wide, lips yummy. "We won't go far, okay. Just get in."

"Must be some picnic."

"It has potential."

He climbed in and she placed the basket next to the railing, letting it teeter on the edge.

"Honey, that's going to fall right in the water and all the great fried chicken I smell will be nothing but fish food." Beau grabbed for the basket, and, as he did, she slipped a handcuff on his wrist and the other on the railing, clamping them both down tight. For a split second Beau was speechless staring at the handcuffs. She was kind of speechless, too, staring right along with him.

"Well, I went and did it. Been practicing all day since I swiped them from Bebe."

"You stole handcuffs from a cop?"

"I gave her my eyebrow pencil and mascara, we're even." His gaze met hers, and she took a step back and jutted her chin. "I'm sex-napping you, Beau Cleveland. It's for your own good. Or maybe my own good. That part's a little fuzzy. Now you just sit right down back here and let me do my thing." She made for the steering part of the boat that was called some name she couldn't think of at the moment.

"Wait. What are you doing? You can't drive this boat, Brie. It's getting dark. There are shoals, jetties." She could hear him yanking on the cuffs, but they didn't budge. Only the best for the Savannah PD. "Why are you doing this?"

She turned and held her arms out wide. "Because I'm baffled. I don't know what's wrong with me? What's wrong with this?"

"Nothing."

"See, there it is in a nutshell, one little word sums it all up. Nothing. That's exactly what happens when we're together. We go out on the town, we have fun, you see me to the door, fidget on one foot, then the other, kiss my cheek, and leave. This time there's no leaving, Beau. You are looking at an overwrought woman here. I'm . . . horny. There—I said it, and it's true no matter how embarrassing it is and, Lord have mercy, I'm going to fix this situation tonight once and for all." She climbed out of the boat and undid the dock lines.

"Look, Brie, I know things between us have been a little strange, but—"

"Little? Strange? You've got the reputation of being the Casanova of Savannah and cities beyond and all I get is hearing about the reputation and I get none of the proof."

"I'm cursed, that's the whole darn trouble, and I'm going to make it right. I've talked to Prissy and we're going to undo this spell I'm under and this here is not some little bass boat you'll be driving. The *Shindig* has four-hundred-sixty horsepower and a fuel injection engine and—"

"And I can handle it." Brie climbed back in. "I graduated first in my Boats-for-Babes class. I took it for just this occasion. The instructor kept hitting on me, so his grading may have been a bit biased, but I'm sure I can do fine." She turned the little silver key, powered up the motor, feeling the big engines rumble under her feet, up her legs, even between her legs. If all went well she'd have Beau in that very position doing some rumbling of his own and it better be a nice big hard engine doing that rumbling. Oh sweet mother, she got hot and sweaty at the thought!

"I'll take you wherever you want to go, Brie, just let me drive."

"You had your chances, Beau. Now it's my turn to do some driving," she yelled over the engine. "I have no intention of going to Milwaukee for some infernal medical convention with a man I don't give two licks for. I'm not listening to you, Beau. Not one more syllable. Lalalalalala," she bellowed to drown out his protests. As she eased the throttle thingie, the boat glided forward too fast. Oh crap, oh crap, oh crap what had she gotten herself into?

"For crying in a bucket, girl, don't hit Ray's Donzi! He'll skin us both."

"You're making me nervous here!"

"Things aren't any better back here!"

Missing the Donzi by a hair, she headed out into the channel and remembered to breathe and be calm. A crane swept low, an osprey stood in the marsh grass, shorebirds scampered over the mudflats, and she could hear Beau snorting and grumbling behind her. Long shadows fell across the water as the sun dropped below the horizon. Her stomach dropped to her toes as the river split into a Y. "Which way? Which way?"

"Where are we going?"

"Cabbage Island."

"Port. That's left. Go left."

"I know it's left." She'd been out here before, but the driver knew the rivers and she hadn't paid any attention. She should have paid attention! She took the right fork and the river narrowed.

"I said left. Left, left, left! Port!"

"I thought you were lying because you're pissed."

"You got the last part right. Dammit, Brie, undo these cuffs."

"I hid the key. It's in my panties. I can't let go of this wheel to get it or we'll run aground."

Holy shit! Beau felt his pissed-offness fade as it was replaced by visions of a little silver key hidden in Brie's panties! The river narrowed again as the boat rounded the bend and then slid to an easy stop, the engines still rumbling, bow up, transom down. Eyes huge, Brie glanced back to Beau. "What just happened here?"

"Kill the engine, Captain Ahab. Land ahoy." If he'd told her to stop the boat a minute ago they wouldn't be in this mess. But then she went and mentioned her panties and he couldn't put two words together and all his thoughts were about areas below her waist.

She turned off the engine; the quiet of the night marsh settled in along with the no-see-em's. Brie smacked at something biting her neck and all Beau could think about was how he wanted to do some biting of his own.

"Can't I just go in reverse and back the boat up to get us out of here?"

"You'll tear off the prop and screw up the out-drive. I can't call someone to pull us off in the dark. They'll just wind up getting stuck out here, too. It's low tide." He glanced around. "And we seem to be in the middle of nowhere, so there's no one here to help get us off this sandbar."

"Well, this is not Cabbage Island and not what I had planned at all." Brie drummed her fingernails on the steering wheel and sighed. "But I suppose it will just have to do. Like my mama always said, bloom where you're planted, and right now we're planted wherever this is." Her tone had a sassy sound he hadn't heard before, making his mouth go dry.

"What's going to bloom?"

"Us, Beau Cleveland, or I'm going to die trying." She pursed her very sweet lips and batted her lovely eyes. "I'm mighty sorry about getting your boat stuck, I truly am. I never did that in boat class." She smacked at something on her ankle. She had great ankles. "These Low Country piranhas are eating me alive."

"I sure can't fault them for wanting to do that."

She broke into a laugh, the sweet sound making his heart dance. Her eyes twinkled in the last rays of sun, suddenly making this whole mess worth while. Hell, maybe this would work? Maybe getting out of Savannah was just what they both needed. He pointed to the cabin. "There are lanterns below that will chase the bugs. Undo me, I can help."

"I can do this. You just stay put." She returned with three lanterns as he stuffed the last of a brownie in his mouth and licked his fingers.

"Hey, that was supposed to be dessert." She lit a lantern, the soft glow cutting into the falling night. "Then again—" she turned and blew out the match with a seductive pucker "—maybe I should be dessert." And BrieAnn Montgomery, the judge's perfect daughter, stepped out of the sexiest sandals God saw fit to allow on this here earth and purred, "Wanna play find the key with me, Beau?"

His heart revved faster than the engines on this boat ever could and when she slipped off her top and tossed it over his right shoulder, leaving her in a tiny little black bra, he nearly passed out right there on the deck.

"You like?"

He'd answer, except there wasn't a drop of spit left in his mouth. Lantern light turned her skin golden and the sound of her unzipping made him hard to the point of pain. He'd wanted BrieAnn for so long the frustration was torture. Then her slacks pooled at her ankles, leaving her in lacy panties, adding to his agonizing situation. It took every bit of self-control he had to keep from jumping her sweet body this very minute . . . except he was cuffed to the railing, so he wasn't jumping anywhere.

"So tell me, Beau Cleveland, does that bulge I see in your jeans mean you're pleased as punch to see me, all of me, though I haven't gotten to the all part yet?"

And he'd die right on the spot when she did!

She sashayed in front of him and bent over, giving him a soft wet kiss and a glimpse of great cleavage with nipples peeking under lace. "You want to come find that little ol' key now?"

"Lord have mercy, Brie, you are something else. You're perfect. Every strand of hair, every square inch of incredible skin. Your eyes, your lips. You are . . ." Perfect . . . the word stuck in his throat and gripped his chest tighter than a churchgoing bow tie. She cupped his erection, least it should have been his erection.

"Beau?" Her eyes went huge and not from passion but disbelief and he felt the same way. Dammit!

"What happened? It's . . . wilted. I don't know what's wrong with me."

He took her other hand and looked her in the eyes. "It's me and not you and this sucks and I have no control over it. You are gorgeous, the most beautiful woman I've ever seen . . . and I've seen some . . . and—"

"Beau I do not want to hear about the other women you've seen and more then likely been ready, willing, and able for." She stepped back and folded her arms. "That's it. I give up. This is never going to work, we're never going to have sex, and I want to go home. I'd say you're gay, Beau Cleveland, except half the female population in Savannah would laugh themselves to tears over that one, because they'd never believe me. And no matter what you say, it is something to do with me, or you and me together. Whatever, but something's not working the way the Almighty meant it to." Her gaze zeroed in on his nonperforming crotch. "Not working right one bit."

"I think it's some voodoo curse," he rushed on to give this situation some explanation. "Ex-girlfriend's went and laid it on me, that's got to be it."

"Do not mention the word 'laid' in my presence." She jammed her right arm into her blouse, then the left, and yanked on her pants. "So what are we going to do all night? I had plans, big plans, and the big part is obviously not happening anytime soon."

"Eat?"

"Eating would have been fine, except not food, and

now all you can think about is food?" She flung a sandal at him. "I hope you choke on that chicken. I hope you get a big old bellyache, Beau Cleveland, because then something will be aching on you as much as I am all over."

She ran her finger inside her waistband and pulled out the silver key, then tossed it to him. "Here. I'm going into that cabin and sleep all by myself and don't you dare wake me up till we can get out of here. And then I'm going to get you out of my life for good if I have to move all the way to New Orleans to do it."

Beau undid the handcuffs as Brie stormed off . . . if five feet to the cabin could be considered off. The storming part she had down pat. He forked a heap of potato salad. He and BrieAnn had chemistry; he could feel it when she walked into a room. She lit up his life like no woman ever had. But when it came to sex and him thinking about her being naked and him the same way . . . That combination left him lifeless as a wet noodle. But why? BrieAnn was perfect. What more could he want? He absently rubbed his left thigh and knee; the dull throb was always worse at night, not that he was complaining. Hell, he still had his leg.

He wouldn't sleep tonight, no matter what. This branch of waterway was out of the main channels leading out to sea. With its sandbars and shallows, no one came back here. This was all Ray's territory, sure enough, but people still got robbed now and then and boats stolen especially if there was no one around to witness. Pirates weren't just from the past, and Beau sure as hell wasn't taking any chances of anything happening with BrieAnn on board.

Leaning back, he crooked his arm under his head and gazed up at the Big Dipper. He remembered looking up to that same sky in Afghanistan, the Milky Way far away and so bright it made a dazzling smear across the sky. That was the good part about that place. The not-so-good parts included roadside bombs, and he knew about those up close and personal.

Gripping the car steering wheel and clenching her teeth in terminal frustration, Brie drove her Audi down State Street, then swung into the driveway behind her brownstone. Not only had she run Beau's boat aground last night, it took almost the whole blessed day to get unstuck because no one could find them and then she had to watch a hot hunky Beau at work with all those lovely muscles bunching and unbunching and not do one thing about it. And oh how she wanted to do something! She was so horny at this moment she could mount a fence post. Just how much worse could this day get?

A lot worse, Brie realized as she watched Mama stomping Brie's way. Aldeen Montgomery would not be paying a visit in her new lavender suit from Macy's at six o'clock on a Saturday night if things were peachy. She'd be home over on Jones Street having a second martini with Daddy on the veranda then heading off to Savannah Bistro or the country club or a benefit at the Mansion. Brie kissed Aldeen's cheek. " 'Evening, Mama. It's a mighty beautiful evening, don't you think?"

Aldeen's red lips thinned and her gray eyes got a little beady. Brie knew this look, the same one she got when committing such cardinal sins as ordering a beer instead of white wine or wearing jeans out in public or taking Alvin Holman to the high school senior prom. Public school boys did not attend private school dances, no matter how nice they were.

"Lord have mercy," Aldeen started. "And Saint Peter save us all, BrieAnn. I think you're trying to put me in the grave, I swear I do." Mama fanned herself with her hand

and sat down on the little stone bench by the azaleas. "What do you mean by being out all night and most of the day on the river with that Beau Cleveland person? Tongues are wagging all over Savannah. This will ruin you to the core. How are you ever going to align yourself to a respectable man, a respectable family like the Laskins, when you associate yourself with the likes of the local gangster?"

Aldeen's brow furrowed, trapping her perfect makeup into little creases across her forehead. "And look at you now, not a speck of color anywhere. Beige is not a color. And your hair is flat as a pancake and you don't have on lipstick. And have you been sweating? Do I see perspiration? Have I not taught you better than this? You're not getting any younger, you know. Thirty is borderline old-maid status."

"Well, you don't have to worry about Beau, Mama. He and I are ancient history."

"Well bless the heavens for that much." She let out an exaggerated sigh. "Your father is a judge and up for re-election, for crying out loud, and you simply cannot go running around with the local riffraff. I'm going to the club tonight and I'll simply tell everyone you were out at the Cove getting a donation for the Telfair Museum auction next month. No one will say anything, heaven knows all their daughters have more sordid pasts than this and I'll be expecting you for supper Sunday night at the usual time and don't be late." She started to get up and Brie pulled her back to the bench.

"Mama, what was that last part you sneaked in there? You got that look in your eye. Did you go and invite Lamont? For God's sake tell me you didn't invite Lamont without even asking me!"

Aldeen tossed her head. "He may just drop by and you need to be thanking me instead of getting all huffy. The man's a prize. You give him a chance now, you hear. Your children would be smart and rich and you'd be living in the biggest house in Savannah, just consider that."

Aldeen's tirade faded, but the children reference was loud and clear. Children meant BrieAnn Montgomery would have to be in bed or another such intimate position with Lamont to have those children. Oh dear God! Sex with Lamont! "Mama—"

"Do not Mama me, young lady. You be on time Sunday and wear that new blue dress with the sweetheart neckline and the pearls your daddy gave you for Cotillion. And speaking of your daddy, he'd be pleased as punch to have you with Lamont and married into the Laskin family. Your daddy nearly had a coronary when he heard you were spending time with a common crook, and Beau Cleveland is that and then some."

"But—"

"No buts," Aldeen cut in. "You know I'm right and you know your daddy only wants what is best for you. He may look the other way to what goes on out at the Cove because of the charitable good that comes from it, but he most certainly does not want his daughter involved in any way."

Brie watched Aldeen head for Jones Street. Deep down, Brie knew Beau was not the man her daddy would have picked for his little princess and no matter how old she was, she'd always be his princess. They had a bond, as if Daddy could almost tell what she was thinking, that he knew her better than she knew herself. And maybe since Brie was adopted and Daddy had been the one who brought her home to Aldeen, he did know Brie better. He and Mama never talked about that time or her life before she came to be BrieAnn Montgomery. Still . . . sometimes she wondered why she preferred beer to white wine and what made her such a neatnik about her clothes and why was she so driven and why there was a hint of rebellion that sometimes seemed to hum in her veins and wouldn't go away.

Brie took the picnic basket from the backseat of her convertible, the handcuffs rattling around in the bottom a reminder of what could have been. But now Mama was playing matchmaker and—

"Mercy!" Brie gasped, dropping the basket. A young woman sat on the bench she and Mama had just occupied. "I . . . I didn't hear you come up the walk. You scared me to death." A chilling breeze not fit for an April evening in Savannah swirled around the yard, stirring the grass and bushes and making Brie rub her arms for warmth.

"Heavenly days now, I think you're quite a ways from death." The young girl gave a tired smile. She had her auburn hair pulled back into a tight bun, her frame thin and overworked. "It's going to be a lovely night. Don't you agree? I just had to get out of the hotel for a spell to enjoy the weather. And I wanted . . . needed to meet you."

"The Magnolia House?" Brie nodded at the stone wall and the line of Savannah Blues separating her backyard from the hotel. "I didn't recognize your uniform."

"Upstairs maid." The girl fluffed the white apron over the black cotton dress and adjusted her maid's cap. "Sure wish Mr. Parish would let us wear pants, but I suppose that's not the thing to do in such a fancy establishment." She bit at her bottom lip and put her hand to her stomach. "Though just because a place is all ritzy-like doesn't mean it's without its own set of problems."

She looked Brie in the eyes; the maid's own were dull and lifeless. "You need to be staying away from that hotel. It's no good for you. There are folks there not to be trusted. You could be in danger. That's why I came here, you see, to warn you." She suddenly looked sad. "It's a shame how people change. They don't start out bad, but they just end up that way." She gave Brie a loving smile, her face suddenly radiant instead of pasty. "You are a lovely girl. Any mama would be proud to have you for a daughter. The judge and Aldeen are fortunate indeed."

Brie felt the urge to touch the girl, give her a reassuring hug. "Maybe next time you want to get away you can come over here for dinner."

"My, my, I'd like that more than you can imagine." She stood. "I best be getting back, but mark my words, there's trouble brewing over at Magnolia House, no one knows that better than me. You and your friends need to keep a good distance." She headed toward the wall.

"Wait. What kind of trouble?"

The woman glanced back. "I can't be saying. Sometimes there's no need to have all the facts. What's done is done and better left that way, but you must take care of yourself now. I'll be looking out for you as best I can." She suddenly giggled. "And don't be giving up on Beau Cleveland just because things aren't exactly the way you want them to be. The man loves you like crazy." The woman disappeared though the narrow archway barely visible through the growth of trees.

"Okay, what in the world was that all about?" Brie said out loud, feeling a little creepy. How'd the woman know so much about her and what was this danger? The missing jewelry that belonged to Charlotte's parents? Their unsolved murders at the morgue all those years ago? Was the trouble that Donovan McCabe guy who had already turned Bebe's life upside down? Was he going to hurt her? Bebe had enough hurt for two lifetimes and Brie was not going to let anything else happen and just why in blazes shouldn't she give up on Beau?

Because she couldn't. She was plum crazy about the big

undersexed oaf and had to figure out what was holding him back from being crazy about her. She also needed to figure out what was going on with her friends and where was this danger. She felt a bit faint. Danger was not her thing at all. BrieAnn Montgomery threw fund-raising galas and arranged the best social events in Savannah and had fine manners and good hair and knew how to be a belle . . . except she couldn't twirl a baton for spit.

Brie headed for the back yard of Magnolia House. She needed a Bloody Mary, then shivered over the bloody part. Lordy, all this commotion was no way to start a fine spring evening. She pushed her way through the tangle of blue flowers and white dogwood at the archway. How'd that woman get through this jungle so easily?

Circumventing the hotel patio, which was adorned in glittering candlelight, fine china, crisp linens, and lucky guests dining on yummy Magnolia House cuisine, she entered the back door of the hotel. The familiar narrow hallway of cherrywood paneling lined with vintage hotel pictures usually made her feel welcome; this time it didn't. Something was different about the place, something was . . . wrong. A bad feeling, dangerous even. There was that horrid word again.

"And just what are you doing sneaking in my hotel," said Charlotte soon-to-be-Missus Griffin Parish. She linked arms with Brie. "Trying to keep a low profile after your day of sex and seduction out there on the water with a certain guy? Well, I want every teeny little detail. I want the vava-voom."

"Right now I'd settle for a vava and to top it off Lamont Laskin's coming to Mama's for dinner and one of your maids just paid me a visit and said we're all headed for a big mess of trouble around here. She has amber hair and blue eyes, a black uniform dress, and white apron, and I think I'm having an attack of the vapors and I have no idea whatsoever what vapors even are."

Charlotte stopped dead in the middle of the hallway halting Brie with her. "Breathe, honey, breathe. You're going to pass out cold. I'm sorry about Beau and even sorrier about Lamont and dinner. That uniform you described isn't ours, but we'll find Mr. Rutledge. Being the manager, he'll know where to find this woman."

"Did I just hear my name," said Daemon Rutledge from behind Brie. He smiled, looking much younger than his sixty-plus years, and took Brie's hand. "How are you these days? And your mama and the judge? You give them my best, now, you hear?" He smoothed back his neat salt-and-pepper hair. Any hotel in Savannah would give five of their present employees for just this one.

"I'm trying to find a certain maid. She's my coloring, black cotton dress with white lacy apron and matching maid's cap."

Daemon pointed to a picture hanging with a group of hotel photos on the wall. "There it is, the very clothes you described, but of course these pictures were from a long time ago. Was the lady you met going to a vintage party? See, that there's a picture of our first staff here at Magnolia House in just such a uniform. And there I am." Mr. Rutledge tapped a younger version of himself, complete with rose in his lapel.

"Holy mother in heaven!" Brie put her hand to her heart to keep it from leaping right out of her chest. "And that's the girl I was talking to. The girl who warned me there was trouble." She touched the maid beside the young Rutledge. "She's the one who visited me no more than twenty minutes . . ." Brie's gaze fused with Charlotte's and Daemon turned the color of mashed potatoes.

Char pulled in a deep breath and forced a tight smile that didn't reach her eyes. "Brie, honey, you're all out of sorts because of Beau and you've been in this hotel a million times, so you just dreamed up this girl, is all. Let's go in the bar. I truly think we need the bar." She turned to Rutledge. "And I believe there are guests at the front desk who could use your expert touch."

Rutledge took another look at the picture on the wall, then cut his eyes back to Brie. "Listen to Ms. Charlotte. You have had a troublesome day and it is likely you imagined this woman. Yes, that certainly must be it, and you can put the whole episode out of your mind."

He hurried off, and Charlotte said to Brie in a hushed voice, "I'm not saying you didn't see this woman, but I don't want to be freaking out the other employees and customers around here." Her voice dropped to a whisper. "Even by Savannah standards, this hotel is beyond strange. I bet Mr. Rutledge believes you, too; he's just trying to smooth things over. He's very good at that with the guests. You can't imagine how many complaints Griff and I get about furniture moving around on the fourth floor . . . and there aren't any rooms up there and hardly a day goes by that the elevator doesn't get stuck and the lights flicker and alarms go off and that picture of Robert E. Lee on the stairway is always crooked as a dog's hind leg, and cell phones ring in the middle of the night and—"

Brie put her hand over Charlotte's mouth. "I get it, but you've got to stop talking about this right now or I'm going to have an aneurysm. But why would . . . whoever . . . or whatever . . . visit me? Why warn me?"

"It's an apparition," Char mumbled under the hand before Brie took it away. "Who knows what the rules are for them, but what you need right now is a little bourbon."

"How about a lot of bourbon? I'll call Prissy and Bebe and you get the hooch. It's no fun to get hammered all by ourselves." She glanced back at the photo and shivered. "Definitely hammered."

With it being Saturday night, the bar was crowded to the rafters and Brie gave a couple at a table by the window fifty dollars to drink somewhere else. She'd never done anything like that before, but life had never been quite like this before . . . a lost boyfriend replaced by a fixed-up boyfriend and a visit from the friendly neighborhood apparition.

Elbowing her way through the throng, Charlotte plopped a bottle of whiskey and four glasses in the middle of the little table. Without saying a word, she splashed out the liquor and the two of them held up their glasses. "To sanity."

Bebe walked up and took the glass right out of BrieAnn's hand and downed the bourbon in one swallow.

"Hey," BrieAnn groused. "That was mine. I've had a really rotten day. And you're in jeans, least I think they're jeans. They're so baggy it's hard to tell."

"I'm packing heat and now I'm a little smashed."

"Right," Brie nodded. "Great jeans. Fit you like a glove. I want some."

"No need to overdo." Prissy sank into the fourth chair as Bebe smoothed her baggy sweater that no amount of smoothing would ever improve, though Brie thought it best to keep that to herself.

"I'll tell you about rotten," Bebe said. "Yesterday I put on those high heels like you all said I should and ended up doing the horizontal hula with McCabe in the mortuary kitchen on the table."

"Holy Hannah," Prissy said. Charlotte and Brie stared, their mouths gaping. "That's some reaction to shoes and the table. How was the hula?"

"I haven't done all that much hula-ing, you understand, but with McCabe . . ." Bebe grabbed two handfuls of her hair, her eyes wild.

Charlotte grinned. "That good, huh."

"And now I can't concentrate on anything but . . . dancing, and I couldn't sleep, so I took the day off. McCabe's been calling me every half hour and Ray Cleveland's going to wind up in jail if I don't get my act together quick and get rid of McCabe. The only good part about me and McCabe is that I'm not starved all the time and I've lost ten pounds." She took a swallow of bourbon straight from the bottle and passed it to Prissy, even though the Magnolia House wasn't exactly a pass-the-bottle kind of place.

"And I thought my life was crazy with the Italian brothers deciding to rehab the morgue themselves and the good sisters having a hissy. Have you ever seen a bunch of nuns running around having hissies? Let me tell you, they're never going to get to heaven that way. They're counting on this money to help with the runaway shelter and now we've lost the job and I think there's something very strange going on with Anthony and Vincent. They can't remodel for beans."

Prissy rummaged around in her purse. "I'm not sure what to do with my rehab problems, but I do have a cure for Bebe in here somewhere. Wait till you see." She pulled out a spiral book. "Here it is, Casillero del Espiritu, this is the Cave of the Spirits. I've learned some fine new spells from grandma Minerva and—"

"No," they all said at once, Charlotte snatching the book from Prissy's fingertips and holding it out of her reach. "Remember the morgue and the casket room when you spelled last week. You nearly burned the place down with us in it. No Casillero del Espiritu."

Bebe passed the bottle the other way, and Prissy grabbed back the book. "Look what you went and did, you tainted my notes with spilled booze. Bad mojo." She turned the damp pages. "Let's see . . . potions, charms, tarot, spells. Here we are, a spell for nonfraternization."

Charlotte hiccupped. "Sounds more like a legal document than some spell."

"Don't argue with the book." Prissy hooked her finger at Bebe. "Give me something from your purse."

"This is crazy. I don't believe in any of this hocus-pocus, and besides I don't trust you."

"Like you have a choice. Are you willing to take the chance of falling for McCabe for real, of Ray Cleveland ending up in jail or you winding up in Boston? Honey, are you truly willing to take a chance on being a Yankee, because if you get it on with that man and you get all serious . . . it's Yankee time for you and the land of beans and Sox."

They all made the sign of the cross and Bebe slid her cell phone to the middle of the table.

"Got anything of McCabe's?"

"No." Bebe did an eye roll. "Well, maybe, sort of." She pulled a condom wrapper from her purse and four pair of eyes zeroed in on the torn blue foil next to the phone.

"Dang. A hula trophy. I guess that will work," Prissy said. "Now I need some jewelry." Rings, necklaces, and bracelets littered the table. No one wanted to see Bebe a Yank. "Too bad we don't have that missing necklace to add to this pile. Bet that would conjure up some serious mojo for this spell." Prissy eyed Bebe. "Do you have any clues at all where the necklace might be?"

"Just thinking of that thing gives me the shivers." Charlotte took a sip of bourbon. "It's probably pretty with all those diamonds, but my parents were killed for it, Otis Parish had to marry Camilla because of it being gone, Ray Cleveland lost his baby daughter over it, and it was the reason Prissy's mama left her on the nunnery doorstep. I hope I never see that necklace as long as I live."

Bebe stared at the pile of jewelry, her eyes going a little crossed. "Not that I believe in such things," she said in a low voice. "But with all the evil that surrounds that necklace and with me being three sheets to the wind at the moment, I'm thinking the dang thing's cursed; there's no other explanation for all that's going on with it. Not one good thing has come from it, only bad. If I found that necklace I swear I wouldn't tell a soul about it. I'd split the diamonds, sell them off bit by bit, and drop the cash on the nunnery doorstep for their shelter."

"Amen." Prissy nodded. "But you can't be doing that if you're far off in Boston doing whatever things Yankees do." She cleared her throat, stared intently at the pile in the middle of the table and read,

*Silver jewels and honey gold*
*Awaken powers young and old*
*With these treasures seal a wish*
*Hearts of fire more to kiss*
*I shall be yours you shall be mine*
*You shall be mine for all of time*

Bebe rubbed her eyes and tried to focus. "That didn't sound right at all."

"We're zonked. Nothing sounds right." Prissy tapped the book. "Trust me, it's all there, just like I read it, word for word I wrote it down from Minerva so there'd be no more screwups." She grinned. "I ran it though spell check. A little soothsayer humor."

They all groaned and Bebe burped. "I've got a really weird feeling." She stood and put her hand to her head. "I've got to go."

"See," Prissy purred as Bebe headed for the door. "The spell's working already. She's forgetting about McCabe."

BrieAnn idly flipped through the book, then stopped. She peeled apart two wet stuck-together pages. "Oh . . . dear . . . heaven. You might want to rethink the working part."

She yanked her cell phone from her purse and hit number two speed dial for Bebe. "Pick up, pick up, pick up. I positively forbid you to send me to voice mail," she pleaded till a phone rang and rang and rang from under the pile of jewelry in the middle of the table.

# *Chapter Four*

Donovan parked his Jeep in front of the morgue. Street-lights cast a yellow glow on the sidewalk and cars. Joggers, families, and couples walking hand in hand meandered through Forsythe Park, and Donovan couldn't remember the last time he meandered or felt anything romantic. Hell, since Sly died he couldn't remember feeling period.

For the last ten months he'd been in a fog, doing the next thing that came along. He'd kept busy, and if life slowed down and he started to think about Sly, he came up with more stuff to do, like putting together the task force on organized crime, going to Atlanta for that conference, and saying yes to that abysmal congressman and winding up in Savannah. Donovan felt as if he were blood and bones held together by skin . . . until . . . until . . . ah, shit . . . until yesterday in the kitchen in this morgue on the table.

He stopped at the wrought-iron fence in front of the morgue and gazed up at the kitchen window remembering Bebe, her head in the fridge and gnawing on drumsticks. And he remembered the sex. Like he'd ever forget. Mind-blowing, all-consuming sex. Had sex ever been like that before? It was always good, but with Bebe Fitzgerald, sex was out of this freaking world. Maybe because sex wasn't casual with her. Friends with benefits was a term Bebe Fitzgerald would never use. Sex with Bebe counted.

And . . . added the voice of sanity under all that freaking . . . Bebe Fitzgerald was the very last person he should get involved with because there was a little matter of Ray Cleveland sitting right between them. And the Ray Cleveland situation was not going to get any better, because Donovan had decided to take Joe Earl up on his suggestion of finding evidence to connect Cleveland with the murder. In fact, that's one of the reasons he was here at the morgue now. The other reason was the thought of going back to a hotel room alone sucked.

The morgue was dark, the only light spilling from the partially open third-floor window. Donovan banged on the front door and yelled, "Hey, anybody home in there?"

A man who looked like an older George Clooney covered in sawdust stuck his head out the third story. "Buon giorno. Can I be of help to you this fine evening?"

Donovan flashed his badge upward. "I'm Detective McCabe. I'd like to take another look at the room where that fire was."

"At this hour of the night?"

"Things look different in the dark. I won't be long." It wasn't hard to tell the guy didn't want any part of a cop snooping in his place, but he faked a smile, probably because pissing off the police was never a good idea.

"Of course, that would be okay. I am Anthony Biscotti."

"Biscotti like the cookie?"

"Yes, the cookie. Why the cookie? Always the cookie." The man sighed as if bored to his toes by the comparison he'd probably heard all his life. "My brother Vincent and I are working up here to . . . to restore. If you find anything . . . I mean if you are in need of anything we will be pleased to be of help to you. The side door is open. There is a post light."

Donovan gave a little salute and headed for the rear of the stone building to get to the other side. Sounds of hammering and sawing drifted from the third floor and then a light flickered across the window on the second floor. A flashlight? Donovan stopped and gazed at the window. Someone was up there, shadows moving in the dark rooms. If it was the brothers, they'd turn on the light. Wanting to see the other windows to maybe catch a distinguishing silhouette, Donovan retraced his steps. He rounded the corner and ran into Bebe.

"What in the heck are you doing here?"

Donovan put his hand over her mouth and drew her against the building. He whispered in her ear, "There's someone on the second floor. I want to find out who it is, and that's not going to happen if they see us first."

She yanked his hand away and glared. "Vince and Anthony live here, second floor and all." That's what her delicious mouth said, but her eyes were lit with fire in the early moonlight, her body pressing closer to his instead of pulling away. Her breasts rose and fell against his chest, turning him on, making his dick hard as the stone they huddled against and his brain put any thoughts of an intruder someplace far away for the moment. "What the hell are we doing?"

"Nothing. We're not supposed to be doing anything at all. Zip. Nada. Zilch. I have a spell on me to prove it, though I don't think it worked. Does anything of Prissy's ever work? You think I'd know better."

She smelled of herbal shampoo and expensive bourbon and he tangled his fingers into her silky hair, the strands running over his palm. He kissed her, the taste of warm alcohol in her mouth and lingering on her tongue as it mated with his. "I'd say the spell worked damn fine."

"It was supposed to keep us *from* doing . . . this, not *to* doing this," Bebe whispered, looking as confused as he felt.

"Tell Prissy not to give up her day job."

Bebe slid her arms around his neck, and her fingertips dug into his shoulders. Her pelvis pressed intimately against his erection and he nearly lost consciousness. God, he wanted her! He had never wanted a woman this much before. The quiet whimpers of desire deep in Bebe's throat as he kissed her again and again assured him the feeling was mutual.

Her sweater was soft under his hands and he pushed aside the material, connecting with bare skin, then full lush breasts. Nipples strained against a thin bra and he released them, the delicate weight resting in his palm. His thumb stroked the tips and she moaned and sank against him.

His muscles tensing, his hands stroked her back, then cupped the sweet mounds of her tight ass. He slid his right hand over her slim hip; his fingers then trailed through soft pubic hair and slipped into her wet heat ready and wanting him. She gasped once, then again at her unexpected climax, her mouth opening wide, and he kissed her harder, longer, deeper as she shuddered, another orgasm taking her again. Her reaction to his impromptu lovemaking was an incredible turn-on and he grabbed at every ounce of self-control he possessed to not take her here on the driveway. Gazing up at him, her eyes cloudy from her orgasm, he said. "Why are you here?"

"Why are you?"

"I was taking a walk and saw your car." She nibbled his chin.

"You're not going to like my answer."

"I really like the result." She kissed him slowly, her lips warm and soft and mesmerizing. His dick was about to explode. He took a big breath to calm down . . . yeah, like that would work. "I'm never going to get that warrant for Cleveland."

"Oh, I like that part a lot, sounding better the more I think about it." Her tongue slid into his mouth, suggesting exactly what he wanted to do. "And I like this part. I think I want more of this part."

"Since the warrant idea is out, I'm here to find evidence to link Cleveland to the murder that happened thirty years ago. There's no statute of limitations on murder."

She blinked a few times, the words slowly sinking in through the whiskey. "Cleveland? Murder?"

"I'll get Cleveland any way I can, Bebe."

"You bastard!" She pushed him away, and he tripped on a rock and landed flat on his ass. That was one painful way to kill a hard-on.

"I never want to see you again as long as I live, and the way my head is starting to pound, that may not be all that long." She stormed off, but he caught up with her.

"We work together. We need to get through this."

"If I don't die, maybe you should. I know the islands; they'd never find your pitiful carcass anywhere."

An SUV pulled out from an adjoining alleyway and headed up Drayton. Bebe's eyes widened, her gaze following the car. Even in the darkness he could see her pale.

"Who was that?"

"It's just a car, McCabe. There are lots of them in Savannah."

"Black, tinted windows and you weren't happy to see it. In fact you were shocked. It was Cleveland, wasn't it? You wouldn't be this defensive otherwise. And what better time for him to snoop around the morgue than on Saturday night, the busiest night at the Cove, when he won't be missed for an hour or two? The man's looking for something, Bebe. He was here for a reason. To find the necklace that went missing because there's more, something that will connect him as the murderer. He's the one behind the hauntings that have kept people away from the morgue all these years. I'd bet on it."

"Then you'd lose."

He held her shoulders so she'd have to look him in the eyes. "Ray Cleveland's into this murder up to his neck. You've got to see that. The evidence keeps growing. You can't protect this guy forever and why the hell are you doing it anyway? What's he to you?"

"Because one night Dara did leave me in the marsh. Ray Cleveland found me and cleaned me up and fed me. He took me back to Dara, but he must have said something to her because she never did that to me again. Cleveland was a friend when I needed a friend really bad and now he needs me and I'm not letting him down and I don't give a tinker's damn what you say and I can tell you've never had a real friend or you'd get it. You don't trust anyone and that's a sad way to live, Donovan McCabe. Fact is, I feel sorry for you."

This time her eyes were clouded with tears she probably didn't know were there and it damn-near broke his heart. He let her go and she ran off, her long legs eating up the sidewalk as if she couldn't get away from him fast enough, her blond hair dancing across her shoulders in the moonlight. "Ah, fuck a duck."

"Bet you can come up with something a hell of a lot better to fuck than a damn duck."

The voice sounded like . . . Impossible! He spun around and faced . . . "S—Sly? Sly! Holy shit, Sly!"

Donovan blinked a few times to clear his vision, but his partner was still there, leaning against the side of the building, smoking a cigarette, the red tip glowing in the dark. His craggy face looked younger than Donovan remembered, but did anyone look good in a casket? He had on his usual attire of worn jeans, beat-up black leather jacket that he was probably born in, and his Sox baseball cap that Donovan had given him for Christmas years ago. "You look good. I can't believe I said that."

"A morgue is the last place I want to be." He laughed. "Hell, I guess it really was the last place for me. But the timing's right, so here I am." He nodded after Bebe. "And knowing you, I bet that's where the fucking part comes in. She is some hot babe." Sly gave a soft whistle, then laughed again. "And she's a cop. Now that's got to be damn interesting."

Donovan sat, mostly because seeing Sly was damn unnerving. "Christ, I miss you."

"Yeah, I figured as much. How are Mom and Pop doing?"

Donovan felt his chest tighten into a painful knot. Their only son was dead and they were old. Shit. "They're doing okay. They started the Sly Monroe Memorial Fund down at the station. That helps a lot, gives them focus."

"And what are you doing?"

"Working the case like always, except this one happens to be here where some gal named Paula Deen is queen and the city has roaches the size of small dogs."

"I mean, what are you doing with your whole goddamn life? You're wasting it, that's what you're doing. Where do you live, kid?"

Donovan shrugged. "Still got my place down on Dorchester and—"

"Not there. Here." Sly pointed to Donovan's heart. "Don't do what I did . . . work, eat, sleep, get in the way of one too many bullets. There's more than getting the bad guys. There's the girl."

"Yeah, well, that's never going to happen, especially this time around."

Sly laughed long and low, pulling drags off the cigarette. "When you're standing where I am, never's one hell of a long time. Don't waste what you got right in front of you. Sure beats cuddling up with your badge every night and coming home to nothing but a gun in your pocket and a six-pack in your hand. She's worth it. You're worth it."

"You came here to tell me that?"

"Can you think of a better reason for me to show up on your doorstep?"

"What about the case? I'm drawing a blank here. There's a bad guy who's not all that bad, and I'm going to send him to prison and there's the reason I'll lose the girl. I could do with a little help. What am I missing?"

"Forget the case, take the girl. You always were the brains of our little duo, but you're acting like you have shit for gray matter now." Sly grinned, this one more big-brother than cop. "Sure good to see you, kid. Keep an eye on Mom and Pop, okay?"

Sly exhaled, and as the smoke from the cigarette dissipated, he faded into the night, leaving Donovan on the bench with chirping crickets and frogs for company. Staring at the empty bench, he felt more alone than ever. He would have sworn on a stack of Bibles he'd dreamed this whole damn thing except for the cigarette on the ground, red tip glowing, and the hollow feeling in his belly.

Was Bebe worth the fight? He could screw anyone who was willing, but being with Bebe was always more. Women came and went, but when Bebe did the leaving, he felt the absence. He didn't want her to go, even if they were arguing. And as much as he hated that she wouldn't give up Cleveland, it was the thing he admired most about her. Bebe was for real. Bebe was from the heart. Loyalty counted more than anything and no one felt loyalty like a cop.

Why couldn't he fall for that cute little waitress at the Pirate House or that blonde who brought him extra towels every night at Magnolia House and made it clear she'd be willing to give him a lot more than fresh linens? No, he had the hots for someone who'd like nothing more than to see his taillights heading off to Boston or have his hide stuffed and mounted over her fireplace.

What to do? Cleveland or Bebe? He couldn't have both. He could walk away from Bebe or he could walk away from this case, forget the whole damn thing. He had vacation time coming, just let this blow over. But could he turn his back on someone breaking the law? And not just any law but the sort that sent Sly to the grave? The day Sly died, Donovan swore he'd make damn sure this didn't happen to another great guy, another friend, another partner. Walking away was not making amends. Then again, Sly was the one telling Donovan to take the girl. "Well, fuck." This is what happened when you listened to a . . . ghost.

Well, dang, this was rock star parking for a change, Bebe thought as she pulled right up in front of her little brick apartment row house. Least something had gone right, because Prissy's spell on nonfraternization sure didn't. They only thing that saved Bebe's ass . . . literally . . . was McCabe confessing his plan of connecting Ray Cleveland to the morgue murder. Did Boston boy expect her to help him find evidence against Cleveland because he was a good kisser? *Sweet thing* . . . she wanted to tell McCabe . . . *nobody's that good.*

Bebe killed the engine, locked the PT, then stepped onto the stoop. No kitty at the window? No kitties meowing pitifully by the door as if she'd been gone a month and they were all a breath away from starving to death? Cats were drama queens in fur coats. They probably got into the catnip. Kitty pot, kept them happy for hours. Bebe unlocked her door and stepped inside, the streetlight illuminating the hallway, broken glass crunching under her shoes. She reached for the hall lamp, except it wasn't on the table but on the floor broken. Catnip didn't do this. Nor had cats torn the stuffing out of her sofa and chair, ripped her picture of Robert E. Lee off the wall, turned drawers upside down.

Bebe pulled her weapon. The cats! What if the asshole who did this to her apartment did something to them? Keeping the lights off so as not to be an easy target, she hunkered down. No one behind the upended davenport or in the hall. Her bedroom? Clear. If you didn't count the clothes on the floor, bed torn apart, and closet contents scattered everywhere. Another crunching footstep sounded from the living room. She edged around the corner and spied the silhouette of a man, gun drawn, flattened against the wall. She jumped up, aimed, yelling, "Police. Drop your weapon," just as Donovan did the very same thing with his weapon pointed at her. Face-to-face, gun to gun.

"Shit!"

"It's me, McCabe."

"Like I said . . . shit." She holstered her gun.

"Who did this?"

"I don't know what it's like where you come from, but in Savannah cops aren't loved by one and all." She headed for the kitchen, the French doors already open. Kicking aside pots, pans, strewn cereal, and a brand-new package of Oreos on the floor, she made it to the light switch, then turned on the can opener, the hum filling the apartment.

"What the hell are you doing?" Donovan asked, framed in the doorway, hands in pockets looking perfectly at ease in her mess making her wonder about his housekeeping skills.

"Herding cats. And here's Mr. Gatsby right now," she said, the calico slinking around Donovan's ankles. "And Carraway and Miss Daisy." Bebe let out a big breath as the trio entered. "All present and accounted for, thank God . . . and I mean that," she said casting her eyes skyward. In unison the fur balls leaped onto the counter for the can opener, except for Daisy, who only made it halfway and fell backward. Donovan sprang to life, doing the quick save and snagged Daisy midair.

"Guess this one needs jumping lessons."

"There's blood on your hand. Did you get cut on the glass in the hallway?"

"Not me." Donovan held up the cat. "It's on her paw and she's holding it sort of funny, not that I'm any kind of a cat—" Bebe grabbed Daisy as Donovan finished, "expert. There's blood on the back leg and it's . . . dripping. Got a towel?"

"They hurt my cat," Bebe hissed, anger nearly frying her hair. "Why hurt my cat? It's a cat, not the goddamn FBI for chrissake! I'm going to kill the no-good motherfucking bastard who—"

"See, now that's how you're supposed to handle Dara." He passed Bebe a towel. "Let's get the cat to the vet. I'll drive."

Her gaze met his eyes dark with concern. He . . . cared about a cat he never met till now. "I just called you shit."

He grinned and the dizzies intensified. "I've been called worse." He put his hand on her back and she instantly felt better. "Let's go."

She stopped in the hallway. "I can manage. You don't have to do this."

"We have a bleeding cat; we'll argue later." He hustled her out the door, then snapped up copies of *Southern Living* and *Police Digest* and dropped them over the broken glass. "No more cut cats."

"You double-parked the Jeep?" she said as she got in, Daisy meowing and hissing like something from Animal Planet.

"I spotted your car, and your door was wide open. No lights on. Not a good sign."

Bebe pulled off her sweater, leaving her in her camisole. She wrapped the sweater around Daisy to try and calm her down. Right now it would take a tranquilizing dart. "The Barkley Animal Clinic's over on Abercorn," she said as Donovan fired up the Jeep.

"Barkley?" That got a chuckle. "You got to be kidding." He cast Bebe a quick look. "Nice duds."

"Kmart special. Just drive, okay. And the vet's name is Rex Barkley and rumor has it he's a werewolf. He's some hunk of a guy and everyone knows werewolves are incredible lovers. Nice combo, least the women around here think so. Bet you don't get stories like that in Boston."

"We have the Sox; that trumps werewolves."

"In your dreams, Yankee boy. There's the place," she said pointing to a white clapboard building up ahead while Daisy squirmed and hissed. Donovan pulled into the parking lot between the clinic and the Garden Tea Room.

"We have an injured cat here," ordered Donovan in his best cop voice, which propelled everyone at the clinic into immediate action. And two hours later, Bebe, Donovan, and one cat in a purple leg cast that covered down to her paw stood in the hallway of the apartment with two other cats meowing and playing rub-the-ankles.

Donovan set the broken lamp back on top; the thing had missing glass and was listing to one side, but it still worked. He draped his arm around Bebe. "Well, kid, somebody was looking for something. This is not just a pissed-off ransacking job for the hell of it."

"How can you tell?"

"No spray paint maligning your parentage or your sweet little body parts. Always signs of a breaking-and-entering job being personal." He took an upset drawer from the floor and dumped the rest of the stuff on the floor. "Use this as a bed for our patient. You check if the cats have food and water; I'll clean up the glass. We'll deal with the rest of this mess tomorrow."

"Really, you don't have to stay."

He ran his hand through his disheveled black hair. He looked tired to the bone, and she knew she looked worse. "In case you didn't get the message, someone wants what you have, whatever that may be. And I'm guessing they didn't find it and they want it bad enough to come back here again. We're partners, remember."

Donovan righted the davenport; it landed on its feet with a solid thud. "I'll take the couch, you take the bedroom." She put Daisy in the drawer, then went into the kitchen and filled the water and food bowls. When she got back to the living room, Donovan was lying on the davenport, eyes closed, shoes off. "Go to sleep, Bebe. See you in the morning."

She studied her little apartment and all her earthly possessions that weren't that much except they were hers. This apartment was the one place she felt secure, at home because it was . . . home. And now . . . She felt so cold. Violated. "This is house rape. You know how many times I consoled victims who had their place broken into by telling them to get a security system and they'd feel safe again. I was an idiot. What a bunch of crap. I don't know if I'll ever feel safe here again and I'm a cop. Do you really think they'll be back?"

Donovan opened one eye and this time his smile was menacing and a little scary without a hint of charm anywhere. "Damn, I hope it's tonight. Got any idea what they're looking for?"

"I'm a cop in a small city; I make squat, so we can rule out chunks of cash." Bebe sat down next to Daisy all scrunched up in the drawer. From the floor Bebe snagged the tartan plaid Christmas tablecloth she'd bought at a flea market but never used and snuggled it around the cat. Gatsby plopped on Donovan's chest, Carraway on his crotch and Bebe suddenly wanted to be a cat. Damn Prissy's spells. "Everything I own is secondhand. I even get my clothes at a thrift store."

"Except for the Kmart camisole."

"After my IRA, Roth, mutual funds, and savings bonds, there's not much left for shopping."

"I sense some security issues."

"Security fetish." She gathered up the brown throw that had been draped across the davenport. Wrapping it around her bare shoulders, she leaned back against the up-turned chair. "There's nothing here worth taking. No antiques, no jewelry. Dara never gave me anything except grief."

"You said you changed your name and I wondered about Fitzgerald. And you took on Daisy and Carraway and Gatsby. You're the loner who never fit in."

"Except Gatsby was rich. I still can't imagine why someone would break in here."

"What about the cases you're working on? Do you keep notes, files? A computer?"

"Computer's at the station. I have notes on the morgue murder. I've been working on it whenever I get a chance, but no one's interested except . . ." Her eyes met Donovan's across the dark room.

"Ray Cleveland?"

"I was thinking *you*," she said softly.

"Now that I'm trying to tie Cleveland to the murder. Yeah, you're right those notes would come in handy. And I did get here right after you did." He yawned and snuggled into the davenport. Now Bebe wanted to be the davenport. She was going to beat Prissy over the head with that darn spell book. "It would have been easy enough for me to raid your apartment looking for a notebook, then when you drove up sneak out the back and come in the front. Act as if it were the first time I was here. It fits pretty damn good."

"On second thought, it doesn't fit at all." She closed her eyes and yawned. "If you'd been the son of a bitch who'd hurt the fur balls, they wouldn't be stretched out on top of you now. Being mean to animals is not much different than being mean to kids, the sign of a sick, sick person. But why *did* you show up here?"

"I'm thinking of taking a vacation . . . to Savannah. I wanted you to know and see what you thought about the idea of me getting off the case, letting someone else go after Cleveland. Any suggestions?"

Of all the things Donovan could have said, never in a million years would she have expected him to say that. Her breathing kicked up a notch, and she wasn't half as tired as she was a minute ago. "Well, Savannah's a great place for a vacation. In fact long vacations here are best, so you can really get to know the restaurants and people, and I think the people would like to get to know you."

"And maybe you can take time off, too." His eyes were still closed, but he smiled, his face relaxed, even happy. She'd never seen him that way since he got here. He was always focused and on the job, doing the right thing, asking the right questions. Donovan McCabe was always the cop . . . till right now. Her heart skipped around in her chest. He was taking this vacation for her, at least part of it, and no guy had ever done something like this for her before. Heck, she was impressed if a guy picked up the tab for a beer on a date. She had some pretty rotten dates, but this was not one of them. This was an exceptional man doing something exceptional for her that had possibilities of growing into *them*. How did this happen? How'd she get so lucky?

At the moment she had two choices—one that kept her

where she was, sleeping against the back of a toppled chair, the other was not to stay here and it had nothing to do with going into her bedroom. She could take a chance. She stood.

Donovan cranked open one eye. "Going to bed?"

"I think so." She took the cats from Donovan and put them in the drawer beside Daisy, then took the throw from her shoulders and draped it over him. "Spring evenings can get kind of chilly in Savannah." She kicked off her shoes and put her gun and badge under the chair, where she noticed his were stashed. Picking up a corner of the blanket, she sat on the edge of the cushion.

"Yeah, chilly." He kept his eyes on her and his went from brown to black. He scooted over, putting his back against the back, his front to her, then she crawled in beside him. Her legs snuggled next to his and she bunched her arms up tight against her chest because holding on to Donovan seemed kind of forward. Duh, like crawling into bed with him wasn't forward? She hesitantly slid her arm around his middle. He had a nice middle, all tight and strong and no flab anywhere. Donovan McCabe was all man, she never doubted that for a minute.

"Don't want to fall off the couch?"

Her nose touched the tip of his, his eyes soft and accepting. "Thanks for all that you did tonight. I'm not used to the help."

"You know, as nice as this is, and it is damn nice, what about the Ray Cleveland issue and us? Ray is still an issue? What if they won't let me off the case? I don't want you to regret anything in the morning."

"I like the *us* part and I really like the morning part." She gave him a quick kiss, then scrunched up her face. "Ray Cleveland? Who's Ray Cleveland?"

"And I like the answer." He kissed her, one of those long lingering kisses that set her on fire and said he forgot who

Ray Cleveland was, too. "You're welcome for tonight. I'm glad I was here to help out." He kissed her again. "I'm hoping the night's not over."

Bebe could feel her cheeks redden. "You should know I don't crawl into bed or onto a couch or especially a kitchen table with just every guy. Two guys, actually, counting you, and I probably wouldn't be here right now if it wasn't for Prissy and her spells that never seem to work right. After the kitchen encounter, I wanted something to keep us apart because . . . well . . . after the kitchen table you weren't going to be that easy to stay away from."

He gave her a sly smile. "Really?"

"Kitchen tables are my new favorite piece of furniture. Anyway, I considered skunk perfume, but then Prissy said she could cast a spell on me to keep us apart and I'm talking too much?"

"Remind me to thank Prissy." He kissed her, this time with tongue to make things more interesting. Not tentatively at all, he slid his strong arm under her waist and pulled her on top of him.

"Am I squashing you?" She tried to push her hair back, but it kept falling down and Donovan didn't mind it being in the way. "I'm not exactly a shrimp."

"How did we get here, Bebe Fitzgerald?"

"Some piece of crud broke into my apartment and Daisy got her leg broken."

He laughed outright this time. It was one of those *I'm glad we have all night* kind of laughs that she never heard from a man before but she recognized anyway, just like any woman would. But she wasn't all that sure what to do next. What were woman supposed to do when they got into this position? What was the next step?

"What's going on? I can tell your brain's working overtime."

"This is virgin territory for me, not that I'm a virgin,

and of course you'd know that. So, what do you want me to do? Not that I'd know how to do it, but I can probably figure it out and—"

He placed his finger over her lips, his eyes staring deeply into hers. "Do whatever you want to. If you want to sleep, we can do that, if not we can do that, too."

He kissed the spot where he'd put his finger. "I'm on vacation; I have all the time in the world, Bebe Fitzgerald. What do you want?"

*Chapter Five*

And he did have all the time in the world, Donovan realized. He was taking time to figure out what the hell
he should be doing and right now being with Bebe was
perfect. "I should have taken this vacation months ago."

"Rough days at the office?" She studied his face, looking into his eyes, rubbing her fingers over his chin and
cheeks. Enjoying him as much as he liked being with her.
And he did, he realized. More than any other woman he'd
ever been with. She was independent and anything but
clingy or needy. "I need to figure some stuff out."

"And you're doing it at the right place," she whispered
in his ear, her hot breath on his neck driving him nuts. "It
is a proven fact that foods made with cream and butter
and fried are best for coming up with great answers to
tough problems. You can clog your arteries with chicken
and biscuits and grits and you'll see the light."

"That would be the EMS unit taking me away with a
heart attack."

She laughed and kissed his chin. "This is fun. Almost
worth getting broken into."

He moved his hands under Bebe's baggy sweater, her skin
smooth and so warm. He unsnapped her bra, the flimsy

material parting across her back, a barely discernible sigh escaping her lips and her eyes catching fire as she stared at him. Then suddenly the fire died, replaced by . . . worry?

"I wish I had my clothes already off, then I wouldn't have to figure out how to go about doing it. I mean, when a girl is with a guy like this, there should be some degree of sexiness in taking off her clothes, not just flinging clothes around the room anywhere."

"I don't think I've ever heard that before."

"You've probably never bedded such an inexperienced woman before."

"Do you hear me complaining?" He bunched her sweater around her rib cage. "Put your hands over your head."

This time she laughed. "Now there's a line we've both heard plenty." She laid her head on his chest and he tugged off her sweater, taking her bra, too. He dropped both on the floor. "I think I'm naked."

"With minimal amount of flinging. I like your breasts where I can see them and touch them."

She folded her hands under her chin and peered at him, her eyes smoky. "I like it, too, and I'm not embarrassed by any of this, and I get embarrassed if I even kiss a guy. You make this so easy, or maybe I'm too tired to get embarrassed."

"It is easy, if you're with the right guy," he said while dragging his fingertips down her spine. He stopped at the small of her back by the waistband of her jeans. Bebe had been around the block, but not by much and Donovan guessed he was responsible for most of that journey. He didn't know that before in the kitchen or he wouldn't have come on like a rutting moose. But he knew now. "Before we go any further, you have to want this as much as I do, Bebe."

She grinned wickedly, then planted a kiss on his chest. He felt the heat of her lips clear through his T-shirt. "I want it more," she said, her breath making him warm all over. "I want you more than anything and I am so glad you're vacationing in Savannah."

She levered her torso up, her sex pressing against his dick and her breasts suspended inches from his mouth. One little taste was all he wanted. Yeah, who the hell was he kidding, he wanted a lot more than a taste. "Are you teasing me?"

"I wouldn't do that. I'm not that kind of girl. You can count on me. I don't like playing games."

"This is a different kind of game, and it's okay to play, since we both win." He licked the tip of her right nipple, because there was just so much temptation a man could take. She shuddered, her shoulders quivering, her eyes not focusing. "You have some dynamite shape."

"I don't know much, Donovan, but I know a B cup is not dynamite." She crawled off him and stood. Moonlight creeping in through the blinds silhouetted her bare breasts, sublime body, and tumbled hair. She belonged on the cover of some fashion magazine that made other women eat their hearts out. She unsnapped her jeans and they slipped right off her hips and over her legs, pooling around her ankles. The advantage of jeans three sizes too large.

"Do you have any idea how incredibly beautiful you are?" Though he'd seen shorts on other women that revealed more then Bebe's white cotton . . . underwear. No way could he call her panties lingerie.

"You don't have to flatter me to get me into bed, Donovan," she said with a nervous laugh, her gaze dropping to the floor as if looking at him made her suddenly nervous as hell. "I think that's a forgone conclusion. I'm mostly naked already." She gave another nervous laugh that wasn't really a laugh at all. Damn, she was doing so well and then suddenly . . .

He got off the couch and stood in front of her. "Look at me, Bebe." He tucked his forefinger under her chin and raised her face to his. "Someone . . . Dara, I'm guessing . . . did a number on you. While you were growing up she saw you were a real beauty, more lovely than any of her other kids, if she had any. She never bought you nice clothes, hand-me-downs mostly, made fun of you in front of the other kids, never got involved in any of your school stuff, barely acknowledged you were alive. Any of this sound familiar?"

She stared at him with a blank look that slowly morphed into understanding the more he talked. "I never really thought about that. How did you know?"

"I met Dara. I'm willing to bet all your friends know, too, they just didn't know how to fix it, to fix you." He scooped her into his arms. "But they never had you alone and naked."

Her eyes widened and she tensed all over. "Maybe this isn't such a great idea. I'm just a girl. It's just me, Bebe the string bean. There's nothing to fix, Donovan. What are you going to do? Why don't we just have sex and it'll be over?"

He gave her another reassuring kiss and held her a little tighter. "I'm going to love you slow and easy at first, then when you get used to that and like it, we'll go on, but at no time will *get it over with* come into play. Lovemaking is not to be rushed."

He stepped over books, pillows, dishes, and a turned-over footstool to the French doors separating the hall from the kitchen. He set her down and stood behind her, the dim light offering a reflection of Bebe.

"What are we doing?"

What he was doing was getting really turned on in spite of the bloomers. But this was not about him. "I want you to look at yourself, really look. I want you to believe to the bottom of your lovely toes that you are a beautiful woman."

"The toes are a size nine-and-a-half, Donovan. I could water-ski on these things if I knew how to water-ski. Can we just get back to the couch? We were doing pretty good back there."

He put his hands on her hips. "These are lovely." He cupped her ass, making her gasp as he gave a gentle squeeze. "This is lovely." He stroked his hands up her sides. "You have the shoulders and long neck of a runway model and your face is incredible. Your eyes are an amazing shade of blue. Your lips are full and lush and made for kissing. Your body is exquisite in every way. I don't want you ever to think of yourself as a string bean again."

"I'm not that much shorter than you, and my ears are huge, that's why I never wear my hair up, Bebe Dumbo, and I have no boobs worth considering and—"

"And you are the most amazing woman I've ever met." He pulled her hair up on top of her head, then kissed one ear, then the other and swore if he ever got Dara in a dark alley he'd strangle her with his bare hands. "And your breasts are faultless." He ran his palms along the sides of each, bringing them together in front, forming delicious cleavage. He rubbed the pad of his thumbs over the nipples, feeling them bead with desire.

Her mouth fell open in simple sexual pleasure and she leaned back into him, staring at him for a second in the reflection. Was any of what he said sinking in at all? Maybe? A little? "I think," she finally said. "What makes me beautiful is you thinking I am."

"What makes you beautiful is you thinking you are."

She turned around and kissed his cheek. "I appreciate this, I really do. I'm over Dara, I just have a few residual reactions. And I'm probably not as ugly as she thinks I am, but I know I'm not as pretty as you think I am."

"I can't undo Dara's poison in one night, but I can start by making love to you the way a man makes love to a beautiful woman." He took her back up into his arms, then placed her on the couch. He sat on the edge of the cushion just as she had done before when she crawled in beside him. "And someday you'll realize everything I'm telling you tonight is true. You'll call me up in Boston and say, 'Hey, Yank, I'm one hot chick.'"

She laughed, her eyes dancing, and it made him feel good all over. He pulled his shirt over his head and did the flinging thing she mentioned before. Then he kissed her, her breasts pressing against his chest, her slender arms reaching around his back and holding on to him as if he were the only guy in the world.

"This isn't fair," she said in a breathless voice, her eyes smoldering, her lips still on his. "I'm naked and you're not." He felt her shaky fingers undoing his belt. "You've stroked and touched and played with every part of me."

He slid his hands under her derriere and pulled her body down to a lying position. "Not every part." His hand slid between her legs, feeling her damp heat. "Not every part at all," his voice low and husky as his brain melted. There wasn't enough oxygen in the room, his lungs straining. He stood and grabbed two handfuls of her panties—enough material to make a damn dress—and pulled them off. Wadding them up, he threw them across the room.

She pushed herself up on her elbows, looking indignant. "Hey, those are new."

"Sweet pea, those are ugly." Did he really just call her sweet pea? He sat down and draped one of her lovely legs across his lap, the other now behind him.

"And you still have on your clothes."

"And you don't and right now let's go with that." He bent his head and licked her clit. Her gasp cut through the silence of the room, her legs at his shoulders, now tensing, then relaxed, then spreading wide giving him full access, her hips arching off the couch with each lick of his tongue.

She was wet and ready and he wanted her more than ready. This was for Bebe, all for her. She moaned, then whimpered, his tongue plunging again and again till an orgasm shook her body, her cries of completion filling his head. She grabbed his shoulders as she cried out his name.

He kissed her, her lips devouring his. "How did you do that?" she finally managed, her voice ragged and broken.

"I'll show you again." Standing, he pulled off his jeans and briefs. Her gaze cleared, focusing on his erection. "You're right, that is some show." She swallowed, her eyes wide and wanting.

He got a condom from his wallet and covered himself. "I don't think I've ever wanted a woman as much as I want you right now, Bebe." He lay on top of her, mesmerized by the feel of her warm damp body moving seductively under his in perfect unison. He smoothed back her hair, amazed she was ready for him so quickly. "You were made for sex."

"Uh, that would be you. I can feel the evidence between my legs." Then she took his mouth in a hungry kiss and he slid into her wide-open wet passage. Embracing his middle with her long legs, she held him tight to her, meeting every thrust. Another orgasm made her tremble in his arms, then she arched higher, taking in his full length and letting him find his own release. No orgasm had ever been like this, so complete, so fulfilling, so memorable.

She cuddled up against him, her face to his neck as he pulled the throw over them together on the couch. She said, "You know all that talk about Southern girls not liking Yankee boys? Well, I think the problem is those Southern girls never slept with a Yankee boy . . . man. Definitely man."

"And I've just made love to the most incredible woman."

"Now what do we do?"

"We sleep." He planted a kiss on her hair as her body relaxed in slumber against his. But there was more, he knew that. Where did they go from here? All he knew for sure was that Bebe Fitzgerald had to fit into his plans someway. He wasn't letting her go, and he wasn't leaving.

And falling asleep in Donovan's arms was the last thing Bebe remembered till she woke, morning sun peeking in through the blinds, two cats meowing as if starvation was imminent and one cat with the smallest cast on the planet looking more pitiful than any animal had a right to. "I should rename you Tiny Tim." The aroma of coffee wafted in from the kitchen and she realized her phone was lying next to her, a note underneath.

*The captain wants to see me.*
*I'll tell him about vacation.*
*New locks on front and back doors.*
*New Oreos in the pantry.*
*Prissy dropped off your phone.*

   *Donovan*

"Good Lord, I slept through all this?" She must have been in a coma. Tucking Daisy under her arm, she stumbled her way to the kitchen as Sunday bells from the Baptist, Methodist, and Catholic churches tried to outdo each other. It was the Savannah way; martinis on Saturday night, repent Sunday morning. If Donovan went to tell the captain about the vacation, Donovan must be really serious about it . . . about her.

She grinned like a teenager after her first real date. And in a way Donovan was just that, except she was not a teenager. Donovan made her feel like a woman. She fed the cats, then poured coffee. "Cop, schmop, the man makes great coffee," she said to the fur balls, who weren't impressed at all. "And he brought me cookies." Took a lot to impress cats . . . like a bowlful of chopped fish guts.

She'd never met a man like Donovan. Doubted if there was another man like him. He stayed with her last night, made wild wonderful love to her, and tried to convince her she was beautiful. Dara may have played mind games, but it was a real stretch to beautiful.

But what if this was all a ploy and Donovan was the one playing her to get to Cleveland? She had the notes on the morgue murders and the fire and she knew Cleveland. Then again, what if Donovan wasn't playing her and he was the real deal and he really cared about her?

Life was a lot less complicated in the celibate state. Of course it wasn't fun. Cleaning up this mess could come later. Right now she had to see Donovan. If she looked him square in the eyes she'd know what was going on, right? It was easy to fall in love with a handsome hunk under the seduction of night, but in the bright of day was another story. And was this . . . love? It was *like,* she knew that. A lot of like. A lovey kind of like. "Crap. I have no idea what the hell I'm doing."

She cleaned herself up, then headed for the station. On Sunday morning it didn't take more than ten minutes to get anywhere in Savannah. Pulling into the parking lot behind the redbrick building, she spied Joe Earl trotting down the back steps in his best golf gear of red polo shirt and green pants. Church wasn't the only place of Sunday gathering in Savannah, but in church they didn't dress like a leftover Christmas tree. "When's tee-off time?" she asked, meeting Joe Earl halfway across the lot.

"Eleven." He pushed his golf hat complete with pompom . . . they really did wear those things . . . to the back of his head, looking unpleasant, or as unpleasant as one could look with a pompom on their head. And Joe Earl was always happy . . . usually. Even on a takedown. If criminals gave nice-cop-of-the-year award, Joe Earl would win. "So," he said. "I'm guessing you and McCabe came to some kind of an agreement. I got to tell you I never saw it coming."

She blushed. "Me, neither. It just sort of happened."

"Never thought you'd give up Ray Cleveland that way."

"Huh? What? There's no giving up Cleveland. He's out of the picture, Joe Earl. In fact everything's out of the picture, except me. Donovan's taking vacation. Right here in Savannah. No more case. No more gambling problem. No more warrant or murder investigation. Didn't Donovan tell you that part?"

"McCabe didn't tell me shit. When was the last time you talked to that guy?"

"Last night. Late last night."

"Well damn." Joe Earl nodded toward the station. "A lot's happened from late last night and now."

"No," she said holding up her hands to ward off the crappy feeling coming her way. "I just talked to him a few short hours ago. It's Sunday, for crying out loud. Nothing goes on around here Sunday."

"You'd be plum surprised. You best go find Donovan. I'll be out at the Cove or the country club if you need me. Things are getting might sticky around here, mighty sticky indeed, and it's looking like you and Donovan are right smack in the middle of it all."

But she didn't want to be in the middle of it all, she wanted to be back in bed with Donovan. Bebe headed for the door just as Donovan came out. "Bebe?"

He had a fistful of official-looking papers that sure as heck weren't vacation travel brochures. "We need to talk."

He nodded to the side of the building. "There's been a . . . development."

"No good conversation ever started with 'we need to talk' and I think *development* is code for 'I screwed Bebe so she'd help me get Ray Cleveland.' " She swatted at the papers in his hand. "I met up with Joe Earl. You creep. You think I'm that desperate for a man in my life that I'd fall for you and help you take down a friend?"

"The congressman who sent me here in the first place came in town this morning for some golf tournament." Donovan held the papers out to her. "He's got some good ideas for the task force."

"When it comes to romance I totally suck. I bet all my romance genes went to that Angelina Jolie person. I get someone feeding me a bunch of manure about how this is perfect and that's perfect and then uses me to get ahead. Well, heck. I can't even land a damn Yankee!"

"The congressman is sponsoring a bill to fund the Sly Gavin Task Force. Sly was my partner back in Boston and this would go a long way in bringing down some pretty bad characters in organized crime. Cops would learn how to handle situations like the one that killed Sly. He was a great cop, Bebe. You would have liked him. He sure as hell likes you . . . would have liked you. And this would mean a lot to his family. He was their only son and we were friends and I should have been there when he needed me and then he wouldn't have died like some rat in the gutter."

The words hung in the air and Bebe's heart stopped dead in her chest as she looked at Donovan stunned by what he'd said. Donovan blamed himself for his partner's death and it was killing him. "I didn't mean to say all that."

"I don't know what happened," she said in a quiet

voice. "And I'm not a big-city cop, but I know that if you were there with Sly, you both would have both been killed. Organized crime is just that . . . organized. If they took out your partner, they would have taken you out, too. I'm sorry, Donovan. I'm so very sorry."

He swallowed, trying to get himself together, and her heart cracked. He hurt so much and there wasn't anything she or anyone could do to make it go away.

"The congressman wants Cleveland no matter what it takes. I think he got a lot of ribbing from losing like he did. He's out for blood."

"So he's bribing you to get him."

"If Ray's guilty, it's not a bribe, it's proof. Last night I was willing for someone else to do the job, but now . . . I want this for Sly, for his family."

"He was your friend and Ray Cleveland's mine. Keeping Ray out of jail is the one thing I can do for him. So, we're right back where we started." They stared at each other, knowing that the last part was a lie. Last night happened and that was way beyond from where they started.

"I'm going to the morgue," Donovan said. "The Italian brothers know more than they're letting on. They've worked in that damn place for months now. They must have found something. If they came across that necklace, it could lead to the murderer."

"Meaning Cleveland. It's back to that infuriating necklace again," Bebe sighed. "Always the necklace. Last night I said if I found it I'd sell the damn thing, give the money away, and not tell a soul, and I haven't changed my mind one iota. It's cursed, I swear it is."

"Where exactly did you make this statement?"

"Prissy was doing that spell that didn't work and . . . and . . ." Her eyes met Donovan's. "Holy crap. I was at the Magnolia House bar with wall-to-wall people and someone heard me and that was what they were looking for at my apartment. They thought I had the necklace."

"Do you?"

"Oh, for crying in a bucket, of course not, but that necklace is the key to a lot of what's going on around here. I'm going with you to the morgue. I don't need you coming across some evidence and twisting it around to suit your purpose of nailing Ray."

"You think I'd do that?"

"Sly was your partner and you're dealing with a belly full of anger and guilt. Enough of that and a guy will do almost anything."

He took her shoulders and stared into her eyes. "I didn't use you last night and I wish to hell this was not about Ray. We may be on opposite sides of this case, but it is the same case. I want evidence to find Cleveland guilty, you want to find him innocent, and there's someone out there who probably doesn't want either of us to find anything. If we don't have each other's back, there's a good chance one of us will wind up with a bullet there and that is not an option. So what do you want to do?"

"I want to roll the clocks back to last night and forget this morning happened, but that's not going to happen, so I'll go with solving this case once and for all and getting you the hell out of my life."

His cop face didn't budge, but there was a hint of regret in his eyes, the same that was in her heart. "It's the best we can do."

He kissed her hard, catching her completely off guard, fire in his eyes replacing the regret. "No, that's the best we can do."

Donovan walked off to his Jeep and she licked her lips for another taste of him. Just when she got it straight in her brain it was all business between them and their partnership began and ended with the badge, he had to kiss her, making things not straight at all. What was she supposed to do with a kiss like that?

She parked behind Donovan at the morgue, the spring morning warm and smelling of azaleas, magnolias, lilies, and jasmine. Together they took the front steps. Windows sat open, letting in the fresh air. There was activity inside; at least the brothers were home. "Is there anything more heavenly smelling than jasmine?"

"Yeah, pie. Anthony baked. Cherry, I think." Donovan knocked and the movement inside went quiet immediately, followed by running footsteps that didn't come toward the front door.

Donovan drew his weapon and tried the front door. Locked. "Someone's in there again who shouldn't be and I'm damn tired of chasing ghosts. This time we're nailing their asses." He said to Bebe, "You stay here, I'll take the back."

Bebe watched Donovan disappear around the corner of the building. Stay here? Fuck stay here. Bad language for a bad morning. She ran down the steps and climbed up on the old tiered iron fountain. Balancing on the third bowl, she lunged for the open window, skidded inside, taking a fresh-baked and still warm pie clean off the counter as she slid across, then onto the floor. See, that's what she got for using the "f" word.

Following scrambling footsteps, she tore for the rear of the morgue, spied Donovan coming the other way, trapping the two suspects between them. "Stop," Bebe shouted, pointing her gun at their backs. "Police. Stay right where you are."

"Don't you dare shoot us," the lady said, turning around. "I'll have your jobs if you so much as harm one hair on our heads." She was older, sixties maybe, not that breaking and entering had an age limit, but the woman had on layers of gold jewelry, a lavender scarf, and matching hat, and the guy wore pressed trousers, a tweed sports coat, and a fedora. Breaking and entering goes to Saks.

"What in the world happened to you," Donovan asked, looking at Bebe as he came up the hall.

"You were right about the cherry part and never cuss on a Sunday morning."

"We have a right to be here," the woman huffed. "And if you were competent police officers like we have in Boston and doing your job the way you're supposed to, we wouldn't have to be here doing it for you now. I've already written a letter of complaint to the mayor's office about the irresponsibility of the police force."

Reluctantly, Bebe put her weapon away. "Who the heck are you?"

"The Raeburns, of course," the woman tsked as if everyone should know the name and if they didn't they should burn in hell for all eternity. "I'm Edwina and this is my husband Shipley. We are Jaden Carswell's grandparents from Boston, not that it matters to her. What a rude girl. I cannot imagine who raised her, she has no manners and—"

"Oh, you mean Charlotte," Bebe said. "You're Char's grandparents and you're the ones who believe you have a claim on the necklace." They were also the ones who wouldn't take in their grandbaby thirty years ago after their daughter was murdered.

"A claim?" Shipley's eyes turned to gray pinpoints. "My dear girl, we own that necklace." Edwina added, "My mother . . . for reasons I will never understand . . . gave the necklace to my daughter, bypassing me entirely. My daughter is dead, so that necklace belongs now to me, and I intend to find it, whatever it takes."

"Uh, that necklace belongs to Charlotte, your granddaughter. Her parents were killed because of it. I think that alone gives her points."

Edwina scowled. "That necklace is the Kent Shelton necklace. It is museum quality. Thirteen yellow diamonds and thirteen white diamonds, over sixty carats in all. It's worth a fortune not only because of the jewels themselves but also because of the history surrounding it."

"Do Anthony and Vincent Biscotti know about you being here? Do you have their permission to look around?"

"We only want what belongs to us, and if you do not help us we will take it up with the governor. We travel in connected circles, and is that cherry pie in your hair?"

"I beg your pardon," came Daemon Rutledge's voice from the side hallway. The man looked mortified and he gave Bebe a pleading look. "I've come to fetch the Raeburns. I used the side door and was looking for them when I couldn't find them outside and—"

Side door? Bebe ate a cherry off her sleeve. She forgot about the side door.

"Well, it's about time you got yourself here," Edwina huffed at Rutledge. "Southerners have no sense of responsibility or promptness and with all the unhealthy food you consume, or wear, you deserve to have heart attacks and I cannot wait to get back home with *my* necklace. Come, Shipley, I've had enough. I think it's time we hired a private investigator who knows the city and the people here. He'll get to the bottom of all this for us."

"Edwina, dear." Shipley took off his fedora and smoothed back his hair. "Perhaps this has gone on long enough. The necklace is gone forever. I think we should get on with our lives and give up—"

"Never," Edwina hissed. "Those diamonds rightfully belong to us and I'll not rest till we have them." She pranced out the front door, Shipley following, Daemon Rutledge looked apologetic.

"A private investigator?" He shook his head. "More problems to deal with. I'm afraid this unfortunate incident is all my fault. The Raeburns wanted to visit the morgue and with them being guests at the hotel and all, I agreed, but I never in all my days dreamed they would let themselves inside without the Biscotti brothers present. They are rather ... difficult guests and Miss Charlotte is at her wits' end with them. The hotel will assume full responsibility for anything broken or missing. We don't want any undue publicity. Our guests are like family to us and we do take care of family even if that particular family happens to be black sheep."

Bebe took Daemon's hand to reassure the man before he had a nervous breakdown. Donovan said, "I don't think they took anything, though with the mess this place is in, who the hell would know?"

"Could it be that they went and found the necklace they were looking for?" Rutledge asked, looking truly concerned about the possibility. "It rightfully belongs to Miss Charlotte, you know."

Donovan picked up a piece of molding pried away from the ceiling. "And the list of people wanting that necklace keeps growing."

"Yes, it most certainly does." Rutledge tipped his hat and left and didn't even mention Bebe was decorated in pie. Always the gentleman. Donovan looked around at the torn-up floorboards and holes in the wall. "What the hell do you think is going on here? What kind of renovations are these?"

He turned around to Vincent and Anthony standing in the doorway looking jumpy as peas on a drum. Vincent asked, "Is there some reason you are in our home? Why are you wearing my pie?"

"You had intruders," Bebe offered, making the brothers more nervous. "But no need to worry, except for the pie. They didn't take anything. They were looking for that Shelton Kent necklace."

"Kent Shelton," Vincent corrected in an instant, but now looking as if he might have a stroke. Anthony rolled his eyes and Vincent let out a long sigh of exasperation. "Oh my, now I have done it and let the cat out of the sack. I am . . . how do you say . . . a dumbass."

"What you are is an imposter," Donovan said, nodding at a hole in the floor. "You know the right name of the necklace, you don't like us being here, and not because the place is in such great shape. You're not renovating anything, you're tearing this place apart. What the hell's this all about? It's the necklace, no doubt, but it's more."

Donovan took a chunk of crust from Bebe's shoulder and popped it in his mouth. "But you are damn fine cooks, that much is true enough. Let's all go down to the station and you can tell us who you really are and what you're doing in Savannah and at the morgue."

"We have amaretto cake," Anthony offered, temptation in his voice. "We could perhaps talk in the kitchen? And we have Colombian coffee and whipped cream with shaved chocolate. We do not want to make ourselves known to everyone, as we are on a mission."

Without waiting for Donovan, Bebe trotted down the hall. "Did you say cake? What kind of mission? Sorry I destroyed your pie, it was great pie."

"I can bake you another," Vincent said. "If you do not lock us up in prison."

Bebe sat at the heavy wood table and cast Donovan a quick look. Was that a blush creeping up his neck? Could be since last time they were in this kitchen she was on the table and being served something a whole lot more interesting than cake. Vincent pulled dishes from the cupboard, Anthony retrieved the cake from the pantry, and Donovan asked, "What the hell kind of police procedure is this?"

"The good kind on a Sunday morning," Bebe said with

a mouthful of cake she'd snuck right off the platter. "Sit down, it's been a rough morning."

"We are not criminals," Anthony said.

"And you are not the Biscotti brothers, either," Donovan said, eyeing the cake.

"That is true. We chose that name because Vincent thought Americans could relate to us because of the cookie and I must tell you I will never eat biscotti again. Every time we introduced ourselves we got, *like the cookie.* I am Anthony Mateo and Vincent and I are indeed brothers and we are here in Savannah because the missing necklace belongs to us."

"Oh for the love of Pete," Donovan said. "Two more to add to the list. We should get T-shirts made."

He raked his fingers through his hair, then plopped down in a chair, grabbed a fork, and started in on the cake. Anthony continued, "We believe this Kent Shelton necklace is Frizzante Gioielli, the Sparkling Jewel that went missing from the local Sorano museum in Italy when our grandfather was the security guard many years ago. Our family has suffered much humiliation and what you here call bad mojo because of this. We want to return Frizzante Gioielli to the museum to redeem our family name."

"How do you know it's the same necklace?" Bebe asked while licking whipped cream and chocolate shavings from her coffee. "Lots of diamonds out there, guys."

"Google. Anthony often searches for news on missing jewelry, and when the hotel owner here in Savannah, Otis Parish, died, there was a missing heir and news articles mentioned an unsolved murder and a missing necklace of years ago. Thirteen white diamonds and—"

"Thirteen yellow," Donovan added around a mouthful. "Distinctive enough, I'll give you that. So the necklace here is the same as your missing one. I'm guessing it was brought to the United States and sold at auction. They didn't quibble over proof of ownership in the fifties. Who had it, owned it."

"We believe the double thirteen has caused a curse and that is why the necklace is still missing for us and ruined our family. We need to break this curse and have summoned Miss Prissy. She is coming Monday night. She will then help us find the necklace and all will be well."

## *Chapter Six*

BrieAnn savored a long lick of the soft-serve peach ice cream cone she'd bought from the Candy Kitchen. River Street was crowded with tourists on a Sunday evening, but she looked forward to her first peach cone of the season no matter how busy the place got. It was tradition, like dyeing all the fountains in Savannah green on St. Patrick's Day, getting kissed in the gazebo at Whitefield Square, and regifting that big purple bottle of bubble bath she, Prissy, Char, and Bebe had passed around for the last ten years never knowing who'd wind up with it next for a Christmas present.

And maybe the ice cream would help her forget about dinner at her parents' with Lamont Laskin. Nice man but so not Beau. That was the real trouble. She didn't need help forgetting about Lamont, she needed help forgetting about Beau. She wanted him, he seemed to want her and then he suddenly didn't. He fizzled and she was permanently stuck with wanting.

She licked again, twisting her tongue one way, then the other, making it hard, then soft, than taking another long lick from bottom to top to the tip, her mouth suddenly covering the long twist of ice cream at the top. Except she wasn't thinking ice cream. Lord have mercy, she was having oral sex with frozen dessert. How desperate was that?

She tossed the rest of the cone away. Too . . . erotic and too painful to think of what she wasn't getting. Was she ever going to have sex with that man? Her body ached for him, her insides felt wet and squishy. Think of something else!

She focused on the boats that lined the public landing and the tourists boarding the *Georgia Queen* with the big red paddlewheel for an evening cruise. A water taxi from the Marriott across the Savannah River pulled up and unloaded guests and one of those long low cigarette boats was parked several blocks down the way by the Waving Girl statue. Ray Cleveland's Donzi? Everybody knew his boat with the yellow and purple detail splashed across the side. There were only a few tourists down that way, but they stopped and admired.

Maybe she could talk to Mr. Cleveland about Beau? Maybe he had some advice on what to do with Beau. If he just wasn't into her, she needed to know. But if Mr. Cleveland could shed some bit of light on her predicament of Beau having a bad case of BrieAnn-itus, she'd be eternally grateful!

"Yoo-hoo," she called at Ray from the dock as she approached the Donzi. This was one of those boats where you strapped yourself in and rocketed across the water. Amenities were all below. She knocked on the fiberglass hull. "Anybody home?" There were drinks in the holders and footprints leading to the cabin door. Mr. Cleveland had to be here somewhere. Slinging her purse over her shoulder, she grabbed hold of the railing and swung herself aboard. Gymnastics 101.

"Mr. Cleveland," she called, heading for the doorway that led to the interior. She knocked again and the door swung open. "It's me, BrieAnn Montgomery. I was hoping I could talk to you?" BrieAnn poked her head inside, her eyes taking a moment to adjust and . . . Oh, dear God in heaven! Someone was lying at the bottom of the steps. A man.

"Mr. Cleveland? Lord have mercy." He must have tripped. What kind of a boat was this? "I'm coming. I'm coming. You'll be okay now, you hear."

Brie climbed down the three steps and gently turned the man over, him staring back, blank and cold and . . . lifeless! The good thing was that it wasn't Ray Cleveland. The bad thing was she couldn't breathe, she couldn't see, and she was going to pass out on top of a dead man. A strange dead man.

She started to scream. No screaming, the gossip would be terrible. Mama would be mortified beyond imagination and the scandal of her daughter with a dead man could cause Mama to lose her first table seating at the women's weekly bridge club.

Shaking her head, Brie slapped her face a few times, her heart beating so fast it was right likely to explode. "I will not faint, I will not faint," she chanted as she fumbled her cell from her purse and speed-dialed Bebe. "If you don't pick up I swear to God I'll—"

"Hey, Brie, I can't come to a party tonight, no matter what the cause. I have to clean up this place, you wouldn't believe the mess and—"

"I'mwithadeadguyonMr.Cleveland'sDonziatthepublic-landing. Hurry." She disconnected because no more words would come out and she had depleted all the oxygen in the cabin and the fainting was coming back. Taking the handkerchief with the embroidered yellow daisies from her purse, she fluffed it out over the man's face. She said a prayer because that's what Southern ladies do, though to be perfectly honest she didn't know any in this precise situation.

Sirens sounded in the distance, then a car skidded to a stop outside followed by doors slamming and then Bebe's face at the door. She'd never get used to Bebe the beautiful being a cop with a gun.

"Sweet Jesus," Bebe said as she came down and put her arm around Brie. "I was hoping you just had one too many martinis and had drunk-dialed me from some bar. Nice touch with the daisies."

"Martinis? Does this looked like I'm having a martini and it's too early on a Sunday night to be drinking and I've never drunk-dialed in my life and you're the one who's supposed to find this stuff and not me. I do garden parties and sundresses and mint tea with blueberry scones and . . . This is not the first time I've recited this litany, my life sucks."

"I know, honey, I know. Take a breath. Do you recognize him?"

"I recognize that he's dead." She grabbed Bebe's hand. "I came here to talk to Mr. Cleveland is all and found the body instead. You're going to have to keep this out of the papers. Mama will have a hissy-fit with me being on Mr. Cleveland's boat with a dead guy."

Bebe picked up a corner of the hankie. "Jimmy Waters. Local PI. I got a bad feeling about this."

"I'm sure Jimmy does, too. Do you ever have good feelings about dead guys? How do you suppose he got this way?"

"I don't see any bullet holes so I'm guessing blunt force trauma, meaning somebody whacked him."

"I'm so glad I asked."

Bebe held the man's jaw, then moved his hands. "Dead between one to four hours, easier to tell if it's not that long ago."

"That you know stuff like this scares the bejeebers out of me."

"What's on the front cover of the spring Neiman Marcus catalog?"

"Bow peep-toe pumps and hobo tote from the Valentino collection."

"We all have our gifts." Bebe searched the man's front pocket and pulled out a paper, unfolded it, and read. Her face stayed placid like those people on the CSI shows, but her eyes looked troubled. She stuck the paper in her own pocket. "When we go outside, don't say anything. Let me do the talking."

"What did the note say?"

"It said life is a piece of crap. Let's get out of here." She squeezed Bebe's hand, and they went up the steps.

"Oh my, more police. Mama is not going to like this one little bit."

"Say nothing, remember?" Bebe whispered. Ray Cleveland and Beau hustled down the dock toward the Donzi. Brie's gaze met Beau's and she nearly fell right out of the boat. That man seriously affected her equilibrium, no matter what was going on in her life, even bodies with trauma. She scrambled off the boat with more agility than she knew she possessed and flung herself into Beau's arms.

"Hi, honey. What brings you down this way? What's going on?"

"Nothing." That got a weird look from Beau, but before he could continue, Mr. Cleveland said, "Miss BrieAnn, Miss Bebe. Gentlemen. Always nice to see everyone on a fine Sunday evening such as this, but I'm guessing this here little gathering isn't a social call."

Bebe said, "Jimmy Waters is dead in your cabin. Any ideas what he's doing there?"

"I believe he's a PI here in Savannah, but I can tell you I have no idea as to why he's here on my boat. Do you happen to know?"

Bebe combed back her hair with her fingers, looking none too happy and worn out clear through. Working with dead bodies could do that to a girl. Brie snuggled close to Beau, his strong arm a protective blanket around her.

"This is a crime scene now," Bebe said. "We can't let you back on your boat, Mr. Cleveland. And please stay in Savannah for a few days in case we have questions. Can you tell me where you were for the last three hours?"

Beau stiffened; Brie could feel it in his whole body. "Wait a minute, Bebe," he said. "Do you think my dad had something to do with this? Are you accusing him of murder? You know him better than that. You two are friends, have been since you were born. What's wrong with you?"

"I'm not accusing anyone of anything." Bebe's eyes said she was pained to her soul and Brie said, "Oh for heaven's sake, Beau, she's a police officer, she asks questions, that's what they do. Don't you ever watch TV?"

"This isn't TV," Beau groused and Mr. Cleveland folded his arms. "You might find this hard to believe, but I was taking a little walk around town. You see, I'm thinking of opening a martini bar over there on Bay Street and I was checking out the property. Surely you don't think I'd be plum stupid enough to leave a dead body around on my boat when I could have just as easily gone out to sea and dumped it over."

"And Beau was with you on your walk?"

"Yes," Beau rushed in. Mr. Cleveland gave his son a grateful look. "Beau's mistaken. He was with clients having dinner at Tubby's." Mr. Cleveland nodded down the street. "I ran the boat into town with them. We saw the sights. Beau drove his car in later on and took his turn with the entertaining. Big clients bring in big money for us, so we do our share of wining and dining, if you get my drift. Now if you don't mind, Beau and I will be over at the Magnolia House for the remainder of this evening if you're needing us for anything more."

Mr. Cleveland started to leave when Bebe asked, "Were you in town two nights ago?"

Beau stepped away from her, and, taking Bebe's arm, turned her toward him. His eyes were hard, his face the same, his expression more marine than Southern good-old-boy. She liked the Southern boy so much better and she didn't like the way this was shaping up at all.

"What are you doing?" Beau asked. "This is my dad."

BrieAnn took Beau's arm. "And what are you doing to my friend? She's your friend, too, you know."

"She sure as hell isn't acting like it."

"Enough, you two." Mr. Cleveland held up his hands. "You're scrapping like roosters in the barnyard. I don't mind answering questions. I was in town and again stayed at the Magnolia House. I was at their nice little bar for a while but went out walking, looking for real estate, just like I happened to be this evening."

"Alone?"

"Alone."

"You drove into town? The black SUV with the tinted windows?"

Beau raised his voice, anger in every word. "That's it. We're calling our lawyer. Don't say anything more, Dad. I don't like where this is going."

The other uniformed police climbed onboard the boat and BrieAnn watched Beau and his dad head down the docks. "Well I never. How rude. What did I ever see in that man?"

"Great body, good hair, cute as hell. He's protecting his daddy, Brie, and you're protecting me, and I'm sorry you

both got in the middle of all this. Like enough's not keeping you two apart as it is."

"And I'm thinking it's permanent. We're like those ships
passing in the night. Close but not close enough to amount
to anything."

"I'm sorry, Brie. I truly am. There's a cab down the way.
Go home and stay there and do not talk to anyone about
anything that's gone on here and I do mean anything. I'll
say I went to visit Cleveland and found the body and you
just happened along should anyone ask what you were
doing there."

"You'd lie for me?"

"It's one of those white lies, honey, like when your
Aunt Zinnia comes to visit from up Beaufort way and you
say how happy you are to see the old battle-ax. Jimmy
was dead for some time before you found him, so it
doesn't matter who did the actual finding." She nodded at
the TV trucks heading down River Street. "Get out of
here now."

For the millionth time Beau watched the flickering TV
at Wet Willies roll news clips from the dock that evening.
The bar was mostly empty and the people there knew
enough to leave Beau and his dad be. "Bebe's looking like
an old hag these days," he said to his dad.

"Don't you be too hard on her now, you hear. She's a
pretty girl and trapped between a friend and doing her job
and there's no easy way out." He took a swig of Moon
River. "I do have to say the Donzi looks mighty fine on
TV. Photographs right well." He laughed. "I'll give her
that."

Beau studied his beer and turned it in circles on the bar.
"I'm worried about you, Dad. I'm betting that body's got
some connection with those missing jewels and that mur-

der a long time ago. Dead bodies don't just show up for the hell of it. Somebody went to a lot of trouble to frame you. Who the hell is this guy anyway?"

"He was hired by Edwina and Shipley Raeburn to find the necklace for them."

Beau jerked his head around. "You know?"

Ray laughed. "Son, there's damn little that goes on in this city that I don't know about, usually before it happens. My guess is somebody who's after that necklace didn't like Jimmy snooping and dumped him on my doorstep. It sort of takes us both out of commission."

"You're looking for the necklace, too?"

"Wondering mostly. You know I was a suspect from the get-go in the morgue murders and the missing necklace. This thing with Jimmy makes it look as if I know where the necklace is or I'm getting close and I did Jimmy in so he wouldn't tell." He took a long drink and was quiet for a moment. "Sometime I just go looking at the morgue, wondering what happened to my baby girl." Ray patted Beau on the back. "Good thing I got you, boy. Least I got myself one kid to boss around. See much of your mama lately?"

"Not if I can help it. She's gotten worse, if that's possible. My life would have been a total screwup if you hadn't fought for custody."

"Hell, I needed someone to help me run the Cove, didn't I?" Ray laughed. "You don't worry about a thing, Beau. We're doing okay here. Everything's going to be fine. This will all smooth over."

"A dead body takes a lot of smoothing."

"I've been through worse." Ray slid off his stool. "I'm tired as a tombstone. I'll head back to the Magnolia House, you take your time here. Maybe pay BrieAnn a call, if you got a mind to."

"I think she's done with me."

"I saw the way she looked at you on that dock. She may have stood up for Bebe, but her eyes were all on you. She's got it bad. Go talk to her, figure out how to make you two work. She's a nice girl, Beau. Her parents, especially her mama, are stuck up, but she's a fine one."

"I love you, Dad," Beau said in a quiet voice without looking up. "You've been the only dad I've ever known." He looked at Ray now. "The only person who gave a damn about me, ever. And not just because you raised me when I was a kid but when I got home from Afghanistan and my leg and through rehab and—"

"Yeah, me too, son." Ray patted his back. "Me, too. You made it, I made it, we've been good for each other all along and we're going to be fine. Now go sweet-talk your girl and don't go worrying about me. I'm a tough old bird."

Ray left and Beau finished his beer, wondering if they would be okay. Dead bodies, gambling, old murders, McCabe, and now Bebe. If enough shit hit the wall, something was sure to stick sooner or later.

He paid the tab, then went outside, the breeze kicking up, a hint of rain in the air. He headed down River Street to the Donzi to make sure none of the mooring had pulled loose and the bumpers were still in place keeping her from rubbing on the dock if it stormed. Next to Beau the river flowed with a chop as a huge freighter from Hong Kong motored quietly upstream on her way to the deep ports.

Yellow crime scene tape stretched across the Donzi, flapping in the gusts. The boat bobbed, but the lines held.

"Nice boat," came a voice beside him. Beau turned and faced BrieAnn's dad. "Evening, Judge Montgomery. I think we're in for a spring rain. Out taking a walk before it hits?"

"Out to find you, and I'm not here for pleasantries. I'm here to tell you to stay the hell away from BrieAnn, permanently." His voice was hard, his face chiseled. He had on a full suit as if going to court. "I won't have my daughter associating with criminals and that's what you and your dad are, common crooks. BrieAnn won't give any other man a chance as long as you're in the picture, so I want you gone for good. I've looked the other way on what Ray does out there on the Cove because he gives back to the town and he keeps lowlife out of Savannah."

"The reason you don't come down on Ray is that you want to get reelected. Turning on my dad is political suicide and you know it. My dad's a great guy. Ask anyone."

"I'm not asking, I'm telling you this and you best pay attention real good. If you don't stay away from BrieAnn, I'll give that Donovan McCabe fellow the warrant he wants. That's all he needs to bust the gambling house out there and Ray will go to jail for a very long time and I don't give a tinker's damn about my reelection. Do we understand each other?"

"I understand that you're a rotten stinking politician willing to sell out his position for his own benefit. You don't uphold the law, you sell it. That's extortion and you sicken me."

Even in the dark Beau could tell the judge's eyes were cold and menacing. "I'll do whatever I damn well need to do to protect my daughter. She's too good for you and I'll not stand by and watch you ruin her reputation and her life. Rest assured, I'm not bluffing. This is not an idle threat. If I even hear of you with BrieAnn, I'll ruin Ray Cleveland and the only way you'll see your father is behind bars."

Anger ate at Beau as the judge walked off. Beau's gut tightened. He started after the judge, wanting nothing more than to beat the living crap out of him. How could that no-good asshole threaten Ray like that? How could he sell out his judicial standing in the community? He was nothing but a corrupt politician. He was also a father who loved his daughter.

Beau stopped in his tracks, the judge retreating into the night. Judge Montgomery had a sterling reputation . . . until tonight. And he was willing to trade on that for BrieAnn. Beau hated the judge, but on some level he did understand, even if he didn't agree. Family was everything; Ray taught him that.

How could Beau give up BrieAnn? He took kissing lessons for her. She kidnapped him. They could make it work, if they had the time. Then again, he couldn't sell out Ray. Beau sat at the base of the Waving Girl statue. What the hell was he going to do? The judge wasn't kidding about the warrant, but Beau couldn't just quit seeing Brie cold turkey. But if he did talk to her what could he say? *I can't see you anymore because your dad's going to have my dad thrown in jail?*

Then BrieAnn would hate her dad and Ray would still go to prison.

The best thing to do was nothing. Let BrieAnn go. He wouldn't call her or return her calls. Their relationship that never really got off the ground would eventually die away . . . at least for her. She'd forget about him; lord knows there were tons of guys in town to take his place. The judge was right about one thing—Beau wasn't good enough for BrieAnn. He'd always known that and then she suddenly got interested in him and everything changed. With enough time it would change back again.

Wind kicked up another notch and the moon hid behind gathering clouds. Beau took the steep steps that led off the riverfront, then crossed the iron walkway where cotton growers once drove their horse-drawn wagons underneath and brokers stood on top and shouted their bids. He headed for Bay, then Broughton, and Magnolia House. Cutting down the alley, he decided to go in the back entrance because he wasn't in the mood to answer a ton of questions on murder from anyone he'd meet up with in the lobby if he went in the front door. He was nearly to the rear entrance when he looked up and caught sight of the light in Brie's bedroom across the stone wall that separated her place from the hotel.

His heart thudded and he went a little crazy because suddenly he was tearing back down the alley in a full run, the first fat drops of the storm smacking his head. He hoisted himself over her back porch and knocked on the screen door. "Brie," he whispered. He knocked again, because if she didn't come quick, he'd lose his nerve and leave.

The inside light came on and Brie scampered out onto the screened-in porch. Turning on that light, she opened the door. "Beau?" She dried her face with the lapel of her fluffy white terry robe. A butterfly clip held her hair up, little damp strands curling around her face. "I just got out of the shower and I'm all wet and what are you doing here? We had a big old fight, remember? I don't think we're talking to each other right now . . . are we?"

He reached in and flipped off the porch light. "I should go. This is not one of my better ideas."

He backed up and she grabbed his shirt and pulled him to her, her mouth devouring his in a kiss that singed his eyebrows and made his legs wobble. They may not be talking, but they sure were doing something. Then her hand cupped his stiff erection and he nearly flipped right back over the railing.

"Oh, baby," she panted. "This . . ." she added pressure to his dick ". . . is a very good idea. I love this idea." She undid his belt and unzipped his fly faster than he ever did. "You came here because you want what I want and we're doing this here and now, Beau Cleveland. I'm tired to death of waiting around. I'm in pain, real female pain. I need sex."

She kissed him again, making him hard as the porch post. "And I can tell you're all frustrated just like I am. In fact, you have a very big frustration going on." Grinning, she ground her pelvis against him. "And I'm aiming to get rid of it for you the best way I know how. Me and sex."

Except they were in full view of anyone coming down the alley and was that a car approaching? Damnation! Stay or go? Could he leave Brie in a robe already falling off her shoulders, exposing the most delectable skin in Savannah? He scooped her into his arms and dove for the wicker chaise longue as the car passed. Thank heavens for the row of azaleas in front of the porch keeping them hidden. Truth be told, he should probably thank Brie's gardener.

"Well, honey," Brie said on a giggle as she lay back against the pillows. "I have to say, that's more like it." Her eyes danced as lightning flashed across the sky. The scent of flowers and warm earth drifted in as Brie's robe parted a bit more, now exposing her lush breasts.

"Lord have mercy, woman, I've never seen a more beautiful picture than you like this."

"And don't you dare say we shouldn't be here, because I'm not believing one word. You're the one who knocked on my door and tossed me onto this piece of furniture."

He wasn't going to think about the judge or later. He was going to concentrate on now. He stood, then tugged off his shirt, his shoes, then started on his pants except then he couldn't, it was if his fingers wouldn't budge.

"Beau? What's wrong. Why did you stop there? Honey, I want to see more. I want to see all of you, my big glorious stud of a man." She held out her arms. "Make love to me, Beau. Let me make love to you. Tell me what you're thinking right this minute and we'll fix it and move on from there and we'll be perfect together."

"I . . . I'm not so perfect."

"Drop those pants, sweet stuff, and I'll let you know. Felt pretty damn perfect a few seconds ago."

His chest hurt; his lungs wouldn't work. She sat up, concern replacing hunger. "Beau, what is it? Tell me, please tell me. If there's something you don't like about me, something I can make right, I will, I swear it. I want us to be together, honey."

She wrapped her arms around his hips and held him tight, gazing up at him, her eyes now pleading. "I'm not letting you go, Beau. Not this time. You have to tell me. I'm not the only girl you've been with, I know that for sure. So, what's wrong with me?"

"You're special. You matter to me more than any woman I've ever been with and . . . and I'm pretty much a mess, Brie."

"You're magnificent. Just look at yourself all big and strong and male."

"But you're not looking at all of me. There's more, the not so good part." He could see it all over again, didn't even have to close his eyes.

"What, honey, what? You can tell me anything. Sit down here beside me and we'll make it better."

He rubbed his leg and then he was telling her, the words spilling out all at once. "There was this place, a checkpoint, outside Khost. We were inspecting cars for bombs before they went into the city." It was right there before him as if he never left Afghanistan, as if no time had passed at all. The blazing sun overhead, the sand in his clothes rubbing his skin, the weight of his boots on his feet, the pressure of his helmet on his head, the M4 clutched in his hands. "A car, dirty, white, drove up and stopped and then it . . ." He could feel the blast, the percussion throwing him as if he were no more than a stick. He jerked back as if hit all over again. "The heat, fire, so much fire, Brie. The screams. My scream," he added in a low murmur.

He couldn't move, as if he were frozen to the spot, and suddenly BrieAnn was kneeling in front of him, tears streaming down her incredibly lovely face as she looked up at him. He swiped a tear with his thumb. "Oh, sweetheart, don't cry. Please don't cry."

"I'm not crying, Beau, I'm not, I promise I'm not." She kissed his eyes and nose and chin; he could feel her wet cheeks against his, her wet lips kissing his. "I'm so sorry, Beau." Her ragged voice nearly broke his heart. "I'm sorry for you, for all of you over there."

"I'm okay, now, but—"

"I don't care about the but. You're here with me, that's all that matters." She embraced his neck tight. "I do love you. I want you to know that."

"You're so perfect and the scars are . . . ugly. I look like a road map, Brie."

"A map that made you better. A map that brought you home here to me so we could be together now."

Then her face slowly scrunched up and her lips formed a sweet little pout. She sniffed and swiped away the rest of the tears with the back of her hand. "You truly think I'm that shallow, that you being injured would turn me off, repulse me in some way? Just because I know fashion and have excellent taste and can recite the book on Southern manners, that's all there is to me?"

She poked him in the chest and looked indignant as hell. "How can you suggest such a thing, Beau Cleveland?"

"Well I—"

"Steel Magnolia is not simply the title of some book about Southern gals facing tough things." She kissed him full on the mouth, sucking his breath away. "It's for real. *I'm* for real. I'm stronger than I look, and don't you go and forget it ever again. I'm not some piece of Southern fluff. I'm tough. I don't run. I'm here and I'm not going away ever."

She sat beside him and kissed him for the third time as thunder shook the earth and a patch of golden moon and silver stars slipped through. She cuddled up under his arm and gazed at the sky. "Oh, Beau, it is turning out to be a fine night indeed. It's the best." She wrapped her arms around his chest, a sigh of contentment escaping her lips.

"Are you okay?"

"Never better. Now that I know why you wouldn't make love to me, it's better than doing the deed itself."

He laughed. "I don't know about that."

"I do. I have you and that's what I want . . . you. I want to spend time with you, have fun with you, get to know you. We don't have to jump into the sex part. We can date, be real romantic, you can bring me flowers and I can bake you cakes and we can shop for dishes."

"Dishes?"

"I love dishes, pretty ones with flowers. And we can take them on picnics to Tybee."

"But just a minute ago you were in the mood."

"And now I'm in even a better mood." She looked up at him. "There are more powerful things than sex. There's us, Beau, and a future together. I love you, and now I know you love me, too." She rested her head on his chest. "There's no need to hurry when you know you have the rest of your life together."

Beau held her close, savoring the moment. Brie was right, there were more important things than sex . . . there was love. And he loved her so very much. And he loved Ray. And that's why tonight was the very last night he'd ever spend with BrieAnn Montgomery.

# Chapter Seven

Sunday night at the station was less hectic than the rest of the week and the thunderstorm rattling the windows meant the place was even more subdued with Savannah evildoers preferring fair weather. Bebe was thankful for that. She needed to think, try and make sense out of her notes on the computer about the morgue murders, the necklace, and now Jimmy Waters thrown into the mix and why she missed being with Donovan even though she felt betrayed by him. Damn the man, he chose his precious task force over her, or, more to the point, chose Sly over her. Of course she sided with Ray Cleveland, and that pretty much made things even . . . except she still missed Donovan.

"How come," came Donovan's voice from behind her. "When you're hunting for someone, you always find them in the last place you look?" Splattered with dust, plaster, and raindrops the man was still mind-numbing handsome. Nothing could tarnish basic good looks of brown eyes, black hair, and killer smile and body. He sat across from her.

"Jimmy's untimely demise had to reach the far corners of Savannah in less than ten minutes and it took you six hours to find your way here? Where have you been, and why are you such a mess?"

"I knew you'd be busy with paperwork on the murder so I spent some quality time over at the morgue with Anthony and Vincent."

"The morgue?" That got her attention and she quirked her brow in question. Donovan slid off his jacket and plopped a rain-splattered brown bag on her desk then sat back.

"Oreos? Coffee? What do you want?"

"I'll tell you what I found at the morgue, you tell me what you have on Jimmy. You first, I brought the food."

Taking a scissors, she sliced open the package of Oreos. "Cleveland didn't off Jimmy."

"He had motive, cupcake. Jimmy was getting too close to the necklace Cleveland thought was his or that he already has. And he had opportunity; getting Jimmy on his boat would be a cinch. I'm sure if we look in the water by the docks we'll find the murder weapon."

"Already done. A stainless-steel fishing rod holder. Found it in the cabin. The only prints were Cleveland's, but then it is his boat, so what would you expect?"

Bebe pulled the cover from the coffee and dunked her cookie. "It's a frame. Everyone knows Cleveland's always taking customers out on his Donzi. Strangers boarding wouldn't raise suspicion and by strangers I mean the killer who waited and Jimmy."

"Can't believe you're a dunker."

"It's a Southern thing, just not in public."

"I'm not public?"

"You're a pain-in-the-ass Yankee who just happened to bring me Oreos. I think the killer lured Jimmy to the boat with information about the necklace. He gets whacked, Cleveland looks guilty, and the killer gets three rivals out of the way at once, Cleveland, Jimmy, and the Raeburns. Jimmy's demise shook Ed and Ship up pretty bad, not the dead Jimmy part so much as it could have been them. They're such sympathetic souls."

She looked at her monitor. "There's no proof that the person who did the morgue murders also did Jimmy."

"There's no proof that they were two separate people and Cleveland fits the MO on both."

She ignored him, even though late at night when she wanted to be in bed with him, the ignoring part was darn tough to do. "The Raeburns could be responsible for the morgue murders. Their daughter was selling the necklace they thought belonged to them. They hire someone to steal it and the plan goes sour. Now they're trying to find the necklace."

"Why was the original sale of the necklace at the morgue? And why was the necklace getting sold in the first place?" He held up his hand as soon as he asked the question. "Don't tell me. I want to hear this straight from Cleveland. The way a suspect gives his story, his body language says a lot. I'll drive out tomorrow and talk to him."

"*We* can talk to him at Magnolia House. He's there. Now tell me what you found at the morgue."

"Nothing." Donovan sat back in his chair. "Vincent and Anthony are going with the idea the necklace was hidden there and they've torn the place to hell and back, sawdust and plaster everywhere, looking for it. If you want my opinion, that necklace is long gone. I think Cleveland already has the damn thing and shows up at the morgue from time to time so no one suspects and they think he's still looking like everyone else. Like the other night when we saw his car coming out of that alley. We were there and then conveniently his distinctive SUV drives off for all the world to see."

"How do you know he was driving and, like you said, it's unique and that brings us back to someone framing Cleveland, making him look guilty."

"You're reaching."

"You're only going with the obvious, but either way everything keeps circling back to the morgue." Another rumble of thunder shook the station. "I can't believe that we're no closer to the answers than they were thirty years ago."

"Actually, things are worse. You got yourself another dead body and a totaled apartment."

"Gee, I feel so much better now." She ate a cookie whole. "Prissy's tarot card reading tomorrow night better turn up something. Her methods may not always work the way they should, but usually they get results of some kind."

He leaned across her desk. "Like that spell she cast on you to keep us apart. I really liked the way that one worked out." He stood and stretched and slid on his jacket. "The rain's slacking off. I'm going back to the hotel. See you to-morrow."

He left and she looked back to her notes and ate an-other cookie and another. Nothing connected and Dono-van didn't have any information that helped. He didn't tell her anything new. Why did Donovan come here in the first place? It didn't make any sense. And then it suddenly made perfect sense.

She gave him information and he gave her none and now he was headed back to the hotel and the last thing on his mind was going to bed. Ray Cleveland was there and Donovan was going to talk to Ray and she wasn't in-cluded. So much for having each other's back and being partners. "That dirty double-crossing rat."

* * *

An occasional car rumbled by on Broughton, but other than that Donovan's own footsteps were the only sound. One of the things he liked best about Savannah—besides a certain female detective who lit up his life—was he didn't need his car that much and could walk anywhere in fifteen minutes. Missing a puddle, he crossed Houston. The night mist cast halos around the lights on the street and the ones in Greene Square named after General Nathanael Greene, Revolutionary War hero, whose remains and statue were over in Johnson Square. God only knew where Johnson's statue and remains were, probably Oglethorpe Square, because Oglethorpe's statue was over on Chippewa Square. In Savannah it was tough to tell where anyone would turn up, including Edwina and Shipley, because here they were with Joe Earl. The three of them slipped into the shadows as Donovan slipped behind a live oak to watch.

What did the Raeburns have to do with a cop? *This* cop? Help them look for the necklace? Or could it have been Joe Earl hired by the Raeburns all those years ago to get their necklace? Is that why Joe Earl was good friends with Cleveland, to keep suspicion on Cleveland and off himself and the Raeburns?

Another piece of the puzzle. Lots of pieces, and somehow they had to fit together. Quietly, Donovan retraced his steps. Suspects who didn't know they were suspects usually led somewhere and right now he'd take all the help he could get. Should he tell Bebe? She didn't think Cleveland was guilty of anything and she'd probably never believe Joe Earl was, either. The good-old-boy mentality ran deep in Savannah and Bebe was loyal as a hound dog.

The red neon of the SCAD Theater sign reflected off the wet sidewalk and a tabby cat sat in the storefront window of Pattie's Hallmark shop. Greeted by the outside doorman at Magnolia House, Donovan entered the double glass doors.

" 'Evening, Mr. McCabe," smiled Mr. Rutledge from the reception desk. "Looks like you got yourself caught in the rain. I'll have extra towels sent straight up to your room; the chambermaid is heading that way now. You have a good sleep now, you hear."

That Rutledge didn't mention Donovan being coated in dust made him wonder what other secrets the perfect hotel manager kept to himself. As Donovan got in the elevator, he caught sight of the Raeburns getting out of a cab. Whatever happened between them and Joe Earl happened fast.

"Sure enough is a rainy night out there," the maid said, interrupting his thoughts. She balanced her towels and hit the "3" button in the elevator.

"I think you're heading my way. I can take the towels."

"Some are for Mr. Cleveland."

"Well, now, I happen to be going to his room for a little nightcap, and I'd be glad to save you a trip." Donovan did his best good cop I'm-on-your-side smile.

"Why bless you," she said in a rush. "We're running shorthanded tonight and it seems that everyone's wanting something at the same time."

She handed off the towels, frowned, and pulled a pager from her apron pocket. "Fact is, they want me back in the lobby for something again. Guess they figure I can be two places at once. Mercy, what a night! Tell Mr. Cleveland I'll be up to check on him in a bit. He's such a fine man, I think I'd do just about anything for him, anyone in this town would."

The door opened and Donovan stepped out. "316 is that way, right?" He pointed up the hall.

She looked at her pager again and absently said,

"Mr. Cleveland's in 324 and it's down the other direction." The elevator closed and, whistling "Dixie," Donovan headed for 324. Lucky break with the maid. He didn't know how to find Cleveland other than banging on doors and pretending he was drunk and lost. He'd used that technique more than once.

"Moonlighting these days, McCabe?" Cleveland said as he answered the door. "Mighty thoughtful of you to be bringing me towels, though from the looks of you I'd say you're in need of them more than me."

"Can we talk for a few minutes? Nothing about Jimmy Waters. I'm more interested in what happened thirty years ago at the morgue."

"You can read all about that in the newspapers at the library."

Donovan stepped inside and put the towels on the bed. "Then you won't mind telling me again."

Cleveland's eyes were tired, but they held a sharp steel glint that said this good old boy could be a first-rate badass even at sixty. He closed the door. "I might as well tell you, because I got a feeling you won't leave otherwise. And since you are here, you should know I happen to have a protective steak for Bebe Fitzgerald. The girl's had a hard time of it. Rotten childhood, worse mama. Bebe used to run away every chance she got with the police dragging her home 'cause they had to. They were nice enough to her; I think that's why she became one of them."

"And the cops were that way because you told them to be."

Ray's lips thinned. "You hurt that girl and you and I are gonna tangle, Boston cop or otherwise."

"Why do you care about her so much?"

"I lost a daughter and have no idea where she is. Guess I figure if I take care of this here child, someone somewhere will take a look-see after mine. What goes around comes around in this world." They stared at each other man-to-man for a moment and just when Donovan knew he was going to be kicked right out the door, Cleveland nodded at a chair by the fireplace, a bottle of Southern Comfort on the table. "So, what exactly do you want to know?"

"Why the hell did Dara adopt Bebe to treat her bad?" That stopped Cleveland in his tracks and it pretty much stopped Donovan, too. He hadn't planned on asking that; he wanted to know about the necklace, but somehow the Bebe question jumped right out of his mouth.

"Since you're spending time with Bebe and Lord knows I think she could do herself one hell of a lot better than the likes of some no-count Yankee, I suppose you have a right to ask."

Cleveland sat and poured out two tumblers. "Best I can figure is one of our lily-pure Southern debs got herself with child. Keep in mind this was thirty years ago and a babe out of wedlock had scandal written all over it. No good match came with a daughter having a bastard child in her arms. So, the girl goes off to boarding school for a year and daddy pays for a new home for the babe and his daughter's reputation. Dara got money as long as she kept her mouth shut. It's how things were done here, we take care of our own. Bebe wasn't the first and I'm guessing she won't be the last."

Donovan took the second chair, rain sliding across the two windowpanes facing Broughton, a faint glow reflecting off the street below. "Dara knows who Bebe's parents are?"

"More than likely, no. Too easy to let things slip up that way and Savannah isn't all that big. A few facts are easily connected. These matters are arranged through a family friend or trusted lawyer, if there is such a thing. Everything hush-hush." Cleveland took a long sip the Southern gentleman's way because Southern Comfort was sipping whiskey, social whiskey, not the get-drunk-fast stuff.

"What's the story with the necklace?"

Cleveland studied his glass. "Like I said, Bebe could do herself a lot better." He took another sip. "My first wife was what you all call a trophy wife. I made some money here in Savannah doing this and that and wanted to flaunt it because I was stupid. Nothing flaunts better than a good-looking woman on your arm, and nothing can use you up and throw you away faster. Savannah thirty years ago was boarded-up houses, gangs, and criminals. Otis Parish got people to take a chance on Savannah and buy back the mansions."

"And you took care of the gangs."

"If you say so. Otis and his partner, William Carswell, bought this here Magnolia House that we're sitting in this very night. It took more money to fix up than they figured on. William's wife had a necklace and my wife fancied it. It would have taken every penny, but a pretty woman has her ways. The Carswells agreed to meet at nine o'clock at the funeral parlor, keep it friendly and we both knew the owner. Except when I showed up with the money the Carswells were dead and there was no necklace. A car had run into the iron fence in front of the funeral home and the owner was out of the place dealing with that. When he came inside he saw me running. I was going for the phone, but there was no way of proving that a fact and not me just running away. There was a scandal. My money went to lawyer fees and my wife went to a rancher from Brazil. She took our daughter. Said I ruined her life and she was hell-bent on ruining mine."

Cleveland took a long drink this time. "And," he added

in a whisper "in a lot of ways she did. When you lose a child, you're never the same. A piece of you dies." For a second, a tortured expression replaced badass, then Cleveland continued in a normal voice, "I married Beau's mama when he was seven. Seems I have mighty poor judgment in choosing good women, but when she left, I kept Beau. In a lot of ways he saved me. Gave me a son to raise."

"You have a nice lifestyle now. Maybe your plan was to get the necklace, keep the money, and ditch a bitchy wife in the bargain."

"The Carswells were friends and down here that counts for plenty. And that plan of yours makes it certain I'd lose my baby girl 'cause she'd go with her mama. I'd never take that chance, but I lost her anyway." He stared across the room, but it was one of those stares that only saw memories. "I remember the color of her eyes, her laugh, the way her hand held on to my finger. Do you know I could put her whole foot in my mouth? I remember everything about her."

"What did the room look like when you went to meet the Carswells?"

Cleveland raised his brow and rubbed at his chin. "Well, I have to tell you no one's ever asked me that before. Let's see now, the casket room was off the main hall and down a few steps in the back of the morgue. Maroon carpet, caskets along the wall, a velvet settee and some chairs and an overhead light of some sort. Do you want to know what I think happened? Something spooked Addie and William and they hid the necklace someplace in the morgue, someplace nobody's looked yet, and the reason I think that's what happened is because that someone who did the spooking is still hunting around."

Donovan finished off the whiskey. "Mr. Cleveland, you

had a good lawyer thirty years ago or you wouldn't be sitting here talking to me now."

Cleveland chuckled. "He cost me a damn fortune; the case never made it to trial with things being circumstantial and all, but the way you're going after me I'm thinking I just might be needing that lawyer all over again."

Donovan put down the glass and stood. "If you say so." He walked to the door and Cleveland asked, "Did you learn anything you didn't know before?"

He eyed the table. "I learned I'm developing a taste for Southern Comfort."

"And it looks like we done killed the bottle. Think I'll head on down and get another."

Donovan closed the door behind him and went for his room at the other end of the hallway. He pushed in his room card, the light going red to green, and when he went inside, he was greeted with, "You're a low-rent no-good creep, you know that, Donovan McCabe."

He switched on the light to see Bebe sitting on the edge of his bed, and was that steam curling from her ears? "That's the second time tonight I've been hit with the low-rent crack and you should know there's no such thing as low rent in Boston and even though you're sitting on my bed looking damn gorgeous as always, I'm guessing this visit isn't going where I'd like for it to, and how the hell did you get in?"

"I'd like to wring your neck and everyone in this hotel knows me, so getting in wasn't a big deal." Bebe was wet, her hair in blond ringlets as if she hadn't taken time to grab an umbrella and had been too pissed to dry off. Neither a good sign. "You went behind my back . . . again. You went to see Cleveland. I give up all I have on Jimmy and you can't even level with me on this and who knows what you really found at the morgue with Anthony and

Vincent. We're done, McCabe, and that's what I came to tell you."

She sliced her hand through the air and stood. "This is one of those user relationships and I'm the one getting used by you. All I get in return is a pack of Oreos and not even the double-stuff kind."

He shoved his hands in his pockets because if he didn't he'd snatch her up and kiss her and probably get decked in the process, not that he blamed her. "If I'd brought you along tonight you'd interject and explain everything Cleveland said because you two are friends. I wanted to talk to him alone, see how he came across on his own."

"You'll do anything, say anything, use anyone to get this memorial project off the ground. You didn't level with me and this isn't the first time. Why should I trust anything you say? You do what suits yourself and the hell with anyone else." Her eyes turned dark and sad and suddenly they weren't talking about Cleveland at all.

"You got this all wrong, Bebe. You're getting the case and what's us all mixed up. What I said to you last night about you is the God's honest truth, I swear it. It had nothing to do with Cleveland or Sly. It was you and me and us."

"I . . . I don't believe you." Her voice cracked and he felt a tightening in his chest that nearly made him sick. "You lie to me, then you say you don't lie. How am I supposed to know the difference?"

"I didn't lie about going to see Cleveland."

"You just didn't do full disclosure. Same thing." She pushed past him and yanked open the door.

"Bebe, stop." He followed her into the hallway. "We need to talk."

"Can you please hold that elevator for me, Mr. Rutledge," Bebe called down the hall to the elevator opening with Edwina and Shipley and Ray Cleveland. Bebe turned back to Donovan. "We just did talk and the whole blessed hotel's hearing us loud and clear and don't you dare follow me."

She had a defiant walk with her chin high and backbone rigid like someone used to being messed over but determined not to show the hurt. Except this time he'd been the one doing the messing and the hurting. In Bebe's eyes he was no better than Dara. Bebe couldn't trust either of them to do right by her. This was not the way he wanted things between him and Bebe. Their relationship had gone from trusting to fragile to in the toilet.

Rutledge held the elevator, Shipley and Edwina and Cleveland staring at the little scenario playing out before them. Bebe stepped in, all the rest got out, and Rutledge gave Donovan a sympathetic smile as the doors slid shut. "Don't you fret now, Mr. Donovan. She'll come around. It'll work itself out."

Donovan straightened the picture of Lee on the wall that was forever crooked, then went back in his room and closed the door. "Fuck this damn job!"

"Last time it was fucking a duck. I think you need one of those sexual awareness books." Sly chuckled as a thin ribbon of cigarette smoke circled to the ceiling. He sat in the club chair, feet propped on the desk.

"You better be here with something a hell of a lot better than your smartass talk. I've got bubkes on this case. I can't nail Cleveland with that."

"What you have is a hard head and you're not listening to a word I've said." Sly pulled a drag off his cigarette. "What happened to my *follow the girl* lecture? Did you get a brain freeze and forget it all? You don't know what Cleveland's guilty of."

"He's guilty of something. The problem is—"

"I'm dead and you're not and you got a bad case of the

'why me' syndrome and you're sacrificing a relationship with the best woman who's ever come your way to make things right." He blew smoke rings. "That task force isn't going to bring me back, Donovan. It's not your fault I caught the bullet and you didn't."

Donovan rubbed his forehead and shut his eyes, feeling bone-numbing tired.

"Didn't you ever watch *Scrooged*? You listen to the ghost, and in this particular story that happens to be me. Somehow I've got to get though to you before it's too late and you throw it all away for nothing." Grumbling, Sly faded into the swirl of cigarette smoke; the last thing disappearing was the rim of his Sox hat. Donovan would have sworn this was aftershock of sipping a half bottle of whiskey in the middle of the night except for the lingering hint of smoke and a shoe scuff print on the mahogany desk where Sly had propped his feet. Donovan rubbed at the smudge.

Sly was right about one thing; Bebe mattered and she was the best thing to come his way. Donovan needed to find her and tell her that and somehow make her understand that what happened with Cleveland was police business and what happened between the two of them was personal and they weren't the same. Donovan took the steps to the lobby, the cute little maid running the vac in the deserted hallway. "Did you happen to see which way Bebe Fitzgerald went?"

The lights blinked and the maid switched off the vac. She looked nervously around, then shivered. "The ghosts get right lively in thunderstorms. Once I was alone in the kitchen and this plate of blueberry pie went flying across the room and . . ." She gulped. "I hate thunderstorms and I haven't seen Bebe. But the elevator went and got itself stuck on the fourth floor, so maybe she's trapped in there."

"I didn't know the hotel had a fourth floor."

"Storage attic. The employees have elevator keys to get there, but that doesn't always work, either. Usually we take the stairs around back. Tonight there isn't enough money in all of Christendom to get me up there in that attic no matter what. It's spooky enough in broad daylight. Lordy, I hope Bebe didn't get stuck in that place."

If Jimmy Waters hadn't been whacked earlier in the day, Donovan wouldn't be thinking much about a stuck elevator on the fourth floor of a hotel older than dirt. But Jimmy was on a slab over at the city morgue and Bebe was God-knows-where and who the hell knew what got her there in the first place. Another rumble of thunder shook the hotel. Again the lights flickered and the maid paled. "A night not fit for man nor beast. You need to be finding Bebe."

The elevator doors closed behind Bebe. Why weren't the lights on? This was not the lobby. Then again, when the elevator went up instead of down, she figured something was screwed up, but this was Savannah and old and screwed up wasn't all that uncommon. Groping the wall behind her, she pressed the elevator button to get the elevator back, but nothing happened. No light flashing overhead as to where the thing was or where it was going.

"Terrific," she muttered, another rumble of thunder rattling the rafters; least she thought it was the rafters. It could be anything rattling, because there wasn't any light except the red glow of the exit sign across the room. Stairs? Stairs would be good. She started toward the sign until something moved across the room. "Hello? Anybody here? Anybody know how to get out of here, wherever here is?"

No answer. If it was a bat or one of those big owls that

could turn their head all the way around and carry off small dogs, Magnolia House would have a new skylight because she'd jump right through the roof. "Hello? Polly want a cracker?" Except she didn't have any crackers.

She took a few steps and a *phoof* whizzed by her head. That was no owl, that was a bullet! Heart racing, she dove for the floor and reached for her weapon, which wasn't there because she left it with her cell and handcuffs and other cop stuff at the station because she was pissed and not thinking. She'd had severe Donovan brain, meaning *no* brain, and she deserved being in this situation now. Men were nothing but trouble, and they didn't even have to be on the premises to cause it.

She started to get up again, then heard, "Heavenly days, child, stay down. You're in a heap of danger here. I told BrieAnn to keep you all away from this here place. She needs to listen to me."

Bebe looked around, but there was nothing but dark. "What? Who?"

"Shh," the voice whispered. "Be real still now if you want to keep your head attached to your shoulders the way it should be."

"We can't stay here forever." Bebe peeked around something large and another muffled shot rang out. She ducked back, calling herself every name for stupid for not having her weapon. Some cop she was!

"Told you to keep yourself put," the voice said again.

"No need to rub it in. Who are you?"

"Someone with more sense than you got." Another sound came from the opposite direction of the gunfire.

"Hey, Bebe? Are you up here? What's wrong with the damn lights? They weren't working on the stairs, either." The red exit sign silhouetted Donovan's fine build, which was also a fine big target.

Shit! Shit! Shit! "There's a shooter. Get down!" she yelled, followed by another *phoof* sound across the room. Donovan jerked back as if hit and her heart stopped dead in her chest. Her lungs froze and the whole world moved in slow motion. She could see Donovan falling, falling back, her head screaming, or maybe she was doing it out loud. "Donovan!"

# Chapter Eight

Bebe tore for Donovan. If someone was going to shoot the man, it was going to be her after he lied to her about Cleveland. Pushing stuff out of the way in the dark, she stumbled over furniture, not able to move fast enough. She heard Donovan fire off a round as he scooted out of the light. Finally she made it to his side and he pulled her hard behind him, his hand gripping her arm to the point of pain.

"Don't move," he ordered in a "Moses delivering the Ten Commandments" kind of voice. She wanted to say, "Don't tell me what to do, you big oaf," but she was so thankful he could talk and wasn't badly hurt she didn't say anything. Plus she didn't have her gun, so she wasn't in the position to offer much of an argument. After tonight she was having the darn gun surgically implanted in her side.

Scurrying sounds came from across the room, then all was quiet. Donovan put his weapon in his pocket. "He's gone. There must be another exit somewhere or a trap-door."

She touched his shirt, a familiar stickiness coating her fingers. "You're bleeding."

"It's not bad."

"Bad? Anytime someone's leaking blood it's bad. I'll call 911 and the police. Give me your phone."

"Where's yours?"

"Don't ask."

"No police. I'll tell you why later. I don't want them involved. The bullet just nicked me. We need to get out of here, the ghost explanation to guests down on the third floor goes just so far and then we'll have company and a lot of explaining to do." He stood, a little slower than usual. Even in the dim light she could see the bloodstain on his shirt and the dull pain in his eyes.

"You're hit worse than you think. You got to get to the hospital."

"Forget it. If we get any more people in on this we'll need our own zip code." They made their way down the steps and Donovan pushed open the third floor door a crack. She looked both ways; people were spilling out of their rooms and heading to the elevators and talking about gunfire. She whispered, "I have a plan. Pretend we like each other, okay?"

"I can do that." He gave her a weak smile and she held on to him tight. Cuddling up to Donovan lover-style, she hid the bloody part of his shirt. "Now you can lean on me. It'll look natural, like we're dopey in love."

"I wish to hell it was that easy, cupcake." He pulled out his room card.

Before she could digest the easy part of that statement, they meandered into the hall and mixed with the others there. Rutledge was telling everyone the noise was simply thunder and a bit of plumbing work being done on the boiler. There was no cause for alarm, and everyone needed to be getting back to their rooms—with a complimentary bottle of wine, of course. That Magnolia House didn't have a boiler got lost in the free wine offer.

Bebe opened Donovan's room, then closed the door behind them. "I'll get this cleaned up." He kissed her fore-head. "Don't look so worried. I've been though worse."

He sunk down on the john seat and eased up his shirt, revealing a gory mess. "That's it. You need stitches and antibiotics."

"What I need is whiskey."

"From what I smelled on your breath, I think you've had your quota for the night." Bebe let out a sigh and sat on the edge of the white claw-footed tub. "If I hadn't left my weapon back at the station, you wouldn't have been target practice. Did you ever notice things between us never go smooth, there's always drama? I hate drama. I'm thinking beachcomber out on Tybee Island." She kissed him on the head. "I'll be back in five minutes. Don't leave."

Slipping back into the service stairway, Bebe made for the main floor, opened the door, and bumped smack into Charlotte. Her eyes went huge and she turned white. "Ohmygod, you've got blood on your shirt. You're the one in my attic causing a ruckus." She grabbed Bebe. "I've got you, honey. Don't worry. You'll be okay. I'll get you an ambulance."

"It's Donovan's blood, but no ambulance. Mr. Hard-head refuses. Lend me your sweater so I don't look like something from a Tarantino movie."

"Donovan? Blood? I know you had your differences, but good grief, Bebe."

"It hasn't come to that . . . yet. But the good news is I think we may be getting closer to who killed your parents." Rain slashed against the front windows. "Wanna go poking around in your attic for a bullet tonight?"

"Gee, I can hardly wait. Isn't that what everyone does on a night like this?"

Five minutes later Bebe was back in Donovan's room with a good bottle of whiskey and an even better doctor.

Donovan was sitting on the edge of the tub washing out his wound when he spotted Bebe and the doctor in the doorway. His eyes were hard and pissed, but they were also edged with more pain than before. "I said—"

"This is Doc Stevens, a mighty fine physician who's a personal friend and knows what happens at this hotel stays here, so watch your Yankee mouth and act like somebody raised you proper." Bebe closed the door, peeled the cap off the whiskey, and took a drink. Keeping the bottle in hand, she went to the window and watched patches of moonlight peep though parting clouds, rain gradually giving way to a warm spring night. She pushed on the casement, letting in fresh air and taking a deep breath.

Where was this going with Donovan? Between the arguing and the lovemaking and outside influences it was hard to pinpoint where they stood. The only thing she did know was that when the chips were down, Donovan was the guy to have on her side. As much as she wanted to beat him over the head a lot of times, she admired him as a cop. He was darn good at what he did and took it seriously. And that was the problem. Donovan the cop was after the bad guys and Ray Cleveland was right in his path.

"He'll live," came Doc Stevens' voice from behind her. She turned away from the window. Doc's kind face was smiling. "I shot him up with antibiotics, but I'm betting you need to watch that man. He's got a stubborn steak almost as wide as yours. He needs to rest, and if he won't, he'll bust that wound all open again and next time he'll be in the hospital on a stretcher and lots of people will be asking questions."

Doc handed her a bottle of pills. "Not to be taken with booze." He nodded at the whiskey in her hand.

"Thanks for the help."

His eyes softened. "After you dragged Preston out of

that drunken brawl and brought him home safe, I owe you."

"That was a time ago, Doc. He's a good boy, just got in with the wrong crowd and didn't know how to go about getting himself out."

"He's a sophomore at Georgia State this year. Premed."

Bebe smiled. "Go Bulldogs."

Doc Stevens tipped his head and left and Donovan came out of the bathroom, shirt off, white bandage on, blood-splattered jeans slung low on his hips. She put down the whiskey, pulled the blue comforter off the bed, and folded it over the chair, then peeled back the sheets. Keeping busy was a good way to keep from salivating, least that was the plan till he pulled off his jeans.

Mother have mercy! How could someone so shot up look so darn sexy? What muscles! What a butt! He had such a great butt. Then again, maybe he wasn't that gorgeous and maybe this was the booze affecting her brain. Yeah, and maybe the Pope wasn't Catholic after all. She needed to stop this obsessing over Donovan no matter how good looking he was or how impressive in bed or how great . . . really great . . . the sex was. They were on opposite sides and those sides kept getting farther apart and wasn't he the one who just flimflammed her over the visiting Cleveland issue? *Remember the flimflam!* "Hop in."

Donovan sat on the edge of the bed. She took his hand and dumped two tablets then handed him a glass of water. "Drink up, Yank. You've been enough trouble for one night."

He stared at his palm. "What is this?"

"Happy pills. You need sleep and I'm going to get some clean clothes. Red's not my color. I'll be back."

He gave her a sarcastic smile. "And you expect me to

believe you're not going into the attic to look for casings or bullets? How'd you get up there in the first place?"

"Take the pills, and I'll tell you and do not hide them under your tongue because I'll check."

He popped the pills and she kissed his cheek, his rough stubble against her lips and the heat radiating from his body a sensual experience and reminder he wasn't hurt worse. She kissed his lips, sliding her tongue against his, his mouth forming to hers kiss for kiss. He slid his hand around her waist, then to her derriere. An act of possession.

"Promise me," he said against her lips. "You won't go into the attic. Someone's after you, cupcake." His fingers tightened for emphasis. And she liked it . . . but not enough to tell the truth.

"Nothing's there that can't wait till tomorrow." Except the bullets in the wall that could possibly match the bullets that killed Charlotte's parents and that information had already waited thirty years and was not waiting another night. What if the shooter had the same notion and got to them first? No way was that going to happen when she was so close. She owed this to Charlotte.

Donovan let her go and slid under the covers. "It would be a lot more fun if you were in here with me, but since that's not going to happen, tell me about the attic."

She sat cross-legged on the other side of the bed all sweet and innocent and accommodating. "I stepped in the elevator and I guess I forgot to push down and it went up. Someone called my name, so I got out and the elevator took off and wouldn't come back and the light switch wouldn't work. That's pretty much it till you showed up . . . except for the ghost."

He quirked a brow that sort of slid down because Donovan was falling asleep. "Ghost?"

"Well, somebody was there and had already told Brie

that we should all stay away. It was a maid, I think, and she showed up out of the blue. Well, actually it was black. But she was on my side and friendly and protective and kind of creepy."

"And maybe it wasn't a ghost at all, but that sixth sense that kicks in to help you survive."

"Obviously you are not from Savannah."

"Cleveland was on that elevator before you got in. He watched us arguing and could have a passkey from the maids, who all think he's Mr. Wonderful. He fixed the elevator and up you go, then he took the stairs. If he knows how to fix the elevator, he knows where the fuse box is to cut the attic electricity."

"Ray Cleveland wouldn't kill me."

"He'd kill me. That's what he tried to do when I showed up. And maybe he was trying to scare you off the case. He's got a lot at stake here. The old murders, Jimmy, the necklace. He wasn't ever tried for the Carswell murders, and there's no statute of limitation on murder. He could fry."

"Your brain's what's fried. Don't forget that the Raeburns were on that elevator, too. They're not above paying to get the job done; they proved that with Jimmy." She cupped his chin and kissed his soft warm lips. God, she liked kissing him even when she was mad at him. "I'm going for clothes and I'll be back and when I get here you better be asleep."

He slid under the blanket and closed his eyes. "You swear you're not going into the attic?"

"Don't worry. I've had enough excitement for one night."

"That wasn't a swear."

"I swear. I swear." *I swear to do as I darn well please.* She waited till his breathing slowed to deep and steady. Carefully she searched the dresser, finding Donovan's knife to use for bullet digging. Inching open the nightstand bit by bit she took his Glock. One trip to the attic unarmed was enough, and this time she'd have Charlotte with her. No one else was getting hurt. She kissed Donovan on the forehead, then headed for the door.

Donovan dunked his head under the cold shower and added shampoo, wondering how long before he could dunk his whole body instead of just washing up. And he needed cold water all over, lots of it, because he was mad as hell. Bebe stole his gun. She lied to him. She went into that attic, he'd bet his life on it, and someone was out to get her. There were a lot of questions about this case, but that someone was after Bebe was not a question at all. It was for sure.

He splashed more cold water, his anger not subsiding one bit. She wasn't picking up her cell, so who knew where the hell she was now? In some dark alley bleeding to death. Dammit! He had to get out of this room and find her and . . . and then he'd ground her or nail her foot to the floor because that was the only way he could keep her in one place.

Drying off, he tied the towel around his middle and headed into the bedroom as the door burst open and Bebe pushed in a room-service cart complete with silver-covered plates and a rose in a vase. "You're never going to believe this," she said, excitement filling her voice. Her cheeks were pink, blue eyes bright and flashing, blond hair long and flowing, and he already knew what was under the frumpy brown suit. Not one damn thing frumpy, just all gorgeous, delectable Bebe. And she was okay. Relief washed over him and she looked at him and gave that smile that turned him inside out.

She lifted the silver cover, revealing eggs and all the trimmings. "Hungry?"

"For you," he said in a soft growl. "In my bed, flat on your back, my face buried between your legs." Relief overload? Is that why he said that?

Her gaze cut to his, stayed there, and she dropped the silver lid onto the food with a loud clatter. "I don't think that's on the menu."

He walked toward her.

"You're hurt and I'm mad at you because you lied about meeting Cleveland and you're mad at me because I stole your gun and knife and I went into the attic, but Charlotte was with me and no one else came along and—"

"Cupcake, I'm not that mad right now. I'm betting neither are you and let's talk about the attic later and me pissed later." He dropped his towel, her eyes zeroing in on his erection as he came to her and undid her pants. They started to slide off her, but she grabbed them.

"You don't want?"

"I want." She pulled a condom from her back pocket.

"I'm not the only one full of surprises."

She eyed his dick. "But you're the one with the bigger surprise. Make that biggest surprise I ever saw." She dropped her jeans, heavy with his gun and knife.

"Black bikini panties?" A smile softened his face. "You did it; you believed me when I said you were beautiful."

She shook her head, her hair gliding over her shoulders driving him crazy. "I like to feel pretty. I like the feel of silk and I never knew that before." She took his dick between her warm fingers. "I like the feel of you and I've known that for a while now. I'm still not sure how we wound up here. This was supposed to be breakfast."

He slowly ran his hands over her bare bottom. "You're not in any shape to be doing this, you know." She looked at his dick again. "Well, actually, you are in the right shape, but Doc Stevens said you had to take it easy."

"There are easy ways."

"Right." She slid onto the cart, dishes of food and glasses of orange juice crashing to the floor.

He smiled. "Your legs are apart, just the way I wanted." He unbuttoned her blouse. "And I'm going to see your breasts in the sunlight and taste your nipples and watch them turn pink with desire and the areolae flush and rosy and know it's all because of me." He kissed her lips. "You're all for me."

He peeled her blouse over her naked shoulders, leaving her in a black silk teddy. "No bra?"

"I'm not big enough to really need one and with the teddy under the blouse and . . ."

"I like it." He grazed his palm over her breasts, her nipples like pearls under the thin material. "I think you got everything you need."

She blushed, then pulled the teddy over her head, and the delicious hard pearls were right there in front of him for the taking. He licked one, then the other, her gasps the only sounds in the room. They were such lovely sounds. "I want you, Donovan."

And that sound was even better. He ripped open the blue foil packet. "I want you, too, Bebe." And then he was sliding into her, her hot wet flesh parting for him, yielding, taking him in, making him one with her. Her legs parted wider, her hips arching and her head dipping back, revealing her delicate throat. Cupping her derriere, he buried himself in her completely, then withdrew so he could take her all over again. Would he ever get enough of this woman?

He plunged back into her. Never. He knew as soon as he climaxed with Bebe he'd want the experience all over again and again and again and again.

"Oh, Donovan," she panted, her head now resting on his shoulder. "I think that was the breakfast of champions, because you are some champion and I hope you didn't hurt your side because trying to explain this to Doc Stevens is more embarrassment than I want to deal with."

"I'm fine." He kissed her neck. "More than fine. But how are we going to explain this breakfast mess to the maids?"

She looked at him and laughed, her eyes sparkling. "I think I'll tell them the truth and let them eat their hearts out. See you tonight." She scooted off the table and collected her clothes.

"Wait a minute. We have sex and you leave? I thought that was the guy's role."

"Times are a-changing, Bubba, and I have to get back to the station, but I'll be at the morgue for the tarot card thing. What are you going to do with the rest of the day?"

"Read about tarot cards. Maybe Prissy can turn up something. Like you keep reminding me, this is the South and things are different."

Bebe pulled on her clothes. "The gun that shot you was the same one that shot Charlotte's parents. The bullet that nicked you was old, thirty or forty years. Forensics could tell by the lead content. No casing, so it's a revolver. .22 Smith and Wesson most likely with a silencer, or the shooter could have used a potato or even a can. .22s are easy to silence."

She ran her fingers through her hair to straighten it up, then headed for the door. "And that means we're looking for one suspect for everything going on. Least it narrows the playing field."

Donovan reclaimed his towel. "Yeah, to Cleveland."

"Or the Raeburns with an accomplice; I just have to find out who that accomplice is and I'll have my case."

"I already have a case."

Bebe faced Donovan, fatigue making little lines at her

eyes and mouth. He felt bad about that. He slept and she'd been working her ass off and she had such a nice one.

"Ray Cleveland may be guilty of running a gaming facility, but he's no killer."

"Cleveland admitted that his first wife was one he could live without. I think he had a plan to get the necklace and keep the money and his plan failed for whatever reason and he ended up killing the Carswells and now he's forced into keeping things going because we're on to him."

"Or the Raeburns hired someone who had access to an old untraceable gun from somewhere and someone who knows this town and the people in it. A professional."

"Then why go and hire Jimmy?"

"Their original accomplice is getting nervous. And another thing you need to keep in mind is that Cleveland's home-grown Savannah. He can shoot even better than me. If he meant to hit you, I'd be picking out funeral flowers and pretty songs instead of having this conversation. He'd have a gun that could pick the gnat off a donkey's butt at five hundred yards in the dead of night. Savannah boys know their firearms, Yank, and getting ones not registered is no problem. He wouldn't be rattling your cage with a .22 peashooter."

"If he wanted to keep the heat off himself he would. He's guilty, Bebe, and I'm going to prove it to you."

She pulled his knife and gun from her pants pocket and put them on the dresser. "Thanks for the loaners. Maybe tonight we'll get lucky and see where that necklace is."

"Sweetcakes, I just got damn lucky!" He watched the door close and sat down. A carafe somehow survived sex-on-the-cart. He took a cup from the carpet and poured coffee. He wasn't a very nice guy. He was screwing Bebe two ways. One way was good, damn good, and one way he wasn't leveling with her. He hadn't told her about Joe

Earl and the Raeburns. That little bit of info would help her case. Joe Earl could get an old gun easily enough, he wouldn't shoot Donovan to kill him—cops don't kill cops—and Joe Earl had been in Savannah for over thirty years.

Except something didn't feel right about the Raeburns or Joe Earl. But everything felt right about Cleveland, and Donovan felt that clear though to his gut. Cleveland had motive and opportunity and he ran a gambling casino. A crook was a crook. And Donovan was a bastard. If he put Cleveland away, he could live with the bastard part.

The question was could he live without Bebe, because that's where all this was heading.

Evening cooled the air as Bebe parked her PT. She was late for the reading and Prissy was going to have a hissy and what else could go wrong today and that was a dumb thing to think because Dara came around the corner. "Heading for the morgue? How fitting. Is that where you're living these days?"

"You know I live on Taylor."

"Oh, that's right. Funny that you should mention it. I had lunch the other day with your landlord and convinced him to make your complex pet-free. Keep down on maintenance, it'll save him money. Guess you'll have to find homes for those mangy felines you pick up, or maybe you'll just have to put the little dears to sleep."

Dumbstruck like she always was, Bebe stared after Dara. Donovan parked his car and got out. "What now?"

"She wants to kill my cats."

"There's some reason she goes out of her way to drive you crazy. It's like she won't let it go. But why."

"That's the way Dara gets her jollies."

"Maybe it's a distraction. Tie you up in knots and keep

the heat off the important stuff. This goes beyond basic dislike, this is premeditated and she knows how to get to you. Are you investigating Dara for any reason?"

"I try and stay as far away from that witch as I can. Always have."

"She's keeping you off balance, Bebe. When you were a kid it was easy, but you're not a kid anymore, so she has to work harder at it. Do you have anything on Dara at all?"

"I'd like to have a cement truck on Dara. Does that count?" He grinned and she instantly felt better. "How are you doing? Did our little exercise hurt you any? We probably shouldn't have—"

He kissed her. "Best exercise I've ever had and we definitely should. I got some information on Shipley and Edwina. With them being from Boston it was easy. They might be greedy, but they're clean."

"There's some reason they weren't left the necklace in the first place. Do you realize we've been here for about five minutes and we now have two more questions to add to our long, long, long list of questions. Think we'll ever get any answers?"

"For crying in a bucket," Prissy said from the doorway. "You're late as can be and here you are chatting away on the sidewalk without a care in the world."

Donovan followed Bebe up the steps. "I'm sorry. I had work and Donovan had work and—"

"I wasn't born yesterday. One look at you two and anyone can tell you're off doing the hanky-panky even with Donovan needing recuperation. You already missed the reading, because it had to be at sundown with light passing to dark being the best time for such things." She led them into the kitchen with Charlotte, Brie, Anthony, and Vincent staring wide-eyed over three red lit candles and pile of cards on a black silk scarf on the table.

Bebe took a seat with Donovan and Prissy. Bebe said, "What's going on? You all look like you've seen a—"

"Do not say the 'g' word," Prissy whispered. "We've had an episode." She looked smug. "I think I'm getting better at this stuff."

The candles flickered, the lights blinked, and everyone gasped. "See," Prissy said. "Good mojo."

"Everything in the reading fit," Anthony whispered, a catch in his voice. "The card that is the Fool turned up. It tells of a long journey with nothing but faith and finding what you seek. That is Vincent and myself coming here, so it is true. The Four of Swords says there is a connection to tombs and cemeteries and here we are sitting in a morgue. The Ten of Pentacles says we will have great material success after a long struggle. We are all happy about that, as we will be finding the necklace. But there was also the High Priestess."

"And that means there are secrets," Prissy said.

Bebe exchanged looks with Donovan. "You are getting good. There are so many secrets about this case there should be a whole deck of those Priestess cards. You didn't happen to get any answers, did you? We could use some answers. Get anything with a gun or bullet?"

Bebe rummaged in her purse and pulled out a slug. "Like this one? The one that got Donovan is with forensics, but Charlotte and I dug this out of the attic floor at Magnolia House. The shooter fired more than once."

Brie held it in her palm. "Well, my goodness, who would think that something so small like this could be so heavy?" She dumped it into Prissy's palm. "Feel."

Prissy gasped and dropped the bullet on the table with a solid thunk. She pushed her chair back, her eyes black as the silk scarf on the table. "Bad bullet."

Bebe looked around for a cookie. There had to be a

cookie here somewhere. "The way I see it, it's a good bullet. It missed me."

Prissy took Bebe's arm and looked her in the eyes. "You're linked with this bullet, honey." Prissy held out her arms. "Looky here, goose bumps. King-sized ones. I get these feelings and they're for real. Remember Griff's check when he first came to Charlotte four weeks ago and everything started to go wacky. I picked up that check and got the bumps then, too. The bumps are not to be treated lightly."

"It's just a bullet," she said to Prissy to downplay the situation because she was right, the check thing was a definite goose bump hit and maybe this was, too. Bebe put the slug back in her purse. "I have to get back to the station and finish up some paperwork." She said to Vincent and Anthony, "I think you're on the right track. The jewels are probably here . . . somewhere."

BrieAnn followed her to the door, Donovan trailing behind. Brie kissed her cheek. "Be careful, you hear? I'm spending the night with Prissy if you need anything. You're looking so tired."

"Dead bodies and getting shot and another Dara encounter makes me grumpy."

"Dara?"

"Don't ask." Donovan joined her on the steps and BrieAnn closed the door. He sat and pulled her down with him. "Do you believe in Prissy's connection theory? You sure got out of there fast enough."

"Psychics can pull off some pretty weird stuff. At the station we've used them to find missing people and they do help steer us in the right direction. Prissy's bumps are all I have to go on."

Bebe stood. "That's it! I am so done with Ray Cleveland as a killer. We're going to go talk to him right now and end this connection idea before it goes any further. I know he's innocent, but everything keep coming back to him and we have to find out why." She got in the PT, Donovan on the other side, and she floored the accelerator, tires squealing. Dodging other cars, she hit seventy, eighty, eight-five across the bridge and into the dense black of sky-over-sea of Thunderbolt Island.

"You could get a ticket driving like this, you know."

"I've got connections at the police department, and, besides, everyone knows the PT. I just want this done with, and the reason you're here is because when I do find out what's going on, I want you around to hear it for yourself." She swung onto the sandy road, fishtailing right and left, the lights of the restaurant looming ahead. She pulled to a stop in the less-than-crowded Monday-night parking lot and reached for the handle to get out till Donovan stopped her.

"We're going in there. I didn't come here for nothing. I want to know what's going on and—"

"Sh." Donovan pointed out the window. "You're going to have to wait in line if you want to see Cleveland tonight. Isn't that him and Judge Montgomery over there on the end of the docks? And they aren't discussing the price of boats and fish." Donovan sunk down, Bebe following. "Cleveland looks pissed as hell. He and the judge, now that's a meeting I never expected and . . . holy crap, he just punched out the judge!" They watched Montgomery stagger to his feet, then leave, and Cleveland storm his way back to the restaurant.

"What the hell was that all about? It was a lot more than 'keep your son away from my daughter.' Cleveland would just have told the judge to go suck an egg and that Beau and Brie could do anything they wanted. Besides, the judge would have taken it up with Brie. Why go to Cleveland? This was something between the two of them. Something personal. Now what's their connection?"

Donovan stroked his chin. "BrieAnn's their link, but why would they be fighting over her?"

Bebe grabbed Donovan's arm. "Oh crap, the reason BrieAnn, Charlotte, Prissy, and I are blood sisters is because we were all adopted at the same time, had no brothers and sisters and were pretty much outcasts at school because we weren't really part of any family. Who your mama and daddy are matters down here. A few weeks ago Charlotte found out her parents were the Carswells, who were murdered, Prissy found out her grandmother is Minerva, I'm the bastard child of some debutante who paid Dara to take me, and that leaves BrieAnn the orphan and Cleveland with his daughter missing at the exact same time."

"Wouldn't Cleveland connect the dots if we did?"

"There were four baby adoptions that year and all of them questionable as to who the real parents were. Cleveland assumed his daughter went with his wife, so there was no reason to narrow it down to BrieAnn. Now the three of us know our pasts and that leaves . . ."

"BrieAnn. She was the one who gave the bullet to Prissy, not me. I'm guessing the judge has known all along and figured with things heating up, he better come clean. He probably got Brie from Ray's wife. She said she'd ruin Ray's life and what better why than to have his daughter right here all the time? The judge figured he'd save Brie from being raised by Cleveland, a crook, someone on the brink of going to jail, least that's what he thought then, and Cleveland's been under a cloud of suspicion ever since. The judge decided to tell Cleveland before he starts to suspect. With all that's happened he'd put it together soon enough."

"What do we do now? Cleveland is in no frame of mind for a little chat. And we can't tell BrieAnn anything yet. We're just operating on speculation here, nothing but circumstantial evidence. It's not like we're sitting on birth certificates or adoption papers. We don't know the particulars of what happened thirty years ago when Cleveland's wife left him, and it could be we got this all wrong. Only one person has all the details. Tomorrow I'm paying the judge a visit and getting some answers." She fired up the PT and headed out of the parking lot.

"How do you think Brie's going to take the news if all this is right?"

"She loves the judge; they'll get beyond what happened all those years ago. After all, he was trying to protect her, do what was best at the time. She and Ray Cleveland have always gotten along, too. He respects her charity work, even had a few fund-raisers out at the Cove, though to tell you the truth I don't see much of Ray in Brie. The girl can't gamble at all. She doesn't know twenty-one from sixty-one, she has no poker face, all her emotions are right out there on her face, and she'd pass out cold if she ever touched a gun. But the kindness and caring for others is there. She's got Ray's good qualities that way, and now she'll have a brother and . . . Holy jumping Jehoshaphat!"

"People really say things like that?"

Bebe swerved the car to the side of the road and hit the brakes. "There's another glitch. Brie and Beau together."

"They don't have the same parents. Ray isn't Beau's biological dad."

"In this town that's close enough. They both have the same father and if they do get married that's what it's going to look like. There will always be talk and tongues wagging and if they have kids that will just add to it. It's not wrong but it sure muddies the waters. Brie has to know what's going on. No wonder the judge and Aldeen have been moving heaven and earth to get Brie to go with Lamont. She's spending the night with Prissy, but tomorrow . . ."

"Tomorrow you visit the judge and see what he has to say and it ain't gonna be pretty. Want me to come?"

"I can do this and you need some rest." She touched his cheek. "Thanks for not jumping out of the speeding car on our way here. I think I'm losing it."

"I think you've got everything you need and more." He kissed her slowly, his lips making love to hers. "I know a nice apartment where three cats are hanging out, one in a purple cast. Maybe we should grab a pizza and cans of tuna and see what happens next."

"You're an invalid, Yank, and you double-crossed me and—"

He kissed her, shutting her up. "Can we not keep score for tonight? It gets you and me farther and farther apart. I don't want to be apart, I want us together and the only thing we have to worry about till tomorrow morning is pepperoni or sausage, thick crust or hand-tossed, and do we really want anchovies and extra cheese?"

She closed her eyes for a moment. A few hours of sleep with Donovan would be heaven. "If we don't do anchovies, three cats will be pissed. Why can't every night be this way? Pizza, cats, your place or mine?"

"It could get boring."

"I love boring." She kissed him. "And I think I'm falling in love with you."

# Chapter Nine

BrieAnn handed her keys and a tip to the valet driver at the Magnolia House. "Morning, Ms. BrieAnn," he greeted her with a smile. It was kind of silly to drive here when she could just as well slip though the back, but the shrubs were terrible overgrown. That might be fine and dandy for privacy, but could very well give a woman bad hair and that was one of the three major sins of a Southern lady. The other two sins were bad manners and bad cooking. But besides all that, she needed to look her best because Ms. BrieAnn Montgomery had set her mind on seducing Mr. Beau Cleveland nice and early this fine Savannah morning and nothing was going to stop her.

She headed for the elevator till she spotted Daemon Rutledge. Just the man she needed. "What an excellent morning it is, Mr. Rutledge," she greeted, hooking her arm though his and guiding him to a nook in the lobby. "I was wondering if you could do me a teensy little favor?" She lowered her voice. "Might you tell me what room Beau Cleveland's staying in while he's here?"

"I believe he's getting ready to check out."

"Then I suppose I should make my visit right quick. And I do have a little something else. With you appreciating the evening spring garden tours as much as I do, I made a reservation for you and a guest followed by dinner at the Pink House. We both know they have the best garlic grits in Savannah, and this month they're featuring California wines. I think you'll have a fine time."

"I do need to be watching my cholesterol; the old ticker isn't what it used to be. All this good Savannah eating. But now and then it can't hurt to enjoy life a bit." He smiled and kissed her cheek. "That is certainly nice of you, but not necessary at all and—"

"My sincere pleasure, Mr. Rutledge. I wouldn't have it any other way."

Rutledge printed numbers on a pad he took from his inside pocket and handed it and the rose from his lapel to Brie. "I know white ones are your favorite, but red's lovely, too. It is indeed a lovely day, almost as lovely as you, my dear."

Brie caught the elevator to the third floor. She stuck the red rose in the buttonhole of her green sweater and smoothed out the matching dress from page one-thirty-six of Neiman Marcus spring catalog, then knocked on Beau's door.

"Brie? What are you doing here?" Beau took her hand and all but yanked her inside, then looked both ways as if the FBI was sure to be on her trail. She handed her fine handsome man the blue box tied in a white bow. "For us."

He opened the box. "Two dishes?"

"From Blue Ridge pottery. The little apples aren't too fussy, so I thought you'd like them and they're perfect for picnics." She put the box on the fireplace mantel. "But you're looking all flustered, sugar." She pressed herself to him and teasingly fluttered her lashes. "And I'm here to make you feel even more that way. In fact when I get through with you, Beau honey, you're going to be downright spent!" She backed him flat against the wall, enjoying all his fine hard muscles pressing against her.

"This isn't a good idea, Brie," he said panting. Nice to know she wasn't the only one excited. "Did anyone see you come here?"

"People at the front desk, of course, and Mr. Rutledge. He is a sweet man. What is your problem? It's no crime for me to be coming up here, now is it? I'm old enough and you're old enough and we're both consenting." She kissed him hard. "In fact I'm consenting all over to the point where I can hardly contain myself." She took off her sweater. "You like?" she asked twirling around, her dress fluffing out in a circle.

"Yeah, right, sure. Very pretty."

"Well, it's going to look a lot prettier on the floor." She unzipped the back and let the dress slide off, leaving red bikini pants and bra. "See," she said putting her hands under her breasts. "Sweet and Perky. I named them just for you." Then she jumped into his arms and locked her legs around his waist, his hand supporting her bottom. "You came to my place two nights ago, sugar, so it's my turn to come over to your place and play. Take me to bed, Beau, and make me a happy woman."

"I can't."

She laughed. "That there bulge I saw a second ago is either some piece of big old hose you happen to be carrying around in your pocket for some reason, or you're as glad to see me as I am to see you. And now that we have all that misunderstanding about you thinking I'd be put off by your injuries out of the way, we can start dating and romancing."

She slid down to a standing position, then tugged him over to the bed, pushing him backward, sprawling across the comforter. "And here comes some romance," she said. "Ready or not and I know you're plenty ready."

She leaped onto the bed, the mattress quivering when she landed beside him, except Beau scrambled away and stood by the side of the bed. He ran his hand through his blond-streaked hair that she loved so much.

"No! This isn't a good idea." He held up his hands. "We're done here, Brie."

"Beau, honey, we haven't even got a good start, but I promise we're going to have a fine finish."

He picked up her dress and her sweater and tossed them to her on the bed. "I mean it, we're through. I shouldn't have come to your house the other night. That was a mistake. Bad judgment on my account, really, really bad judgment. What the hell was I thinking? You have to go right now and not come back and I'm not coming to you, either."

She knelt on the bed, her heart pounding. "You have someone else?"

"Well, sort of, that's one way of putting it. There is another person I'm involved with and—"

"Another! Someone else besides me? How could you! I hate you, Beau Cleveland!" She hopped off the bed, stomped up to him, and socked him in the jaw. He stumbled back, knocking over a chair.

She held her hand. "That hurt! It never looks like it hurts in the movies; they just do it."

Holding his jaw, he said, "Let me see your hand."

"No!" She yanked it away. "I'm fine. Don't you dare touch me." She snatched her dress up and pulled it on, then retrieved her cardigan and started for the door, stopped, and turned. "Is LulaJean back in the picture?"

"It's not LulaJean, it never has been. It's another interest, like you said."

"You betrayed me, Beau Cleveland, and I hope you rot in hell! I hope your big old do-da falls off. I hope you become a girl and then you'll know how it feels to get messed over by a guy. I hate you and we are finished for good. You can toy with a girl's heart just so many times before she throws in the towel! Well, I'm throwing."

Brie stormed out of the room and slammed the door behind her. How could she be so wrong about Beau? She kicked the door, putting a scuff on her taupe strappy sandals.

"Ohmygod, there you are," Bebe said, running down the hall full tilt. She flattened herself across Beau's door, looking like a big old spider with her arms and legs extended out. "You can't go in there."

"Too late."

"What!" Bebe turned the color of Brie's sweater. "Why didn't you pick up your phone? I called and called and you were spending the night with Prissy, so I thought I was safe especially since you said you and Beau were quits and so when I couldn't reach you this morning I came here right quick and Donovan went to your house to see if you were there and why didn't you pick up your blessed phone?"

"I had other things on my mind like a special morning with a certain someone, but that sure didn't work out the way I planned and I'm taking away your Starbucks card. You are on double espresso overload. You're acting downright nutty as a fruitcake."

Bebe squinted her eyes shut and gritted her teeth. "Did you and Beau . . . do it?"

"Once and for all, we are done broken up for good." She lowered her voice. "And that we never did the nasty is probably for the best and why in the world are you so concerned about all this that you'd come over here in the first place?"

"Let's get out of here."

"Amen to that." BrieAnn stomped to the elevator that was already waiting. When it shut, she said, "Beau finally opens up to me about things and why he can't perform and now he doesn't want to perform and has someone else in his life, which makes no sense at all, but since when did men make sense and what is wrong with you? Honey you look like you're going to have heart failure right here in this elevator."

Bebe held out her trembling hand. "Aftershock."

"We'll get you something to eat and you'll be better in no time. Soak up some of that caffeine. I think it's already starting to curl your hair, it looks a bit fried today. What kind of conditioner are you using?"

The elevator doors parted to, "Why, Daddy, what are you doing here?" Her father's creased forehead morphed smooth and he beamed the way he always did when he looked at her, as if she were the finest prize in all Savannah. "Bebe and I were going for breakfast; she's in need of nourishment. You simply have to come join us."

"I should go," Bebe said. "This isn't a good idea for me to be here." She looked at the judge. "But if you're free later on this morning I'd like to stop by and—"

"But we're all here right now, so there's no need for later on," Brie said, feeling better by the minute. "Nothing like having family and friends around to make a body feel better." She took Bebe's hand. "Some Magnolia House blueberry muffins will fix you right up."

"I'm in total agreement," the judge said, draping his arm around her and guiding her toward the outdoor patio where other guests were brunching under the blue umbrellas.

The judge held her chair the way a true gentleman does for a lady and the way Beau always did, too. Forget Beau. Beau was a creep, she reminded herself. The judge took his chair and draped his napkin across his lap. "So you two were here visiting Charlotte, I suppose?"

"Not exactly." Brie huffed. The waiter left a basket of muffins and Brie selected one. "You might as well know it all. I was here to see Beau, but before you get in a state you need to hear that it didn't work out and now Beau and I are through and this time it's for real and I'm not going back. He's made it crystal clear he wants nothing more to do with the likes of me. For a while there, I thought we could truly make things work, but that's not going to happen, so you can rest easy and tell Mama the same thing."

The judge arched his brow and selected a muffin. "Is that right?"

"And . . ." Brie watched her daddy methodically butter just the way he always did, a bit here, a bit there, not too much, just the proper amount. "What did you go and do?"

The judge smiled at Brie. "Excuse me?"

"I know how you and Mama feel about Ray and Beau and that me having anything to do with Beau was driving you both over the edge to the point where you were ready to marry me off to Lamont for a seat on the Telfair Museum board and voting privileges at the Oglethorpe Club. Then I tell you Beau and I are through and all I get is an 'Is that right?' "

"Well, sweet pea, I am mighty thrilled, but—"

"You should be thrilled to your toes, grinning like a cat lapping cream, kissing me on the cheek, and telling me how I'll have men lined up from here to Beaufort and I'm not to fret any over the likes of Beau Cleveland. You'd make a big deal of this, but you didn't." She folded her hands in her lap. "It was like you knew before I told you. And why were you here in the first place, Daddy? What is going on? I know there's something. You got that look about you like when you're trying a big case and can't tell a soul what you're thinking, but you're thinking plenty."

"BrieAnn, you're making entirely too much over this breakup and in the presence of company." He nodded to Bebe, who hadn't moved since she took her chair but kept her eyes on the judge. He put down his muffin and took

Brie's hand. "Another man more to your liking *will* come along, I promise."

"You mean more to *your* liking, and I'm thinking that with you being a judge and Ray Cleveland . . . well, being Ray Cleveland, and Beau suddenly not being Beau at all, you somehow got your fingers in the pie. Am I right? This is my life we're talking about here. You can't arrange it to suit you even if you do think you're doing the right thing."

"Lower your voice, now, you hear? Since the day I brought you home, I've looked out for you, only wanted the best for you, and Ray Cleveland isn't the best at all."

"Even if he is your father," Bebe blurted out in a rush.

Brie dropped her muffin in her lap and stared at Bebe. The judge froze in place, his knife poised in midair. Brie managed, "What are you talking about?"

"Last night I saw the judge talking with Ray Cleveland out at the Cove and it wasn't a friendly kind of talk. You're their only link, Brie. The judge couldn't have you running after Beau if he was your . . . It just wouldn't be right at all."

Brie felt her world start to unravel. Like a piece of yarn on a sweater, pull it and all the stitches that took so long to make simply vanish into a long meaningless line. She looked back to the judge. "Mr. Cleveland? Me? That's why you and Mama were so adamant to keep Beau and me apart?" She could barely get the words out, she could barely breathe.

"I don't know where you're coming from," the judge said to Bebe, his face more angry than Brie had ever seen. "Or where you got your information, but I can only hope you are a better police officer other times than you are now. I don't want Brie to have anything to do with the likes of Beau Cleveland because he and his father are criminals. Period, and that is a very big period in my book. I will not have my daughter mixed up with crooks and thieves. And since BrieAnn seemed too smitten to understand the situation, I intervened, and that is all there is to it."

Brie gripped the edge of the table. "Define intervened, daddy."

"BrieAnn, your mama and I are overprotective, I know that, but this situation had to stop."

"Tell me what you did."

Almost in a whisper that was laced with steel, the judge said, "I made it very clear to Beau that if he did not stop seeing you on all accounts I would give Detective McCabe that warrant for the Cove he so badly wants and then Beau's daddy would wind up in jail just where he belongs. That's what I was telling Ray Cleveland last night. If he didn't get Beau away from you I'd see he went to prison for a long time."

"You threatened the man I love? And you threatened his family?"

"BrieAnn, you do not love this man."

"More now than ever knowing what he had to endure to protect his own father from you. You are reprehensible and I no longer want us to be in the same room. In fact I don't want to be in the same city with you."

She stood and tossed her napkin in her chair. "Bebe, we need to go." She said to her father, "Do not follow us or I will throw the biggest hissy Savannah has ever seen, and, as we both know, that covers a lot of territory."

"BrieAnn, please." Her father's eyes were sad and tired, but no more so than her heart. She choked back a sob and somehow made it across the patio and out the back exit, then she ran to the line of trees, found the overgrown archway, and fought her way though the brush, not caring diddly about her hair or shoes or anything else except putting distance between herself and her father, the hero of her life. How could he?

"Wait up," Bebe huffed from behind her. Covered in

leaves and sticks, she caught up with Brie and took her arm. "Dear God, Brie, what was I thinking? It just came out. I should have waited till I had all the facts, that's what I wanted to see the judge about today, to confront him and make him tell you that you were Ray's daughter. I'm so sorry. I thought you had a right to know and then it turns out I have it all backward. I'm never going to figure out the answers to anything. I keep getting it wrong and this one was huge and hurt you."

"And you thought I might be sleeping with my . . . not that Beau was my brother for real but plenty close enough to cause a fine scandal." In spite of all the mess, a little laugh bubbled up her throat.

"Yeah, and there was that."

"I can only imagine what Ray Cleveland told my father he could do with his warrant." Brie sat down on the little bench and Bebe sat beside her. "Do you forgive me? I didn't want to say anything to you until I talked to the judge and then he was there and I opened my big mouth."

"Good thing you did or I wouldn't have known about Daddy's threatening Beau. Besides, you thought you were protecting me and you stood up to Daddy for that reason, and not all that many people can stand up to that man." She kissed Bebe on the cheek. "You had the right intentions, just the wrong conclusion."

She picked a pink tulip and studied it. "So on a happier note, you and Donovan were at the Cove last night spying on my father and I'm guessing you didn't go home alone. When you were at the morgue last night I saw the way he looks at you and the way you look at him. He's a keeper, Bebe."

"Honey, he's a Yank!" They both giggled the way they used to back in high school when they shared a secret about a boyfriend. "You'll just have to convert him, is all. Now I'm going inside that house of mine and pack a suitcase and get out of here. I'm done with this town and my parents. I can't stay one minute longer."

Bebe's eyes rounded. "What about me and Prissy and Charlotte? Pinky swear? Blood sisters forever? Sound familiar? For crying out loud, you can't just up and leave us."

"I'm going to find Beau. Thunderbolt is fifteen miles away. I'm a Savannah belle; we don't travel all that far from our roots. I'll text and let you know what's happening, well some of what's happening." She pursed her lips and batted her eyes. "Beau Junior is a cute name, don't you think?" She rocked her arms as if holding a baby.

"BrieAnn!"

She went to the top of the stairs and held her arms wide to the world. "You're looking at a woman in love who finally . . . and I do mean finally . . . intends to get herself some satisfaction that she so richly deserves."

Afternoon sun and a sea breeze wafted through the back kitchen screen door. Beau laid out two pieces of toast, topped them with thin slices of turkey, then ham and tomato, and covered it all in Ray's special cheese sauce. Savannah hot brown, was there anything better? Southern comfort food at its best. After lying to Brie about there being another woman in his life he needed some comfort. He felt lower than a snake's belly, but what else could he do?

Picking up the platter with one hand, he opened the oven with the other as BrieAnn stepped through the screen door looking more lovely than ever.

"You know, sweet thing, if you keep eating that stuff you got there, you'll have a heart attack before you're thirty."

"I'm already thirty-two. Brie? What are you doing here? You can't be here. You have to go right now and—"

"I talked to my daddy."

"Oh, crap." Beau kicked the oven closed and put down the platter. "This warrant thing is nothing to fool with. Your daddy's not fooling around here. He's serious and if he gives the warrant to Donovan—"

"He'll never see his daughter or his grandbabies again and he may not see them for a very long while as it is." She held out her suitcase and dropped it in the middle of the kitchen with a solid thunk.

"Grandbabies?"

She sauntered toward him, twitching her hips and strutting her stuff and Brie never strutted, except for now . . . and when she tried to seduce him on the boat. That was a great saunter. She slid her arms around his middle and reached into his back pocket, taking out his wallet. Opening it, she retrieved the condom he had there, dropped it on the floor and stamped on it. She looked him in the eyes. "Grandbabies."

She brought her mouth to his. "Lots of grandbabies. Unless you have any of those sexually transmitted diseases you hear about. I want you, Beau Cleveland, just the way God made you all unencumbered, and I'm damn tired of waiting to have you. Where's *your* daddy?"

"Ray? Minding the lunch crowd. I do dinner. We split it up that way so we both get some time off and I don't have any diseases and . . . grandbabies?"

"You expecting anyone else to come calling?"

He shook his head, because he didn't have any more words. She smiled and winked. Then she kicked off her sandals and shrugged out of her blouse, revealing her tiny pink bra. "Good thing," she purred. Then she pushed aside the hot-browns and slid herself up onto the table and held out her arms. "Lunch is served."

"I can't." He scooped her into his arms, the feel of her bare skin taking his breath away. "I mean I can't do what you want to do here right on this table. Honey, I'd never be able to eat another bite off this thing from thinking about . . . us doing what we want to do."

She buried her face in his neck, her hypnotic perfume filling his head, her giggles making his heart sing. He never had a singing heart before. In fact when he heard someone say such a thing or heard it in a song, he thought it was just plain stupid. Now Brie was really here with him smelling like sinful seduction and feeling like heaven. He got the singing thing. Kissing her all the while, he walked up the flight of steps to his room and gently laid her down in his bed. Seagulls cried outside his windows, the sound of the sea gently lapping carried up from below, the sky the bluest blue he'd ever seen in all his years.

"Come to me, Beau." She looked up at him, her auburn hair flowing out across his white pillow, her pink nipples pressing against lace.

"I want to remember you like this. Everything perfect because I swear I never thought it would happen. There was so much keeping us apart and yet, here you are."

"Here we are."

He sat beside her, the bed giving under his weight. He touched her cheek and as her delicious lips parted he kissed them, the sweet taste of BrieAnn Montgomery warming him all over as if he'd taken a bite of sunshine.

Her arms circled his neck, bringing his chest to hers, and he slid his hand under and unsnapped her bra. He kissed her neck and cleavage, then eased up her bra, taking her left nipple slowly, deeply into his mouth.

She sighed, the sound turning him on all the more. He licked her right nipple, making it hard and exquisite. "You're wonderful and I have to see all of you. I can't wait another minute, sugar. Seems I've been waiting forever." He peeled her bra from her shoulders, then ran his finger down her middle, across her delicate navel, and un-snapped her slacks. The waistband opened to a thin ribbon of matching pink. Kissing her navel, he inched her pants open more to lace panties guarding the small dark patch of curls beneath he desperately wanted. Bending his head, he kissed there, the hot scent of sex surrounding him and driving him wild.

"I need you, Beau," she pleaded. "I need more."

He pulled off her slacks, taking the panties and revealing the small triangle, smooth thighs, then calves, then she was gloriously naked. "You're mine, all mine, I can't believe it. How'd I get so damn lucky?"

She giggled. "You haven't gotten lucky yet, sugar, but if you keep flattering me that way it could just happen."

He slid his fingers over her thigh, parted her legs, then touched the lips of her wet sex, waiting for him, wanting him, opening for him. Her breath caught and she grabbed his arm, her legs parting wider, giving him full access to her delicious secrets. "Oh, Beau, what you do to me. I'm so hot for you, honey."

A scorching fire roared through him as he slid in two fingers, stroking her faster, pushing deeper with each caress. Three fingers, her eyes glazing. He rubbed her clit with his thumb, applying more pressure, then covered her soft whimpers with his mouth, his tongue promising what was to come till she climaxed, her body quivering and tensing, her arms grabbing him so tight.

"Oh, Beau," she panted, her hot breath on his neck. "How could you and I didn't get a chance to do you and that's not right at all."

He gazed down at Brie, his Brie. "It was perfect. You are incredible and making love to you is a dream come true for me. I've laid in this bed thinking of you, wanting you with me forever and now . . ."

"I want to make love to you, too." She gazed at his body stretched next to hers, and she squirmed out from under him and sat up.

"Going somewhere?"

"Oh, I hope so. And this time I'm taking you with me." She pushed him over onto his back and straddled his thighs, her delicious hot sex open and wide and wet across him. She unsnapped his jeans and before he could consider his legs and the scars there, she grabbed his jeans and yanked them and the briefs clean off him with more strength than a woman her size should possess. She tossed the jeans on the floor. And there he was in full view with all the scars he'd warned her about. But warning and seeing were two different things, and if she ran away he wouldn't blame her one bit.

"Well now, it looks like the doctors stitched you together pretty darn good, Beau Cleveland."

She put her hands to her hips. "But what went and happened to your do-da? It's looking all pitiful at the moment and you have to know I'm not in the mood for pitiful. I've waited much too long, been through too much drama for plain old limp-dick pitiful."

"And I got to tell you this is embarrassing as hell."

"You? You! And what about me? I'm the one begging and pleading here. But I'm thinking not for long." She took his limp dick between her silky hands, massaged and stroked, the limpness quickly fading.

"Well I'll be. You see that. It's coming back to life fine and dandy. Raising from the dead, it is. But it's still in need of some special Southern belle kind of resuscitating." And she took his erection into her delectable mouth, driving every ounce of oxygen right out of his body.

"Dear God, Brie," he hissed, his fists tangled in the sheets, fighting for control. "What are you doing to me, girl?" Her mouth was magic, her tongue and lips driving him to the brink.

Finally she said, "I'm firing your engines, honey, the best way I know how. And you know what, I think you're liking it." Then she licked the full length of him. The sensation was out of this world and watching Brie make love to him more erotic than anything he'd ever experienced.

"BrieAnn, honey. I'm only human."

"Amen to that, Beau Cleveland." She smiled wickedly. "Feeling a bit better now? Some would say you're looking downright frisky. I think I like the frisky part, Beau." She smiled and bit at her bottom lip as if hiding a secret. "Why, I think we have a new name here. Beau, Brie and . . . Frisky."

Never in a million years would he have thought the prim and proper Miss Montgomery would . . . name his dick! Just when he thought he knew everything about the South and the people and the women, this woman came into his life. "Where did you learn . . . How do you know just what to do?"

"Instinct. We women here in Savannah do know how to please our man, and sometimes it takes a bit more than fried chicken and cream gravy." Then she took his full length into her mouth again, making every cell in his body throb and his head nearly spin clean off his shoulders.

"Enough, sweetheart, enough."

Her eyes were pools of fire. "Never enough, Beau. And I'm thinking from here on out it's your turn." She gave him a sexy pose with her arms folded under her breasts pushing them up and out like some offering. "So come and get me, big boy, and I am emphasizing the big part." She eyed his dick. "Are you man enough?"

"I've never been one to back down from a challenge, BrieAnn, especially this particular one and especially now here with you."

Sitting up he snagged her unexpectedly around the waist. She yelped and giggled as she tumbled into his arms, the wonderful sound making him feel more alive than he had in a long time. He brought her down beside him. Kissing her, he leaned her back, her silky legs locking around his waist. Slowly, because he wanted to savor the moment and the look of love in her eyes, he eased himself into her.

His heart soared, the sounds of war fading, replaced by sunlight and ocean and BrieAnn. She was with him now and forever. At last he was home.

*At last,* Brie thought as she cuddled up close to Beau, listening to his heart beat slow and steady. "I love you," she whispered.

"I love you, too. We're going to make this work, I swear it."

"Especially if I happen to be pregnant. And if the culmination of our lovemaking is any indication of conception we will surely add to the population of Savannah. You are not lacking in the virility department. You do know how to fill a woman right nicely, Beau Cleveland."

He felt himself blush and she rolled over on top of him. "You do want babies with me, don't you? I guess this a mighty poor time to be asking."

"It's a great time. I can't imagine anything better than you and me and kids and all this great sex and—"

"Beau?" came Ray's voice from the kitchen. "Where are you, boy, and I'm hoping you're here? One of the cooks got sick and we're shorthanded in the kitchen and whose suitcase is this? Beau, are you heading out? Why in blazes did you buy a pink suitcase and a blouse? Is there something you're trying to tell me here, boy?"

"Well, dang." Brie grinned. "I do believe Grandpa's in the kitchen."

Brie giggled and Beau jumped up and snagged his jeans. "Don't go away now, you hear." He left and Brie pulled on her dress and went downstairs, listening to Beau and Ray talk about her. She went into the kitchen and snuggled up against Beau and said to Ray, "I have only the most proper intentions concerning your son. Fact is I intend to marry him and move in here with you two if you'll have me."

"Well I'll be." Ray grinned ear to ear and came over to Brie and kissed her on the cheek. "What a fine surprise right here in the middle of the day. You know I love you like a daughter, BrieAnn, and this is mighty good news, least that's the way I see it, but what do your mama and daddy think of your idea?"

She pushed back her hair. "Don't rightly care. You see, my daddy, with my mama's blessing, went out of his way to keep Beau and me apart. Of course you already know about that, since Daddy was here conversing with you last night on that very subject. I don't take kindly to someone controlling my life in that particular way, even if they do it all in the name of love and they are my parents. If they loved me, they'd love Beau, too. I can't abide living so close to them right now, so I'm moving out to Thunderbolt with you, where the company is far more pleasant to be around. Beau and I need to be heading off to Vegas tonight to get ourselves hitched, but after that I'm part of the family. And I want you to know I have no intention of being a freeloader and I will pull my weight around here. I'm right good at organizing dinners and serving guests."

Ray combed back his short hair that didn't need combing in any way at all and looked from Beau to Brie. "I can't image a better couple than you two, but you can't get married the way you said."

"But—" Beau started.

"Hear me out now, son. It's not that I don't want you two hitched but not in this fashion. It would be a big mistake, the kind that can't be undone once it's done and you have to live with the consequences forever. First off, BrieAnn has to go back home."

Brie folded her arms and held her chin high. "I most certainly will not go home."

Ray took her hand. "I know what it's like to lose a daughter, honey, and Lord knows there's no love lost between the judge and myself, but you and Beau can't build a future on his pain and your mama's. I can't be a part of having another man lose his baby girl on my account and deep down you both know that's no way to start married life. You want happiness, as much as you can possibly get. BrieAnn's parents will not cotton to this marriage, but if it's done proper with all the trimmings that will go a long way to smooth things over."

"I don't want to talk to either of them, and if they don't get over me being married to Beau, the man I love, it's their loss, not mine."

"You need to go home and live in your house and Beau needs to live here with me and you both need to go to the judge and Aldeen and tell them your intentions, preferably with a nice big diamond so Aldeen Montgomery can brag the size to her card club all the while acting indignant over such a match. And when I was out walking the other day I happened to notice that the Patterson-Wright house on East York is for sale, three or four million I suppose. A mighty fine old Savannah house if there ever was one. Make anyone right proud."

Beau's eyes covered half his face and Brie felt her tummy drop to her toes. Beau said, "Ray, I can't be affording something like that."

Ray grinned. "But I can, and it would be a proper wedding present and Aldeen would mightily approve even though she'd rather die than admit it. This is Savannah, and if things are done the right way and rather lavishly to boot, she and the judge will come around. They are pillars of Savannah and want their daughter to be that way, too, and money talks, sometimes as loud as pedigree."

Brie sighed. "I don't care a fig about being a pillar and pedigrees, all I care about is Beau."

"But you do love your mamma and your daddy, no matter how mad you are right now. You don't want to be getting married out of spite, sweet pea. Enjoy your engagement time together and the parties and the fuss and your big reception at the Telfair Museum or the country club with pictures taken at that gazebo in Whitfield Square like all the other brides do."

Ray kissed Brie on the forehead and then he kissed Beau the same way. "Everything's going to be fine." He turned to Brie. "Now you better be getting on back home. Your mama and daddy will be worrying themselves into a state if you're not on their doorstep by sundown and you're both going to need plenty of sleep if you're planning on showing them an engagement ring tomorrow."

Ray laughed. "And I best be getting back to work. After you two say your good-byes, I'm still needing you in the kitchen, Beau." He winked, then his eyes turned serious and a little misty. "I want you both to know this is the best news I've had in quite some time. I couldn't be happier for you and for me." He laughed out loud. "Because now I get to start thinking about all those grandbabies coming my way. I think Ray Junior is a fine name, don't you?"

BrieAnn pulled to the curb in front of her parents' brownstone. The live oaks lining Jones Street extended their long evening shadows. She took off her scarf that protected her hair when she had the top down on her convertible and slid out of the car. After climbing the brick steps, she used her key and let herself into the Montgomery family home. Daddy would be on the back veranda at this time having his martini before cook served dinner.

"BrieAnn," Daddy said, surprise brightening his eyes as he looked up from his *Wall Street Journal*. "Thank God, you're home. I thought you might not . . . It's mighty good to see you." He came to her and kissed her cheek. "I'm afraid your mama's not here right now."

"It's the monthly garden club dessert and lecture series and you should be thanking Ray Cleveland that I'm here. You need to know he's the one who sent me back to you. He said he knew what it was like to lose a daughter and he wouldn't wish that on anyone. If I had my way, Beau and I would be in Vegas tonight toasting our marriage. Mr. Cleveland made me promise to have a proper wedding in St. John's Church with all the trimmings. So tomorrow when Beau and I come here for dinner and I have a big ring on my finger and a fine house close to yours and a wonderful man at my side, I expect you and Mama to mind your manners and do the proper thing. And I also expect you to remember who to thank that Beau and I are in this house on Jones Street and not in a hotel room at the Bellagio." Then she turned and left.

*Chapter Ten*

Bebe glanced over at Donovan all big and hunky, still sleeping beside her. Getting shot had taken more of a toll on the man than he realized. He tired faster and slept more, but it sure didn't affect his good looks.

"Hi," he said, smiling up at her with dreamy eyes and looking very cuddly.

She whined and nibbled her bottom lip. "I think I'm a blooming saint. Fact is, they should build altars to me. Last night in the name of helping you heal and get well I refused this." She slid her hand under the sheet, down his muscular thigh, and cupped his morning erection all nice and hard. "And I want it."

He leaned over and gave her a deep kiss that reminded her of the deep, deep other thing she had on her mind. "There are many ways to make love, cupcake."

"And if you get all physical on me and break that wound open, I get to explain it to the ER nurse. I have to live in this town and I'll never hear the end of it. Things like 'Ball-busting Bebe' come to mind, and there are those who'd love to make that one stick. I suppose I'll have to live with Saint Bebe for a while."

She put on his shirt and went to the bathroom to brush her teeth and suddenly Donovan was behind her, his handsome need-a-shave face next to hers in the mirror. His dick pressed hard and firm and long against her left derriere cheek as his fingers slid between her legs, then beyond. She nearly swallowed her toothbrush. "Donovan."

"Spread your legs for me, sweetheart." And his fingers ventured farther still.

"I've never played around like this and . . . ohmygod you feel so good." Her legs parted more and she leaned back against him as he fondled her breasts through the shirt. She was barely able to stand as his fingers performed more magic.

He withdrew and turned her around and sat on the closed commode, his dick covered and ready.

"You're a fast worker."

"And this way there's no 'Ball-busting Bebe.' You get to do all the work. Provided you're in the mood."

"Any more in the mood and the mood would be over."

He unbuttoned his shirt she was wearing and kissed her navel, then took little bites along her waist. "It's going to be fun learning something new, I promise."

"Looks kind of big standing straight up there at attention like that, Yank."

"Boston boys grow 'em bigger."

"I think you're right. I'm just not all that sure about Southern girls being able to accommodate." She straddled him, one leg on each side. "You sure I'm not going to hurt you? Wanna give me some pointers on what to do here?"

"What feels good to you."

She eased herself down till the tip of his penis touched her intimately and suddenly hunger for the rest of him bolted through her like lightning. She could feel herself getting wet, her muscles relaxing and opening, her insides pulsing as she thought about what was to come.

Slowly, so as not to put any strain on him and because she wasn't exactly sure of what the heck she was doing, she inched herself down over him, her body yielding to his. As her breasts came level with his mouth, he kissed one nipple, then the other, making her insides hot and wild, her legs tremble. Then his mouth consumed hers as she straddled him, making him a complete part of her.

"Oh, Donovan." Her chest pressed tight to his and she twined her arms around his broad shoulders. Her eyes wouldn't focus, her heart beating faster than she could count.

"Do you like this?"

"I can feel you so deep inside, every inch of you. It's different this way than in bed." She swallowed. "I like it." Slowly she rose up, only to settle back down again, stroking his erection, stroking herself, his penis against her clit driving her insane.

"That's just right." His eyes glazed. "You sure you've never done this before?" His breaths came faster, his skin hot and damp next to hers. As terrific as this lovemaking was, the best part was pleasing Donovan. She made sex good for him just as he made sex incredibly good for her always.

Legs wider, one last time she took his length again. Her mouth mated to his and when she climaxed it was more than physical but a bonding of souls, one caring for the other, one wanting to please the other. She could give to him as much and as good as he gave to her and in that way they were truly one together.

She rested her head on his shoulder, the pulse in his neck keeping time with hers, both ebbing out of the heart attack zone. "I hope I didn't hurt you."

"What a way to go, sweetheart."

"That isn't funny." Her forehead touched against his and she looked him in the eyes and grinned. "Well, maybe a little funny, especially if we both croaked right now and this is how they found us. The gossips would love us forever. But right now I'm starved, are you starved? You get a shower and I'll get food."

"No way, I'm coming with you. You'll get me some sissy latté with mocha and extra whipped cream with cinnamon concoction and call it coffee."

"Mocha's good and who doesn't like whipped cream, but I was thinking more like a caffeine-free South African botanical carefully blended with vanilla and spices."

"Never ever mess with a man's coffee, especially if it includes the word botanical. Besides you have to help me shower; I'm too weak to do it alone."

"Are you going to milk this injury?"

"If it gets you into my shower, hell yes."

She laughed then kissed him. "I've never been happier in my life, Donovan McCabe, than I am right now." She kissed him again from the sheer joy of him being here with her. "You're Christmas and Halloween and the Fourth of July all rolled into one. You are amazing and I don't know how I got this lucky, but for once in my life, I did. God didn't forget my address, after all, it just took him a while to remember it, and then he sent me Donovan from Boston."

His eyes danced. "That's probably the nicest thing anyone's ever said to me. You make me happy, too, Bebe from Savannah." He stilled for a moment. "And after losing Sly I didn't think I'd ever feel that way again. I was just doing the next thing out there and trying to move on and not doing it very well. And then I came here."

"Do you think it'll last, that *we'll* last, in spite of all our problems?"

He kissed the tip of her nose, his brown eyes dark and sincere. "I do."

Those two words filled Bebe's head as she ran the shower. It wasn't a wedding or marriage *I do,* but it was a commitment all the same. He liked her. He really, really liked her with her ugly suits and frumpy shoes and baggy jeans. It didn't matter, because he thought she was beautiful just the way she was. She pulled her hair on top of her head and looked down at her body. She really looked. Maybe she wasn't a size twelve. Maybe a little smaller and then she wouldn't have to safety pin the waist. That made sense. And if she didn't have all that material hanging off her she wouldn't be so hot in the summer.

He climbed in beside her, water plastering his hair to his head and dripping off his nose. She handed him a loofah and a bottle of body wash.

"How about Dial soap and a washcloth?"

"I have that, but Brie gave these to me for Christmas. They look kind of fun." She squirted the apricot wash on her shoulders and across her breasts. "Feels kind of fun."

"Thank you, Santa." He made little round strokes across her breasts and over her navel, her front covered in bubbles floating into the tub. He turned her around.

"What about the rest of me in front, huh? There are some very interesting places up here, pal."

"Patience, Grasshopper." He stroked the loofah seductively over her shoulder, and then all the way down her spine to the small of her back, then he stopped.

"I'm not going to get clean this way, though I am getting really turned on."

"Did you know you have a birthmark?" He touched the indent of her backbone.

"I can't see it all that well. Is it looking weird?"

"Didn't anyone ever say anything when you wore your bathing suit?"

She looked at him over her shoulder. "That would be me in a two-piece suit. I barely have two-piece underwear. Besides, my skin in the sun gives a whole new meaning to lobster red. What's wrong? Is the birthmark getting all puffy?" She twisted her neck for a better view, but it didn't help.

"Should I have a doctor look at it? Is it still the shape of two petals together?"

"Or the shape of a seagull in flight. Where else is there a seagull?"

She turned around and kissed his chin. "Honey, this is Savannah. The little darlings are everywhere you go, pooping their brains out on the cars and statues and sidewalks. If we could just potty train them this town would be a lot better off."

He took her hand and led her out of the shower. "You should take a look. Do you have a little mirror?" She got one from the vanity and he swiped a towel across the bathroom mirror to remove the steam.

She focused the mirror and touched the birthmark. "I think it's okay, Donovan. It doesn't feel swollen and pretty much the way it's always looked to me, though I don't pay much attention. It's kind of out of the way there. I don't think I've got a problem."

"Think again, cupcake." He took her shoulders and looked her in the eyes. "There's a sign with a gull that looks exactly like this one. Exactly. We've both seen it many times. A trademark."

Bebe's gaze met Donovan's and suddenly all the air got sucked right out of the little bathroom. She couldn't breathe or move and she dropped the mirror, watching it shatter into a million silvery pieces on the tile floor and then everything went black.

Bebe gulped deep breaths as she stood on the wood dock in front of the screen door. Donovan had wanted to come with her, even insisted, but she needed to do this alone. This was about a father and a daughter and no one else . . . maybe. She'd gotten it wrong with BrieAnn and Ray, Bebe could be dead wrong this time, too, but this time there was more than a fistfight and a wayward bullet involved.

She could see through to Ray's kitchen, all neat with Windsor chairs around the big maple table the way it had been as long as she could remember. The lazy Susan in the middle was the one Beau made in shop in high school. It always held a jar of honey, salt and pepper, sugar bowl, and stack of napkins waiting to be rotated around at mealtime. All so . . . homey. Home. All this time. Home. Her home.

She knocked. "Mr. Cleveland? Are you there?" She knocked again out of sheer nerves. Her hand was shaking so bad it knocked all by itself.

"I'm coming, I'm coming. Just hold your britches on now, you hear, I'm getting dolled up in my work clothes." She heard his footsteps, then he hustled into the kitchen while tying his tie. He smiled when he spied her. "Well, now. Miss Bebe. To what do I owe the pleasure of you gracing my doorstep this fine Savannah morning?"

He held the door open, and she wished she'd brought Donovan. Suddenly she didn't know what to say, even though she planned it in her head for as long as she could remember. She swore she didn't want any part of parents who didn't want any part of her, yet, in the quiet of night when she was all alone, she wanted them more than air. "I . . ." She stood there, not knowing what to do.

"Why don't you come on in now that you made the trip all the way out here. You're looking kind of wan and puny, if you don't mind me saying so."

She felt her eyes tear and he said, "Honey, whatever it is, it can't be that bad." She stepped in, the door slapping closed. Then all was quiet except for her heart beating so loud Ray had to hear it, too.

"You know," she blurted to drown out the drumming. "That year we tied for the marksmanship trophy out at

Wilson's Park at that tournament. Did you ever think that was strange?"

"That I got my fanny kicked by a gorgeous blonde half my age?" He laughed. "I thought it was mighty embarrassing. You are some shot and everyone in Savannah knows it. I bet when those bad guys see you coming they just throw down their weapons. Did you come to rub it in?" He laughed again.

"Remember that Monte Carlo night last year at the Policeman's ball?"

"And you walked off with the grand prize of five hundred dollars? You bet I remember. I kept thinking I'm plum tickled you're a cop and not into frequenting my establishment. You could cost me a pretty penny if you had a mind to. You sure got a touch for blackjack."

"And you quit playing an hour before I did to let me win. We were neck and neck till you did that."

"Well now, I had some business calls to make is all."

"You've always been nice to me."

"You're easy to be nice to. Are you in trouble, sweetheart? What can I do to help? I'm pretty good at fixing things. You can count on me."

*Count on him.* Her eyes filled with more tears and her throat burned. "You . . . you could have looked for me harder. You could have tried harder. You shouldn't have given up so fast. I was here. Oh my God, I was here. All along I was right in front of you and I didn't know and you didn't know. You shouldn't have given up so fast. Why did you give up?"

"Give up what?"

"Give up on me and piggyback rides and good-night stories and being there when I won that spelling bee and on father-daughter dances. Things could have been so much better. There's all this." She waved her hand over the table. "And there's Beau and you." Her voice cracked. She turned around and lifted her blouse. Then she turned back slowly, because maybe she had this all wrong for the second time. "And there's . . . me?"

Ray seemed frozen in place. Not breathing. His gaze fused to hers and she knew from the shock, sorrow, and love all mixed together in his blue eyes so much like hers she didn't have things wrong at all. It was if a hundred-pound weight lifted from her shoulders. Surreal, as if she were seeing this happen outside her body.

"Lizzy?" It was barely a whisper.

"You named me Lizzy? Like in lizard?" She laughed through her tears because she was happy beyond words.

"Elizabeth. Your mother's idea after that Elizabeth Taylor person."

She had a name, a real name . . . even if it was after a movie star . . . from a real parent. "Least she didn't go with Cher."

She wiped away tears and Ray wobbled. Pulling out a chair, she sat him down. He blinked as if trying to wake up from a dream. Boy, did she know that feeling! "I . . ."

She sat down across from him and took his hands in hers. "You what?"

"I think Lizzy's a stupid name, too, always did." He held her hands tight enough to hurt, as if when he let go, she'd go, too. "Keep Bebe." He closed his eyes for a second, his broad strong shoulders sagging. "All this time," he said in a tortured voice that squeezed her heart. "I never knew, never suspected. Your mama divorced me for some cattle rancher in Brazil. Babies went with the mother. I tried to find out about you but got nowhere. Even flew to Brazil myself, but it was as if you vanished. Boarding school in Switzerland, someone said, but that's all I got. And the whole time you were . . ." He took a breath. "Your mama died about thirteen years ago."

"That would make me seventeen, when Dara threw me out of the house."

"Dara," Ray said, a menacing edge in his voice. Anger replaced sorrow. "When your mother stopped paying her to keep you."

"Do you think Dara knew?"

He sat there for a long moment, just staring at her, his eyes a bit brighter now, his face a little younger. He kissed her left hand, then her right. "No need for you to worry about Dara now, you're here with me. I'm sorry, honey. I am sorry for both of us. I never forgot you even for a minute, down to the little birthmark on your back. You've always been a part of me." He pulled a green poker chip with a white gull from his pants pocket and placed it carefully on the table. "I always kept you with me."

"And why would you want to keep Bebe with you?" Beau said as he came in through the back door. He loomed over Bebe. "What are you here to accuse my father of now? I should call our lawyers and get this straightened out. She has no business harassing you like this, Dad."

A tear slid down Ray's weathered cheek and Bebe started to cry and Beau looked from one to the other. "Good God in heaven, what have you found? What's going on? Did Donovan get that damn warrant? Ever since that guy came to town there's been nothing but trouble. Fuck."

"Watch your terminology, son. There's a lady present." Ray pulled in a deep breath, then got three glasses and a bottle of whiskey from the cupboard.

Beau rubbed the back of his neck. "We're drinking at noon? It's that bad, huh?"

Ray poured. "Not bad. Good. Damn good and you better sit down." He put a glass in Beau's hand. "You're going to be needing this and probably the rest of the bottle to boot. There's news."

* * *

Bebe looked from Charlotte's bugged eyes to Brie's dropped jaw to Prissy fanning herself with a napkin off the table at the Magnolia House restaurant. "It's true, I swear it." She looked around the patio at the scant three o'clock crowd to make sure she wouldn't scandalize anyone. She lifted her blouse like she'd done for Ray . . . for her dad . . . a few hours ago.

"Lord have mercy and saints preserve us." Prissy flattened the palm of her hand to her forehead. "All this time you've been walking around with this tracking device right there on your back and nobody knew. And if you had worn a bikini like the rest of us we would have noticed it long ago. See, that's what happens when you ignore the fashion gods, they poop on you. The moral of all this is everyone needs to shop and be happy and I do have to say, you do look mighty happy at the moment."

Squealing as if it finally sank in, Prissy jumped up and hugged Bebe, Charlotte kissed one cheek, and Brie kissed the other, and suddenly Daemon Rutledge appeared with a bottle of champagne. "Well now, is all this excitement over the new engagement I just heard about?"

They all looked at each other and Charlotte said, "Uh, not exactly. Bebe just found out she's Ray Cleveland's daughter. All this time no one knew. Can you imagine?"

"Like in some Gothic novel," Prissy added laughing. Rutledge nearly dropped the tray and Prissy steadied it. "That's pretty much the way we all feel."

Rutledge composed himself and cleared his throat. "Well, I do declare, that is some kind of news. All these years his little Lizzy's been gone and Ms. Bebe ends up being her. How . . . How long have you known?"

Bebe looked at her watch. "I've had a father and a brother for five whole hours."

"And that is indeed wonderful news," Mr. Rutledge said, still looking unnerved. "You must be very happy, and I'm guessing Mr. Ray is tickled now on two accounts. Mr. Beau put in a call to me saying to bring over this bottle of champagne to Ms. BrieAnn. He knew you all were meeting here and would want to toast his lovely bride and some other fine news and that must have been the news about Ms. Bebe being his . . . sister. Mercy."

This time all of them stared at Brie with their mouths open.

"I was going to tell you, but we were all in shock over Bebe, and now Beau beat me to the finish. Isn't that just like a man to get there before you do?" She winked.

"We're thrilled to pieces for you," Charlotte said, and Prissy added, "And your mama had a heart attack and the judge wrote you out of the will."

"That is entirely up to Mama and Daddy, but I'm marrying Beau and that's all there is to it."

Mr. Rutledge nodded. "And I must say a fine husband he'll be to you, Ms. BrieAnn. My sincere congratulations. I wish you every happiness." He left still looking confused and Bebe had the same feeling. She raised her glass. "To a Vera Wang wedding dress for Brie."

"And to better times ahead for you," Brie toasted back. "And they got to be better with Dara out of the picture." They drank down the champagne and Prissy said, "Do you think Dara knew who you were all the while?"

"Ray thinks so."

"Oh Lordy." Charlotte put down her glass, looking concerned. "That is indeed unfortunate. Ray Cleveland is not a man to be crossed. He has two things you don't mess with, his family and his money, and family has always been first. I remember the time in high school when that biology teacher was giving Beau a hard time for no good reason. The man quit his job and left Savannah in less than a day, not even bothering to take his clothes with him, and we all knew why."

"You don't think Ray would . . ."

"I think you should warn Dara to get out of Savannah and not leave a forwarding address and do it right quick and one of us should go with you."

"I think you all need to talk bridesmaid dresses, wedding colors, and flowers and think about getting Anthony and Vincent to do the wedding cake and if you put me in pink chiffon I'll strangle someone. For once in my life I believe I can handle Dara. There may even be laws broken here. Maybe I can arrest her. Can you imagine Dara in an orange jumpsuit cleaning litter from the side of the road? I believe today is going to be a really good day. I'm going to tell Dara to get the heck out of Savannah and never bother me again."

Buoyant to the point of not feeling her feet touch the sidewalk, Bebe headed for St. Julian Street. She hated Dara, no doubt about it, but she had a family now and that took the sting out of anything Dara could say. Bebe had Beau and Ray and soon Brie would be her sister-in-law. There would be family parties and family dinners and Thanksgiving and there would be Christmas and presents under the tree and she could use that tartan plaid tablecloth she'd bought and she hoped Ray liked cats.

Dara's Audi sat at the curb and Bebe took the brick walkway between the English boxwoods with the purple flowering ornamental pear on one side and the bubbling stone fountain on the other. This time she'd see Dara on her terms, when Bebe was the one in charge. She raised the brass knocker once, then twice, and when no one came she knocked a third time. Maybe Dara was already packing?

"Dara," Bebe called while opening the door to a mess of a house that resembled her apartment when someone broke in. "Dara?" The back door stood open. All was quiet, much too quiet. Bebe pulled her weapon and crept up the stairs. She inched open a bedroom door to more mess like downstairs. She looked across the hall into another toppled bedroom and to Dara's body on the floor, beady gray eyes that looked evil even in death staring at the ceiling. And there was a bullet hole right in Dara's forehead.

It wasn't just the good who die young, after all. Sometimes the bad got it, too. And Dara took bad to a new level. Weren't villains supposed to have some redeeming characteristic? That Buffalo Bill guy in *Silence of the Lambs* had that cute little dog he loved. Even the dinosaurs in *Jurassic Park* ate the bad guy and Darth Vader ended up being Luke's father. Dara did have kids, five mean-as-catshit brats. She didn't cook or clean. She did watch *Oprah,* but Bebe wasn't going to hold that against Oprah. Nope, not one single good quality. Dara totally sucked . . . but not anymore!

But as many times as Bebe imagined such a delightful scene did it have to be now? Dead Dara would lead straight back to Ray being Bebe's dad and him not being thrilled with her keeping her little secret all to herself. Ray's protection of family was legendary and Dara's death made Ray look like the killer. Why couldn't someone have plugged Dara twenty years ago when it would have done Bebe some good?

Bebe felt kind of bad about not feeling bad, but it only lasted a few seconds and was gone. She called dispatch and gave the information and resisted the urge to dance fearing she might wind up in hell for such a thing, though maybe she could sneak in a little skip. Maybe God wouldn't mind a little skipping, or at least look the other way while she did it.

"What are you doing?" came Donovan's voice from the doorway.

"Savoring the moment, wanna join in? She was dead

when I got here, but why the heck are you here? I didn't hear you come in."

"Back door was open. It occurred to me that Cleveland may not be too thrilled with Dara keeping his daughter from him all these years. I thought someone should have a little chat with her and let her know what's going on. I tried calling, got no answer, and came over." He nodded at the body. "Looks like Ray already expressed his disapproval."

"Okay, wait a minute, Sherlock. How do you know for sure it was Cleveland? I came here to tell her to get out of town because Ray may be upset. I didn't see him when I got here and I didn't see him running away from the house."

"Upset?" Donovan rolled his eyes.

"Why would Ray rifle through her house like this. What could Dara have that Ray wanted? Proof that I'm his daughter? That card's been played. What else is there?"

Sirens sounded in the distance and Donovan said, "Tearing up the place makes it look as if someone was here other than him. This has Cleveland written all over it down to his own personal signature." He pointed beside the dresser and her eyes followed to a green chip with a white gull in the middle. No. No way. Not now. She grabbed it off the floor as if she were picking up a found penny.

"What the hell are you doing? This is a crime scene. That's evidence."

"No. It's not evidence. It's just a chip that must be mine that I happened to have dropped when I was skipping around. You know skipping, up and down as in doing the happy dance for dead Dara and shaking everything loose like the chip and it came right out of my pocket." She dropped it in the front pocket of his jacket. "There, now it's safe with you and it won't get dropped again."

"You're lying through your teeth."

"No, I really did skip. It may not be the politically correct thing to do, but I had the right."

"This is not funny. You're a cop. You can't mess with the facts."

"I'm also a daughter and if you think for one minute I'm giving up my father for the likes of Dara you are so wrong. If it isn't my chip, then someone dropped it on purpose to frame Ray. He's not that stupid."

"You can't prove it's a plant."

"My theory is as good as yours and I will prove that I'm right and I'm not having you drag Ray into the police station on the grounds of one poker chip." Footsteps sounded below in the hall and then Joe Earl came into the room.

He let out a soft whistle when he saw Dara, then said to Bebe, "Well butter my butt and call me a biscuit. If this don't beat all. And if you did it, honey, I don't blame you, but I don't want to know the details."

Bebe said, "I'm just guessing, but I bet the slug that did in Dara is an old .22 from the same gun that got Donovan and killed Charlotte's parents."

"And that would be a gun owned and operated by Ray Cleveland," Donovan said, looking mad as hell.

Bebe felt sick. This was not the way it was supposed to be today. Today should be a good one, the best to make up for all the un-good ones she ever had. All her life she'd wanted a family. Most of her life she wanted a boyfriend. Then she got both at once and in less than six hours she had to choose between them. God had a very warped sense of humor. "My father is not the killer and I'm not letting you lock him up for something he didn't do. He wouldn't have finally found me only to throw it all away over something like Dara. He was pissed. I'm pissed. We're all pissed but not to the point of committing murder."

"Rage makes a man do a lot of things and to have thirty

years of it all come together at once could result in almost anything."

Joe Earl looked from Donovan to Bebe like following a tennis match. "Father? What's this about a father? What the hell's going on with you two?"

She pointed to Donovan. "Ask the Yankee. He's got all the answers." Then she walked out of the room to keep from putting another bullet in Dara for causing all this trouble. Even from the grave the woman was determined to ruin Bebe's life and the worst part was the bitch was succeeding.

Donovan watched as the last of the coroner's department and the forensics people filed out of Dara's room. Not much of a crime scene to process. No sign of struggle or forced entry. Someone she knew pointed a gun at her and shot and tore up the place. Of course the missing gull chip would have been a major find. How could Bebe just pick it up?

Joe Earl gazed around. "The woman sure enough was a first-class pain to Bebe, but she had a mighty nice place here. Who would have ever thought Dara of the projects would wind up as Dara on St. Julian Street living in the William Bird house on the historical registry?"

"This isn't where Bebe grew up?"

Joe Earl laughed deep in his barreled chest. "Dara lived in some two-by-four apartment with a bunch of kids all about the same age. Couldn't tell one from the other and none of them worth two cents except for Bebe. Then the kids left and she suddenly got class and moved on up to here. Said an uncle in Florida left her money. So what's this about Bebe having a father? Who the hell is it? Some rich guy over in Garden City finally found Bebe?"

"Ray Cleveland."

Joe Earl stared, then sat down hard on the tussled bed.

"Sweet mother of pearl. I never suspected for a minute. Bebe just blended in with all those other kids. Everyone figured she was some bastard child of a deb." Joe Earl looked tired to the bone. "For Ray to have his baby girl so close, my oh my. He searched everywhere for her and here she was all the while. Now that I see all the pieces, it fits. When Ray's wife moved on, I suppose she paid Dara to take her baby. That rancher guy probably didn't cotton to her bringing her kid along." Joe Earl ran his hand over his face. "If that don't beat all."

"Would Ray do something like this?" Donovan nodded at the scene.

Joe Earl shrugged. "Well, there're the facts to consider, that's why police have to look at things. She took his kid, Donovan. What would you do if somebody went and took yours? But Ray had to know that he'd be first on the list of suspects and he's already lost thirty years with Bebe. Then again, if he was riled and in a state, who knows what he's capable of, what any of us are capable of doing."

Donovan nodded. "I'd be in a state all right and it wouldn't be pretty." He was amazed he said that but it was true. If someone took his baby from him he'd go nuts. How did a man live with it all these years and then come to find out he'd been played for an idiot and a kid's life had been the price? He looked at the spot where the chip had been. But the law was the law, and Bebe should not have tampered with evidence. She was a cop. "What do you know about the Raeburns?"

"They want their damn necklace. Tried to get me to do some work for them, but Jimmy got his head bashed in when he got involved and I'm not that hungry for money. I bet they went and found somebody. Those jewels must be worth a fortune and I'm sure the price has gone up considerable in the last thirty years."

"Bebe thinks the Raeburns could be responsible for the

morgue murders because they wanted the necklace then. And now whoever has it killed Jimmy because the Raeburns were getting too close."

"I suppose it could work that way and then I went and got you involved and now you think it's Ray doing all this because the necklace and the money belonged to him. I should have kept my big mouth shut, but I figured you'd find something to clear Ray, not implicate him."

"Well either Ray or the Raeburns are responsible. There's no one else in the ballgame."

"Unless there's a pinch hitter hiding somewhere and we're looking right through him." The front door closed and light footsteps sounded in the hall. Joe Earl studied the bloodstain on the carpet. "We sure got ourselves a lot more dead people in this here city than usual."

"But I do think it's just one killer," Bebe said from the doorway. She looked at Donovan and he felt his chest tighten. How could two people find each other and be falling in love and then have all the powers in the universe be perfectly lined up against them? It was bad enough for him to come between Bebe and Cleveland when he was her friend but to come between Bebe and Cleveland with him as her dad . . .

She said, "Thought you'd both like to know that the slug that did in Dara was the same that nicked Donovan and did the morgue murders."

Donovan nodded. "That proves that it's Cleveland all the way. He's guilty, Bebe. Give it up. There's no place else to go with this."

Donovan watched Bebe pace the noncluttered part of the bedroom. He remembered her bedroom just this morning where things between them had been so damn good as if they were the only people on earth, least for a little while. Was that really just this morning? Seemed like a lifetime ago. And for Bebe it was. Her whole life had changed.

"You're looking at this upside down," Bebe finally said

interrupting his bedroom thoughts. "You're going from the old murders to getting shot at in the attic to now here at Dara's. If you go backward, start with Dara, you get a different answer."

Joe Earl stood. "You two are making my head swim. I'm tired as the dead and it's five o'clock and it's Tuesday, meaning the missus has fried chicken and corn bread waiting for me, so I'm letting you two battle out the cerebral stuff, and I'm going home to eat my supper. I'll mosey out and talk to Ray this evening and tell him about Dara and see what he has to say about all this."

He kissed Bebe on the cheek. "Welcome home, sugar. Mighty glad you're here, mighty glad indeed. We'll get this situation with Ray all straightened out now. Don't you be fretting over your daddy."

Donovan shook his head, hoping he didn't hear what he just did. "What a minute, you don't believe Ray killed anyone, do you? Dara? The morgue murders? The shooting in the attic? None of it?"

Joe Earl looked at him as if he'd sprouted two heads. "Hell, no. The way you look at things when you're on the job isn't always the way they are for real. Ray didn't do anything other than miss his daughter and go to the morgue now and then and try and rethink that night when his whole life changed. Just like you probably went to where your partner in Boston was gunned down to try and make sense of that. But now we got Dara living beyond her means and dead in a house torn to hell and back and someone trying mighty hard to pin it on Ray. The murders are connected. Too many and too close together to think otherwise. That connection has to be the necklace, but the question is who and why?"

He looked at Donovan. "You got to remember, Ray's a smart man. He's not going to kill Dara in her own house and leave her here when he sits out there on the big old Atlantic Ocean with enough inlets and outlets he knows by heart to get anything he wants lost for good. And that reasoning goes with Jimmy's body left on his boat. It doesn't wash."

Joe Earl left and Donovan sat on the bed. "This is nothing but the good old boys club."

"It's Savannah, and everyone knows everyone, just like I told you when you first got here. That hasn't changed any in the last ten days just because you landed on our doorstep. We all know Ray's not guilty. We need to figure out how Dara fits into the rest of the killings. What did she have to do with the necklace?" She headed for the door, calling over her shoulder, her very lovely shoulder, that he wasn't going to be kissing any time soon, "And that means I've got a busy night ahead of me trying to come up with something."

Donovan listened to Bebe's footfalls on the steps, the door closing, leaving him alone. He didn't mind alone, he minded lonely, and that's pretty much how he felt when Bebe wasn't around. They talked, figured things out, argued, and managed to find a way to be together . . . till now. Why did she have to pick up that chip? He pulled it out of his jacket pocket where she'd put it, then he slid it back.

And why in the hell couldn't someone else be her father?

# Chapter Eleven

Donovan balanced his supersized morning Starbucks—that some kid with glasses kept calling a grande something—in one hand and a no-caffeine latte mocha sissy drink in the other as he stepped over the yellow crime scene tape at Dara's house and let himself in. The tape would probably come down sometime today. He wished the problems between him and Bebe would go away that easily.

He took the stairs to Dara's room, her belongings still scattered everywhere. The closet door stood open. Someone was rummaging around inside. Bebe came out, pushing strands of mussed blond hair from her face. She looked more beautiful than ever with a glow of self-confidence that comes from having someone in your corner, someone who loves you beyond time and words and any kind of trouble that might come your way. Donovan always felt the love of family. Bebe never had it. Oh there was BrieAnn and Prissy and Charlotte to get her through, and they probably did, but that wasn't the love of a parent. That kind of love changed a person.

"So, why did you want me to meet you here?"

"I . . . I missed you and I'm guessing by the circles under

your eyes and the big high-octane coffees in your hands that you slept about as well as I did."

He handed her the mocha. "No caffeine, so you got that wrong, but the rest is pretty much right on." They stood there looking at each other, not knowing what step was next, so he went with business because he had no idea how to begin to sort out their personal mess. "Your text message said you found something important."

"Thanks for this." She took the drink. "Do you really want to know what I think or are you just here to find more nails to hammer into Ray's coffin?"

"I'm here because I want the truth. That's all I've ever wanted, and from where I stand Ray's guilty. But you obviously got something else or you wouldn't be digging around in that closet. If your latest idea has legs, I want to hear it, but if it's another verse of the *My daddy can do no wrong* song, then you're on your own, cupcake."

"One of the reasons I like you, even when you're being a big Yankee ass, as you so often are, is I can always trust you to do the right thing. Always. No matter what the outcome's going to be, you cross the t's and dot the i's and you see things the way they truly exist. Emotion doesn't get in your way. You're a good cop, Donovan, and I'm going with that." She took a crumpled paper from her suit pocket, the ugly blue suit today, and tossed it on the bed.

"Real estate listings?"

"Dara wasn't that great of a Realtor, which means she was definitely getting money from somewhere. She didn't have stocks or bonds or a sugar daddy in the wings."

"Blackmail? I agree with Joe Earl that all these murders are connected, but it wouldn't be blackmail over knowing where the jewels were. If she knew, she'd get the necklace and run. If it's not that, then maybe she knew the murderer. That's possible. We can check her bank statements for large regular deposits and then track them back to—"

"Hold on. You're thinking Boston, New York, where business is business. Here in Savannah your business is everyone's business. If Dara was depositing regular sums of money, the word would get out and the same if she frequented a safety deposit box or was wiring to an offshore account. Everybody knows where Dara came from. The gossips take note when things aren't quite what they should be. Cash doesn't require a signature, it doesn't have a monthly statement, and gets passed from one hand to another and then it's gone. If Dara kept my secret, she kept others."

Bebe nodded at the room. "Whoever did this didn't find what they were looking for. This place is a mess, no doubt about it, but not excessively so, kind of a quick toss."

"Cleveland covering his tracks and making this look like burglary."

"Except Dara knew her killer. She didn't try and fend him off. Heck, he was in her bedroom. That is not Ray Cleveland; they hated each other."

Donovan drank more coffee and drank again. "So we're looking for something big enough to hold bills and probably fireproof. It has some weight to it and is about the size of a small suitcase."

"Or a large suitcase, depending on Dara's greed, and did you just say *we*?"

He looked at Bebe, the smartest, most gorgeous, most fun, and most loving woman on Earth and thought he might die if he had to give her up. "You said I was a good cop. I respond to flattery."

"You're going to stay and help me? Well, that's more than I hoped for. I just wanted to talk. Try and salvage something between us and give you my latest theory on Dara and see if it had any holes. I knew you'd be objective."

She rubbed her forehead looking exhausted and not just

from lack of sleep. "I hated what happened with you and me here yesterday. A bad ending to what should have been a great day. I guess there's no day where everything is just the way you want it. So, Yank, on a scale of one to ten just how mad are you at me?"

He said in a quiet voice, "You shouldn't have taken the chip, or at least you should have explained where you were going with all this."

"If you recall, you weren't exactly in a listening kind of mood. You didn't even want to kick Dara, this from the guy who offered to lend me his gun at one time. And the police were coming down the street. Being a cop is a job and Ray's my dad and I'll pick him every time, Donovan. That's my decision, I know it's not yours."

He didn't want to ask but he had to. He had to know where they stood. He liked Bebe too much. If they were over it would hurt like hell and he didn't want to be blind-sided. "What about you and me together? Where is this taking us? We get caught in the middle and have nowhere to go. Is that what we're doing now, going nowhere. Are we . . . through?"

She kissed him on the mouth. "The big reason I wanted you here is because looking for this blackmail money puts us on the same side." She kissed him again, longer this time. "We both want to find it, and I wanted to spend time with you and not be arguing. Today we can do that. I want to be with you. I miss you, a whole lot. I love my job, always have, but I love Ray more."

She put her drink down. "It's the way I'm wired, Donovan. You go with the evidence and follow the facts and see everything in black and white. I follow my heart and defend those I care about. Even before I knew Ray was my dad, I protected him. It's who I am."

He threaded his fingers into her long blond hair, loving the feel of her in his arms and her arms slipping around him. This time he kissed her and she kissed him back, allowing him to relax a little, the fear of losing Bebe that ate at him all night subsiding. Except this wouldn't last. There was a lot of evidence stacked against Ray. What would happen between him and Bebe if he had a part in arresting Ray? How could they ever get beyond that?

They wouldn't. Deep in his heart he knew it was true. There was nothing more sacred than family, just ask the girl who didn't have one for thirty years.

"I'm so glad you're here." She hugged him tight, her cheek on his chest, her body warm against his. He forced himself to think about Bebe now and not what might be. "It's easier to be facing this with you and not against you. But the question now is—where the heck did Dara hide that money and does she have any cookies around here? I'm starved."

The clock on Dara's nightstand blinked ten p.m. as Donovan came back into the bedroom. He shoved the mattress up onto the box springs and all but collapsed on the pile of covers. Bebe scooted the antique dresser back against the wall and joined him, both of them staring straight ahead in an exhausted stupor. "I've look behind and under and in and between every piece of furniture in this house."

He handed her a chocolate chip cookie and ate one himself. "I went into the attic looking for trapdoors and passageways and all the other things old houses are supposed to have. I found two dead bats and rotting timber. Dara has termites. I tapped on walls and floors, but no space to hide a suitcase. I'd say Dara planted it in the backyard, but that meant every time she got money she had to dig it up, and with houses here being close someone was sure to notice the difference between a silver box and a red rosebush."

Bebe flopped back on the bed. "I want food, real food with protein and vegetables and not sugar food. I'm getting fructose jitters. Let's order in Chinese. Are you a chopstick kind of guy or do you fork it?"

"Fork's cheating. Face it, cupcake, there's nothing here. No blackmail, no evidence, and no money. Joe Earl said Dara got an inheritance, so maybe that *is* how she afforded this place. The uncle was in Florida, she could have an online account there to keep people and her rotten kids out of her business here. And that leads us back to Ray as our number-one suspect. The district attorney is starting to build a case against Ray and he's got a lot of ammunition. It wouldn't be long before they arrest him."

"We're missing something." She was quiet for a minute, then continued, "What if we're reading too much into Dara's murder? What if it's just another attempt to frame Ray? Finding Jimmy on Ray's boat set Ray up. Dara's murder adds to it, letting the real murderer go about his business looking for the necklace. Someone's covering their tracks and we're looking right at them and buying every word they're feeding us and this has gone on way too long and we're getting nowhere. We need a change of action. This is all about finding that damn necklace. Period."

She sat up. "We need to find those diamonds and do it now. Then the killer will come to us. That would be really nice for a change. I'm so tired of looking for that bastard."

"It would be different, I'll give you that." Donovan sat up beside her and she rested her head on Donovan's shoulder. He needed that. He needed her with him because life was so much better with Bebe in it. He kissed her hair and he felt her relax against him. Somehow he had to find a way to keep them together just like they were now. Somehow . . .

"Most of the activity involving the necklace is at the morgue, so our chances are best for finding it there. We'll do a search the police way. No more hit-and-miss looking around the morgue, we divide the place into quadrants and methodically cover every inch. The more people we have, the better and more thorough job we'll do."

She laughed "For once I get to play the sisters-forever card. We can count on BrieAnn and Prissy and Charlotte and now they have Beau and Sam and Griff. With you and me and Vincent and Anthony that gives us ten people. I can get Joe Earl, he'll help."

"How well do you know Joe Earl?"

She gave a nonchalant shrug. "He's lived in Savannah forever and been a cop just as long. He was my mentor when I first joined the force. He and Ray are tight as twins. Do you know something I don't?"

"That he and Ray are tight as twins and he's a cop." And that he met with the Raeburns in the park and it looked a lot more involved than simply turning down a job offer. Before Bebe could ask any more questions, he hooked his arm around her and brought her close. "We've got a plan for tomorrow, so that leaves us the rest of the night and for now we have that same-side thing going for us. Any ideas?"

Her mouth met his. "Come home with me. The cats miss you. Daisy was complaining, '*He doesn't write, he doesn't call, he doesn't send flowers.*' You're giving men a bad name."

"There's Chinese All-Night over on Abercorn. I'll get extra dumplings."

"And don't forget the flowers."

Bebe scooped out cat food into crystal bowls, Daisy me-owing at the top of her lungs, Carraway dancing figure eights at her ankles, Gatsby just looking pissed because food wasn't served now. "I'm scooping as fast as I can, give me a break here, will you?"

She set the bowls on the floor to expressions of *what, no*

*tablecloth and candelabra*? All three darlings sniffed, fluffed their tails, and walked away, stubby noses in the air. "Do not give me the pout look. I spend more on your food than I do on mine."

There was a knock at the door. "Please be Donovan with lots of food." And it was Donovan, but there were no bags in his hands or yummy smells of shrimp egg rolls or spicy General Tso's chicken drifting her way. "Chinese All-Night was closed? I'm so hungry my stomach thinks my throat's been cut and . . . and oh my goodness," she said forgetting her empty stomach and egg rolls as a white carriage pulled by two black horses, the interior filled with red roses, came to a stop in front of her apartment.

"But I remembered the flowers." Donovan took her hand and helped her into the carriage. She sat next to him surrounded by so much loveliness and that included the man at her side.

"How did you do this?"

"Yankees have their ways. Happy Birthday, cupcake."

"It's not my birthday."

"It was a three-hundred-and-sixty-five-to-one shot that I'd get it right, so we'll just pretend." He called to the driver, "Home, James." And the carriage started off, the rhythmic clip-clop of hooves on cobblestone chasing away the tedium of the day. The romance of Savannah settling over them.

"Where's home?" She snuggled up to him and kissed his lips, letting hers linger so he knew she meant it.

"Someplace that's not your apartment or Dara's house or the police station or the morgue or Magnolia House. Some place where no one can find us for the rest of the night. I want this to be about us."

"Even after we had that big fight today?"

His dark eyes got darker still. "Especially because we had the fight and we did make up and this is an extension of that." He put his arm around her. "I have to say these squares are a lot nicer when you're not trying to get some-where."

She gazed up at him and smiled wickedly. "I'd say you're trying mighty hard to get somewhere, Mr. McCabe. In fact I'd say you have designs on my virtue."

"And you have mighty fine virtue and a lot of other fine parts that I intend to pay particular attention to." The carriage meandered under the massive oaks, the moss so close she could reach out and touch it as it drifted in the night breeze. Lamplight cast a warm glow over the city, the whole place moving at an even slower pace than it did at daytime.

"I can't believe you did this all for me."

"I did it a bit for me, too. I love seeing you happy and with what's going on between us I don't see you that way very often. It's the job. It robs us of being human. We deal with the ugly so often we forget there's more, better, that life can be fun." The carriage drew to a stop.

"The Planters Inn? It's spring in Savannah with garden parties and garden tours. There's not a vacant hotel room within fifty miles."

"Yankees can be very persuasive. This is home for tonight. I've left word nowhere, called no one, turned off my cell, and you left yours in the apartment. If something happens tonight it'll damn well have to get solved without us."

He helped her down like a true Southern gentleman, the way she'd seen other men treat their ladies. "It must be close to midnight. I feel like a princess. Except for the clothes. I don't have princess clothes." She pointed to the carriage. "What about all my flowers?"

"Verge here will take them back to your apartment."

She smiled up at Verge and grabbed two armfuls of roses and buried her nose in the heavenly bouquets. "I never got flowers before, except from the blood sisters

when I made detective. I never got flowers from a man."
She could feel herself blush. "And you've made up for so
many nevers all in one night that started out to be a real
sucky night."

They walked across the little iron footbridge bedecked
with white flower boxes. "Here we are." They stopped next
to a white door with a brass knocker and lit by an old coach
lamp flickering in the night. Donovan took a brass key
from his pocket . . . a real key and not one of those so un-
romantic plastic door card things . . . and let them into a
room overlooking the Savannah River and more flowers,
yellow roses this time, and a linen-draped table with pink
candles and dotted with white Chinese-food cartons and a
silver champagne bucket.

In the room beyond, a gentle fire crackled in the hearth
beside a canopy bed with white eyelet topping and matching comforter. "I always wanted to see the rooms here.
Thought about telling the innkeeper there was a distur-
bance and as a cop I needed to get inside. And now I'm
here inside and with you and the last thing I want is a dis-
turbance."

She laid the roses across the bed and took Donovan's face
between her palms. "You are a most remarkable man."

She could see him blush. He did that a lot for a big
rough Yankee detective.

"You are a most remarkable woman, and whatever happens with Ray and the necklace and warrants that's never
going to change."

They sat at the little table by the window, the river
rolling lazily along, lights from tugboats and the docks
casting wavy lines across the ink-black water. Bebe bit into
an egg roll, declaring it delicious, then offering Donovan a
bite. He fed her a dumpling and she shared her glass of
champagne because it was a night for two people sharing.
Just two, no more.

Donovan kissed her, the taste of the champagne lingering on his lips making her dizzy drunk even though she had but one glass. Then he carried her to bed, their bed, drenched with the red roses, and undressed her as if they had all night, because they did. One night, one perfect as can be night just for lovers.

They did make love, then again, and again. He held her close, the only sound the beating of his heart mixing with the final sputters of the dying fire in the hearth, a hint of morning transforming the world from the magic of night to the reality of day. They didn't talk; there wasn't anything to say. They had this time together, and it was special beyond words. She fell asleep, her hand on Donovan's chest, their bodies entwined, and when she woke he was gone, one red rose on the white lace pillow where he'd slept beside her.

Maybe she was still dreaming. Then again, no dream had ever been as wonderful as this one night with Donovan.

Morning sun drifted in and out of the trees as Brie stood at the Patterson-Wright House on East York with the judge and Aldeen. Aldeen checked her watch for the millionth time and all but tapped her foot. "That realtor is late and wasn't Beau supposed to be picking her up? And here we are pacing the sidewalk. The only things we're missing is a monkey in a red vest and a tin cup."

"But Mama," Brie gushed. "Don't you agree this is a most exquisite house, the finest Georgian east of Atlanta, and we're facing Wright Square, one of the original squares. What could be better? There simply isn't anything."

"I suppose it is a fine enough place here on the outside, but who knows what it looks like inside. It could very well be a termite-infested dungeon for all we know . . . because we can't get ourselves inside because the precious realtor and your fiancé are late just like you and Beau were late for dinner. You'd think that when a man goes asking—"

"Telling," the judge added. "Not asking at all, but telling us that the two of you were getting yourselves married and we had no say in the matter."

"And it was *us* doing the telling," Brie added, "not just Beau, so you can't go holding that against him any more than you can hold it against me, and if you choose to do so—which I sincerely hope you do not—but if you're of that mind-set, then it can't be helped. But you are not ruining my happiness, you both need to understand that. All you'll be doing is ruining it for yourselves."

"Well here they come at last," groused Aldeen.

" 'Morning, Mrs. Montgomery, Judge," Beau offered looking nervous as a cat on hot coals. "I apologize for us being late, but—"

"Hi, sugar." Brie swung her arms around Beau's neck and kissed him on the cheek, a completely proper public greeting between a fiancée and her beau even her mama couldn't throw a hissy over.

The realtor pulled out the key and they followed her up the walk while she said, "Mr. Cleveland's already signed the papers, so you just take your time and look around and get acquainted." She turned to Brie. "I must say you are indeed a lucky lady to have not only this fine Savannah house to start your married life but a fine Southern gentleman for a husband and remarkable father-in-law who is responsible for saving much of our fair city. Being a Realtor of fine homes here in Savannah I appreciate him every single day."

Mama scoffed under her breath as Southern women are known to do when irritated and they know they have no real reason to be.

The realtor opened the double doors to the wide foyer.

"The chandelier is from the DeSoto Hotel before those money-grubbing scalawags razed it all those years ago. The Chinese-style wallpaper in the parlor was reproduced from fragments found in the wall when the house was restored to its original grandeur. There is original random-width pine flooring throughout the house except where there's Italian marble brought over special when the house was built. The master suite has a mahogany-and-brass bed used in India during the British campaign in the 1800s that Mr. Cleveland purchased with the house. A special wedding present to the bride and groom. Now I will leave you to enjoy your treasure and it truly is that."

Brie did a slow twirl, taking in the grand staircase and row of windows facing east to capture the morning sun and avoid the scorching heat of the afternoon. She went into the living room, her father wandering behind her, their footsteps echoing in the emptiness. "I can see the Christmas tree here in front of the windows, all our friends singing carols and you and Mama sitting by the fire and Elgin sleeping peacefully by the hearth."

"Elgin?"

"Our golden retriever, of course, and the cradle will be right beside him with little Montgomery sleeping there all nice and peaceful. Montgomery Cleveland is a fine name. We'll call him Monty and maybe he'll be a judge like his grandfather. I want my name—" she looked at her daddy "—your name to be passed on to the boys. And then we'll have Beauregard Montgomery Cleveland. We could call him BM but that just won't work at all." She laughed and threw her arms around her daddy. "Be happy for me."

"Your husband may have other ideas about what to name your children."

Beau came into the room and kissed her cheek. "If my darling wife wants Monty, that is fine with me, and if law school is in the cards, then that's fine, too." He gazed at her the way every wife dreams of being appreciated.

"Such silly talk," Aldeen huffed. "You'd think two people never got married before."

"And I think our marriage should be next month."

"Lordy!" Aldeen puffed out a disapproving sigh. "That is much too soon for a proper wedding. How could you even think such a thing."

"It will be a proper wedding, Mama. I booked the Telfair and St. John's for a Sunday-afternoon affair."

"It should be a Saturday night wedding and you are well aware of that."

"I'm aware I have a fiancé I want to marry and the afternoon will give us a wonderful wedding picture with all the flowers in bloom and guests will be thrilled to not have yet another Saturday wedding on their schedule."

"There is that, I suppose."

The judge checked his watch. "I have to get to court."

Aldeen followed him to the front door. "And I have a meeting at the museum and I don't know if you heard the latest," she said to Brie. "But Lamont Laskin has taken up with that LulaJean person who sings jazz at the Blue Note of all places. Not only is she older than him, she is also of questionable parentage."

*And so am I,* Brie considered adding, but that would upset Mama and truth be told Brie had always thought of herself as a Montgomery through and through.

"LulaJean's a great kisser," Beau added absently while looking out the window to the garden. "Uh, so I've heard . . . that she's a great kisser and—"

"And they are going to a medical convention . . . the one Lamont asked BrieAnn to," Mama threw in with a tsk. "I declare, the medical profession will never be the same."

She hustled out the front door without looking back and the judge left right behind her. Beau circled his arm around Brie from the front door as they watched them leave. "I don't think they were impressed."

"And I don't think I give two hoots in hell if they are or not. This is our house." She looked up at him and fluttered her eyes then added in a very Southern voice, "Why, Mr. Cleveland, I hear you have a big old bed upstairs in this fine house. Whatever do men such as yourself do in such fine beds? It sounds most sinful for an innocent like me."

"Innocent?" He laughed. "This from the girl who thought up Frisky?"

He scooped her into his arms and kicked the door closed. His hand maneuvered under her dress, his warm palm resting very nicely against her bottom, his fingers creeping under the thin strap of lace panties right to her skin. "And I'll just show you what men do to women in such fine beds."

"Oh, I was hoping you'd say that." She giggled as Beau took the curved stairs two at a time and found the master suite. Unceremoniously, he tossed her in the middle and grinned devilishly. "I'm getting to like this house more all the time. I've heard they crack champagne bottles over a ship to christen it, but I'm thinking this is a very fine way to christen a house."

He undid his tie and unbuttoned his shirt, the material falling open to such a fine firm chest. His dropped pants exposed all his delicious fine firm stuff there, and it tickled BrieAnn to no end knowing she'd be seeing that very fine stuff every day for the rest of their lives.

"And now about that innocent part." He sat on the bed and flipped up her dress. "Those are not the underpants of an innocent. Damn, girl. You have the best underwear."

"My sweet man, at these prices they call it lingerie."

"I'd rather just call it not necessary." He slid her panties down, slowly. "And there it is, that little patch of heaven all for me."

"And a nice big do-da all for me." She giggled. But as he slid into her, giggles melted to sighs, then gasps, then sheer happiness. She'd waited for and wanted Beau and finally made a stand for the man she loved and then at long last BrieAnn Montgomery was home.

At noon Bebe parked the PT in front of the morgue, the reality of murders and mayhem crowding out memories of carriage rides, soft beds, and very fine lovemaking. When she slammed her fist against the dash, the car turned off. Why this worked she had no idea, but it solved the problem and it helped to relieve a lot of pent-up frustration.

Vincent swaggered out the front door in perfectly pressed jeans and button-down shirt. No one swaggered quite like Vincent. "I am in my work clothes from the Gap. Very reasonably priced. Do you think we will truly find the missing necklace today?"

"I'm betting we find something." She hooked her arm through Vincent's. "And whatever you're cooking, it smells like heaven on a plate."

"The chicken Marsala, garlic focaccia, and espresso crostata invertita, that is an upside-down cake with a cocoa glaze."

She stopped on the front porch and hugged him. "Forget Spider-Man and Batman, I'll take Food Man. You're my hero." Vincent gave her the you-are-a-crazy-woman look as they went inside.

Donovan sat at the kitchen table with Prissy and Sam, Charlotte and Griff, Brie and Beau. Anthony stirred something on the stove behind them, little wisps of steam scenting the air. Normally Bebe's stomach would do little flips of joy because of the scenting wisps and stirring, now the flips were over seeing Donovan.

He winked, and she wanted to jump him right there in the kitchen and take up where they left off last night. Of course that couldn't happen, because they weren't alone and it wasn't night and she wondered if there'd ever be another night between them like last night. Donovan said, "We're ready to get started."

"And I'm here to help," Joe Earl said as he came in the side door, forcing her to think about the purpose of the day instead of the hunk of the day. "I heard what you all are up to, I suppose everyone in town has by now, and figured you could use an extra hand in the search."

The lights blinked and Prissy gasped. "Uh-oh, it's starting already. The ghosts don't like us being here on their territory."

Anthony shook his head. "That is Mr. Cleveland reconnecting the electricity in the casket room and the hallway. He's been here all day cleaning out the mess from the fire." Anthony smiled at Bebe. "I understand he is your father. You are a lucky girl."

"Thank you. I think so, too, and in some way it's like getting reborn."

She exchanged looks with Donovan. Gone were the memories of a great night replaced by the business of he day. What did she expect, romance forever? Well . . . actually . . . yeah. As long as they could be on the same side of finding evidence and it not implicating Ray, she had a good shot at the forever romance thing. "I'll go help Ray," she said. "You all start the search up here when you're ready." And that was code to Donovan for "I'll watch what Ray's doing because I know you think he's guilty as homegrown sin."

Bebe took the stairs and short hallway to Ray standing

on a ladder screwing in a lightbulb. Temporary lights hung off the sides of the ladder, an orange extension cord stretched out the open door probably to a power source beyond.

He grinned when he saw her. "Well there you are, sweet pea." He climbed down and kissed her cheek. "Beau said you were going whole hog today, looking for those jewels, so I thought I'd come on over and help clean up a little and maybe work on getting some light on the subject and see if anything showed up that way."

He gazed up at the one lit bulb. "Been a while since the electricity's been on. The funeral parlor closed right after the murders, bad press does that to a place. New owners never stayed long enough to fix it proper. They said it was haunted." He laughed. "But Vincent and Anthony never said anything about ghosts or with all the racket they made tearing the place up they never heard anything else."

"I'm betting it's all that garlic around. The ghosts never stood a chance." They laughed together and for a moment she nearly imploded with happiness. How could something so simple as a shared laugh make her feel so good? Being with Ray now and Donovan last night was almost too much to take in all at once. It was like eating oatmeal her whole life and suddenly finding Lucky Charms and Cocoa Puffs. Euphoria! At least for now. "You didn't have to come, you know."

"I wanted to. You pretty much grew up without me being around, but I am now. And there's another little matter we needed to discuss. I heard about Dara. No one deserved to die more, but I want you to know it wasn't me who pulled the trigger. You and I just got ourselves together and I wouldn't chance us being separated again for all the tea in China. I didn't do in Jimmy, either, or any of the other things going on around here. Someone's going to a powerful lot of trouble to make me look damn guilty."

He took her hand. "You're a cop, so I don't have to go spelling this out for you in great detail, but your daddy here isn't looking all that good in the eyes of the law these days. The gambling's one thing, but these murders are serious and they're all pointing straight at me. I don't want you to do anything to jeopardize you being a police officer and get yourself in the middle of some ugly trouble. I didn't come into your life to ruin it."

This time she kissed his cheek. "You couldn't ruin my life if you tried. Just having you around makes me happy all over. And the plan for the day is to not have any bad things happen to you or me."

"From your lips to God's ears, sweet pea." He handed her the bulbs. "You finish up there and I'll scrape up the rest of the grime. Maybe that necklace fell between some floorboards or Addie and William stashed it behind a panel that's come loose by now."

He picked up a shovel. "We pretty much tore apart all the caskets and furniture here after the murders but never found anything."

Bebe took a roll of paper towels and container of spray cleaner up the ladder with lightbulbs as Ray shoveled debris, stirring up the ashes, the place smelling like fire all over again. She screwed in another bulb, making the room brighter and dismal at the same time. She could imagine what the place looked like once a long time ago and with some serious effort the morgue could look that way again.

Voices came from outside. "And now we're late as usual and we would have been on time, but you had to have that second piece of apple pie. You've gained ten pounds since we got here." Edwina and Shipley hustled into the room, Daemon Rutledge behind them, looking proper as always, though Daemon's expression at the moment hinted he'd rather get boiled in oil than be with these two.

"Well where is everyone," Edwina asked in a huff, looking around. "Where is this all-out effort to find my jewels?" She peered up at Bebe. "This morning you were at the hotel talking to Charlotte about that and I insist on knowing what you've found so far. Mr. Rutledge was kind enough to bring us over here so we could get to the bottom of this situation once and for all."

Bebe screwed in another bulb. "We haven't found anything yet, but you're welcome to help." Ray and Daemon both did an eye roll as Charlotte and Prissy and Brie came into the room. Brie said, "What's all the noise down here? Did you all find something?"

Bebe sprayed cleaner. "Edwin and Shipley found us." She sprayed more, soot and grime sliding from the light. "We can settle who owns the necklace once we find it so you all better quit standing around like sparrows on a cow pie and get cracking."

"Donovan!" BrieAnn yelled. "You better get yourself down here. You're not going to believe this."

Good grief, Edwina and Shipley weren't all that bad. A little mouthy perhaps, but Brie didn't have to go yelling her head off for Donovan. Bebe sprayed again, watching dirt give way to crystals glistening in the light.

Donovan, Beau, and Joe Earl hustled into the room and stopped dead. Anthony and Vincent followed and did the same thing, all of them mesmerized by the emerging chandelier. Bebe added another blast of cleaner. "I think this piece should go in the entrance hall." She sprayed more. "I've never seen anything like it in all of Savannah."

No one agreed or disagreed with her comment, and with this crew someone always had an opinion about something. She glanced down to a whole lot of eyes staring right back up at her.

"Bebe," Donovan said. "Look what you're doing. It's damn amazing."

"Good to know. If I don't cut it as a cop I can do housekeeping." She smiled and sprayed a few more times, all the crystals coming into view now. They swagged around the chandelier in graceful loops, one glistening more than the other like strands of sparklers going off on the Fourth of July. She climbed down the ladder, then looked to the light to get the full effect and . . . "Oh Lordy!"

"I'll be damned," Edwina Raeburn said on an appreciative sigh mixed with a good deal of awe.

"And if you don't do exactly as I say, that's what's going to happen to Charlotte here."

# Chapter Twelve

Daemon Rutledge's voice came from the back of the room, though it sounded like weird-Rutledge and not usual polite hotel manager Rutledge. Robot Rutledge. All eyes cut to him now . . . and the gun in his hand pointed to the back of Charlotte's head. Bebe's blood went cold and Prissy and Brie looked as if they would faint.

"That necklace is mine," Rutledge said, bitterness dripping from each word. "I've looked for it for thirty years, thirty long years, and now you find it and it's not fair. Not fair at all."

"Put the gun down, Daemon," Griff Parish said, sounding a lot more calm than Bebe felt. "We'll give you whatever you want, just don't hurt Charlotte."

"I want the necklace. I killed the Carswells when they wouldn't tell me what they did with it, and here it was all the time." His voice broke and he looked deranged. "They hid it in the crystal chandelier right over my head. It just blended in with all the glass. As many times as I looked down here and scared folks away so I could look more, I never saw it. The jewels belong to me, dammit, me." He waved his hand, the old .22 still on Charlotte. "Everyone against the wall and you best move fast."

Edwina huffed, "That's enough. You are completely insane. It is most certainly not your necklace, it's ours, our daughter's, and—"

Daemon fired a shot above Edwina's head, making her eyes bulge and mouth snap shut. Never call an insane person insane, but then maybe Daemon wasn't all that crazy; he got Edwina to finally shut up. Bebe could appreciate that a ton more if he didn't have a gun on Charlotte. Charlotte looked afraid but not in panic mode. Guess she was leaving that to Prissy, BrieAnn, and the resident female cop, who had to do something but didn't know what.

Daemon grabbed Charlotte's arm and steered her toward the ladder. "Nobody be doing anything dumb now or the blood sisters here will be minus a member and Griff can forget all his fancy wedding plans. You cops put your guns on the floor real careful like."

Donovan put down his weapon, followed by Bebe, then Joe Earl. They all moved to the edge of the room. Bebe said, "You can't hurt Charlotte. She's been your friend all these years. We all have."

"I'll be doing whatever I want to do for a change. I've fetched and carried for you all. Took care of Magnolia House like it was my own and it should have been mine. None of you can manage it like I can, and with that necklace I could have bought it. It should have been mine."

He put Charlotte in front of the ladder as he climbed up. "You hold right still, missy, if you want to keep breathing. I'm a mighty good shot. I got Donovan easy enough in that attic, could have done him in but I didn't need the police crawling all over the hotel and asking questions. I figured Donovan would keep his mouth shut since he didn't know who to trust."

"What about Dara?" Donovan asked making an attempt to keep Daemon focused on himself and off Charlotte. "Why did you kill her?"

"I figured I'd give the police someone to keep them

busy, and Ray Cleveland fit the bill since McCabe came to town and stirred things up against him."

Daemon deftly unwound the necklace from the chandelier while keeping the gun perfectly aimed. "He was the prime suspect after I killed Jimmy. Our daddies collected guns, and he remembered the .22. I told him I was selling the necklace to Cleveland and would cut him in if he kept his mouth shut. After I took out Jimmy, Cleveland was your man. I added Dara to make him look guiltier still to give myself more time to look for the necklace. No one suspected me. Then you all got this idea for getting together today to look for the jewels and I figured you'd find them. I've come to get what I should have had all along. You were all rich and it wasn't fair. I needed a break, too. It was my turn, dammit. The necklace was my turn to get what I wanted, what I deserved."

The necklace twisted around other crystals in the chandelier. "You're never going to get out of this," Donovan said.

"I've been in tighter places. Got out of that attic, didn't I. After I killed Addie and William I got out of that. Now I'm taking Charlotte with me and if any of you follow us I'll—" He yanked the necklace, making the ladder wobble, then grabbed the chandelier to steady himself. Suddenly, he shook violently all over, then fell to the floor in a heap.

Prissy tsked, "Well dang. We never give ghosts enough credit."

Donovan felt the pulse point in Daemon's neck. "Nothing." He quickly rolled Daemon over and started CPR as Bebe dialed for an ambulance.

Joe Earl sprinted toward the door. "I'll meet the paramedics and lead then back here."

Vincent looked to Anthony. "We'll get dinner."

BrieAnn stood close to Beau, Griff held on to Charlotte as if he'd never let her go, and Prissy had her arms around

Sam. Shipley held a weeping Edwina. Who would have thought he was the strong one in that relationship? Brie said, "How could Daemon do this? Treat us so poorly and threaten Charlotte? We all liked him, he liked us."

"Apparently not so much." Bebe watched Donovan work. "Daemon was obsessed with the necklace. I think after all this time of looking for it and not finding it, it drove him mad. It's like he was two different people, the Daemon Rutledge we knew and loved at the Magnolia House, and Daemon Rutledge the killer and thief who would do anything to get a necklace he really thought belonged to him."

The wail of sirens drew nearer, then stopped, giving way to the clatter of a gurney as the paramedics rolled it and their equipment into the dismal room. They started in on Daemon, hooking him up to machines and oxygen.

"We have a pulse," one of them said. He turned back to Donovan and gave a thumbs-up. "Nice job, buddy."

Bebe stood by Donovan and they all watched the paramedics usher Rutledge into the ambulance. Sirens screaming again, the sound faded into the distance. No one said anything, each of them trying to figure out what happened.

Prissy looked up at the diamonds dangling over her head. "So did the ghosts get Daemon? Is that why he fell?"

"Looked like a heart attack." Ray touched the dripping wet ladder. "A heart attack brought on by a dose of electrocution. Old wiring mixed with all this here water and a metal ladder thrown in for good measure and you get yourself a sizable charge. That and a weak ticker and—"

"You get toast," Prissy said, then made the sign of the cross. "I'm never going to get to heaven with this mouth. I'm doomed."

Bebe held up her hand. "Wait a minute. I think the ghosts had more to do with all this than you think. I was up there on the ladder, even doing all the spraying, and I didn't get electrocuted."

"You didn't touch the light after you added water, sweet pea." Ray picked up the half-empty bottle of cleaning solution. "I think you damn-near drowned the thing. And even if you did happen to brush against the light, your unique taste in fashion saved your pretty self. Your Hush Puppies have rubber soles, nice thick rubber soles. You were grounded. Rutledge and his perfect appearance of immaculate suits and fine leather dress shoes let the electricity pass right on through his body, sending his heart into overload."

Prissy looked bewildered. "You're kidding." And Bebe added, "Well, there you go." She stuck her nose in the air. "After taking all this grief all these years I have finally been vindicated. The fashion gods have smiled on me at last."

"I don't believe this," Brie said, "Now we'll never get her out of those ugly suits. And we get the poster girl for Hush Puppies-r-me."

Prissy studied Bebe's gray suede shoes. "Personally I'd rather be electrocuted."

The lights suddenly went out, and Ray came in the room with a flashlight. "Thought I'd cut the power before any more damage was done." He climbed the ladder and unwound the necklace from the chandelier. "Hard to believe one piece of jewelry can cause so much trouble." He came back down and dropped the stones in Donovan's hand. "Fire and ice and they've brought nothing but sorrow and heartache to everyone who's been involved with them."

He shined the light on Charlotte. "Her mama and daddy were killed for it." The light went to Prissy. "Her mama went and left her on the nunnery doorstep because she couldn't find the necklace. Bebe's mamma wanted revenge because she couldn't have it. Even the Raeburns gave the necklace all that love and attention that rightfully belonged to their daughter and granddaughter and Anthony and Vincent's family was disgraced over its loss. Now I'm not one to believe in ghosts or curses, but this time it sure seems true enough. If ever something had bad mojo, this necklace is it."

"Well, I don't care about mojo or curses," Edwina said. "Shipley and I have waited years to get that necklace back. I intend to have it."

"No," said Shipley with more force in his voice than Bebe thought he possessed. "We will not have those diamonds in our home. We lost our Addie over it and I almost lost you; Mr. Cleveland is right; the necklace poisons everyone who touches it. It's eaten up enough of our lives, and it's time to quit, Edwina."

"But . . ." started Edwina until Shipley interrupted. "The necklace needs to go back to where it came from, the town in Italy. Perhaps that will bring an end to all the evil and no one else will suffer."

"That is very nice of you," Anthony said from the doorway. He came in. "Even after all these years, my town still offers a reward for its return. It was a big tourist attraction, like your Disney World but no rides, and we have better pizza."

Ray picked up a strand of the jewels, their blaze of color amazing even in the weak beam of a flashlight. "That reward smacks of blood money and just as cursed . . . if you believe in such things and I'm guessing right now after all that's gone on over the years we all believe a little bit."

"After the police are finished with it as evidence and the necklace is returned what if some of the reward goes to Daemon? He's probably—"

"Completely off his rocker," Prissy said.

"I was going to say mentally unbalanced but you get the idea. Money could go for his care. The necklace messed up a lot of lives, including Daemon's. Seems fitting for the money to go for some good."

Bebe cleared her throat and made the sign of the cross. "And," Donovan added. "The good sisters and their shelter. Lots of good there, too."

"Amen," Prissy said as Donovan passed the necklace to Anthony, adding, "I hope this brings your family much happiness in the future."

Anthony took Donovan's shoulders and kissed him on both cheeks. "It is finished. Our family name can be restored. It is a fine day for the Mateos."

"Does that mean you're going back to Italy?" Bebe asked, thinking of all that great food leaving the country and having the sudden urge to weep.

"As you say here in Savannah . . . not a snowball's chance in hell. Since the gossips have already been talking Vincent and I have had five calls to come see the chandelier where the necklace was found today. We have decided to open the morgue as a restaurant. Crystals." He beamed. "We will make what is called a fucking killing. But now we have much good food upstairs waiting for us. *Permette di mangiare*, let's eat!"

The parade of people filed toward the stairs, but Bebe took Donovan's arm and pulled him toward the outside door. "Okay, it's just us now. So why did you suggest using the reward money for Daemon and it wasn't because you saved his life or that the money should be used for good . . . though that might figure into it some way. I think there's more."

"And I think you're overthinking."

"I know you . . . well." She kissed him. "Very, very well. I can see the *more* part in your eyes. We've shared getting shot at and finding bodies and Dara alive and dead and chocolate chip cookies. We can share this. Spill it."

"Sometimes ignorance is bliss and I want you to trust me in that this is one of those times. I'm not just saying that to be cryptic. I mean it. Trust me on this one, Bebe."

"I've lived with this necklace and what's surrounded it all my life. It's defined my life, and I'm not letting this final part go."

Donovan took a wallet from his front pocket, but it wasn't his wallet. He opened it and pulled out a newspaper clipping about a benefit garden party with BrieAnn's picture as the hostess. "Daemon's wallet. When he fell, it slid from his pocket."

"Maybe he just had a fondness for BrieAnn. He's known her for years, and they've always gotten along." Bebe read the article. It was recent, only a few weeks old. She felt sick and cold like when she used to take a test in school and was afraid she didn't know the answers except this time she was afraid she knew the answer all too well. "I've heard talk about how long ago Daemon and this maid at Magnolia House had a thing for each other. It was talk, gossip talk. Brie's adoption was private, so there's no way of checking. The papers are sealed and a new birth certificate issued at the adoption. Yesterday at Magnolia House when we all learned Brie was engaged, Daemon was thrilled, over-the-moon thrilled."

"And he has her picture. Something BrieAnn said or did recently must have gotten him thinking about this, tipped him off to who she was. What do you want to do with the article?" He tapped the paper.

"Brie's happy and in love and has a diamond the size of Rhode Island and a mama and daddy who adore her beyond words even if they're not thrilled about who she's marrying. To throw this information into the mix when all we have is an article would serve no purpose and more than likely cause a lot of pain." She ripped the clipping into tiny pieces and scattered it out the door.

"Do you really think Daemon's her dad?"

She kissed Donovan and took his hand. "I think it's over and it should stay that way and we should get some chicken Marsala before it's gone." She started off and he held her in place. "Donovan, if you've found something else, I don't want to hear it. My brain is oatmeal."

"You got the necklace and we found the killer and you have a dad. Things are pretty good . . . except for the oatmeal brain . . . right?"

"Agreed, especially with you here." She stood on her tiptoes and kissed him

"And that's the problem."

She knew what was coming and had refused to even think about it, hoping that if she didn't send those brain waves out into the universe they simply wouldn't exist. "Not now. Not yet. I don't want you to leave, not when everything's so good. It's not fair."

"If I hang around here, it's back to your side, my side. Not over Ray as the killer, but Ray and the gambling, and that one's not going away. I'll get that warrant sooner or later and then what? Arrest him? You're right, he's a great guy and I'm not going to be the one to put him in prison, especially when I get to watch you hate my guts while I do it. The problem started when I got here, and if I go, the problem goes with me."

"What about Sly? The task force?"

"Not if it costs you your dad. I'll tell the congressman there wasn't enough evidence for a warrant. He'll find something else that will get him votes and make him look good and move on."

"I'm not ready for this. I don't know if I'll be ready. I . . . I love you. I really do."

"And you love Ray. If I go, I just go back to Boston. If I stay, Ray goes to prison. No one ever gets it all, cupcake. It just doesn't work that way."

"When do you . . ."

"In the morning. I have the room at the Inn for another night. Stay with me."

She looked at him, knowing that this time tomorrow he'd be gone and she'd never see him again. She crossed her arms over her chest to stop the hurt. "Other than Brie, Char, and Prissy there's never been anyone in my life I care about or who cared about me. I found Ray and I found you and I can't just let you go."

"Hey, Bebe? Donovan?" Ray said as he came into the room. "We're all wanting to toast you two up there. Quit your necking and smooching and come on up."

She started up the stairs with Donovan following her, and she realized she was listening to his footsteps, trying with all her heart to remember them so when he wasn't with her some part of him would be even if it was simply the sound of his footsteps behind her.

Everyone clapped and wolf-whistled, including Edwina and Shipley. They sat beside Charlotte. The age of miracles was not over if the three of them were talking. Bebe and Donovan took chairs between Joe Earl and Vincent. Bebe was not in the mood to be Little Miss Sunshine right now. She's rather go home, eat popcorn, and lose herself in re-runs of *Lost,* so she didn't have to think about Donovan going. But these were her friends, who deserved better than Bebe moping.

"Now this is a really great dinner." Bebe smiled and waved her hand over the table piled high with chicken and eggplant and bread and bottles of red wine.

Anthony stood and raised his glass. "To spring nights, new friends, and good food to share." He grinned. "I am getting very good with the English."

And they ate and ate more and talked and drank till dark fell across the windows and Bebe thought for sure she'd turn into a pumpkin or whatever happened to people at midnight when they were really tired. The fearsome foursome that had morphed into eight thanked the brothers and Joe Earl and wished Edwina and Shipley good night, then shuffled out of the morgue and onto the sidewalk.

"Well, here we all are," Prissy said. "It's nearly midnight and we found the necklace today, the necklace that brought the blood sisters together. So you know what that means, don't you?" She looked at Brie, Char, and Bebe.

Bebe shrugged. "We're thirty and getting old."

Prissy huffed, "We have to renew blood sisters forever. Our lives together started with the necklace lost, now there are eight of us, and new lives begin with necklace found. Who's got a knife?"

Donovan reached into his pocket and pulled out the one Bebe had used to dig the bullet out of the attic floor at Magnolia House. Prissy beamed. "That's perfect. We'll meet at Bonaventure."

"And why are we doing this?" Donovan asked as he drove the two of them through town toward Skidaway Island and the cemetery. She'd pretend this was just another drive with Donovan and not the last drive. That she'd see him tomorrow and they'd work on some other case and find clues and bad guys and eat Chinese and talk about how they had to write teeny-weeny to sign Daisy's cast.

"Because Prissy wants us to do this, and the trip is a small price to pay to keep Prissy happy. No one wants to piss off the priestess or whatever she is. Her grandma Minerva is responsible for some pretty wacky stuff around here and who knows what gets passed on in the great gene pool of life. Take a left there," Bebe said. Donovan did, then stopped the car in front of the double gates. "Well, it's closed. Now what?"

"It's not iHop. We have to improvise. There's a space down by the river where the wrought-iron fence ends. We can shimmy through the break, although I have to tell you shimmy at ten is a lot easier than shimmy at thirty, and we have to hide the car in the bushes or we'll get arrested and I hope you have a flashlight."

"Is it really worth it?"

"How do you feel about being a werewolf or growing an extra ear? Family photos will never be the same."

Bebe had no problem finding the right gravesite, mostly because Charlotte and Griff were already there, Griff looking as enthused as Donovan. Brie came around the corner with starry-eyed Beau, who would obviously go anywhere with BrieAnn, and Prissy and Sam arrived a few minutes later, Sam looking as if he were used to the world of Prissy.

They all sat on the granite slab, a crescent moon reflecting in the polished surface, the river lapping the shore, a nightingale calling in the distance. Prissy dumped a paper bag upside down on the slab. Skittles, Sno-Caps and gummy worms fell out.

"Better than eye of gnat and hair of dog," Griff said, the other guys nodding.

"We were ten," Prissy said. "Who else would choose a grave inscribed with *I'll Be Back* on it? And people wonder why Savannah is haunted, the whole place is loopy. And since we're renewing the blood sister bond that will now be the blood-sister-and-brother bond, we need continuity." She opened the Skittles, ate one, and passed the bag. She lit a white candle, then put eight white stones in a circle around it. "Donovan, the knife, if you please."

"If I didn't love you all so much," BrieAnn said, "I'd never consider doing this, you know. I hate blood, especially my own." Brie nicked her pinky, stifled a yelp, then passed the knife to Beau, who did the same without the yelp till the knife got all the way around the circle to Donovan. "I'm leaving tomorrow, guys. Maybe I shouldn't be part of this."

"You're leaving?" Brie sounded almost as forlorn as

Bebe felt and Beau added, "You're already part. You've been a friend and at times you've been a pain in the ass along with it, but we got over it. Good God, now we'll have Yankee blood." They all made the sign of the cross.

Prissy pressed her pinky to Beau's, who did the same to Charlotte to Sam to Brie to Griff to Donovan to Bebe, then back to Prissy while she recited . . .

> *Sister to brother in blood that is mine*
> *We'll be for each other till the end of time*
> *To this we will pledge, to this we'll be true*
> *That nothing can harm us because there is you*

"Now everyone, take a stone." Prissy clapped her hands together. "I did it. I did it right. I can feel it in my bones. Good mojo abounds."

Donovan felt the side of his head. "Hey, I think I'm growing an extra ear."

They finished off the candy except for the gummy worms, all agreeing that the taste for gummy worms diminished with the arrival of adulthood. Prissy blew out the candle and Bebe brushed Savannah sand from their clothes like she did when she and Donovan first landed in that pile at the morgue.

"Well, I guess this is it," Beau said and shook Donovan's hand. "There's always a Moon River waiting for you at the bar, Yank, if you get back this way." Donovan shook hands with the guys and cheek-kissed the girls, then he took Bebe's hand. They strolled back to the hidden Jeep and started toward town.

"Come to Boston," Donovan finally said, his voice tight. "I'll take you to a Sox game."

"Forget the Sox, how about Filene's Basement?" A stupid response, but if she didn't keep things light, she'd lose it. They needed small talk, the kind that passes time and gets you where you need to go without anything meaningful. She couldn't handle meaningful now. They'd been through too much meaningful already.

Donovan gazed down at her, moonlight in his brown eyes, his black hair needing a cut and mussed from the top down on the Jeep. "Shopping? Fashion? You? Do Prissy and BrieAnn know about this latest development?"

"And no one's going to tell them. I figure I'll have to wear a dress for Brie's wedding, so I'll take some baby steps toward the land of chiffon and satin and heels and . . . and don't go." She rested her head against his strong arm. "I swore I wouldn't say that."

He slid his finger under her chin and brought her face to his. "I hate this. I hate what will happen if I stay more. Tell Daisy I'll write, I'll call, I'll send flowers."

He pulled the Jeep to the curb by the PT still parked in front of the morgue and kissed her, his lips lingering, his arms holding her tight, then tighter still. She finally broke the kiss and slid from the seat before she cried. "Be safe, Donovan McCabe."

"You too, cupcake." He looked at her, his eyes sad. Then he gave her a half smile and a wink and she watched his taillights fade down the street and felt her heart break a little more. It was really over, and for a minute she thought she might die from the sheer agony of Donovan driving out of her life. She understood what he was doing and why, but it just hurt so very bad.

She was not ever going through this pain again. No more falling in love. Even though women have probably been reciting that line for as long as humans have roamed the earth, she meant it. No more trusting a man with her heart to have him up and leave no matter what the reason. It wasn't worth it. That saying of "better to have loved and lost" was crap. If you didn't know what you were missing, you didn't miss it. Like never eating peanut butter out of the jar with chocolate poured on top. If you never did it, you'd never know how darn good it was.

She fired up the PT and headed for home. Forget men, she had cats. Daisy, Gatsby, and Carraway didn't argue with her, didn't criticize her driving and none of them had a police badge to get involved in her business and none of them called her "cupcake." Amen. Cats were better than men . . . except when considering the sex angle, and there Donovan was spectacular. And to tell the truth she really didn't mind cupcake. How could she not like a nickname about food? Damn.

Instead of heading home, she turned the PT for Thunderbolt. She needed to drive. Maybe because she wanted to see Ray, or maybe because it was a beautiful night or because if she didn't head somewhere out of town she'd wind up in Donovan's bed and that would be heartbreak, round two, and one round of that was enough.

"Bebe," Ray said as she came into the restaurant. The place was closed and he was sitting at a table, the blue tablecloth still in place, white gardenias with trailing green ivy in the center. He was looking at what were probably the night's receipts and working on his laptop. The doors and windows of the restaurant stood open, night ocean air wafting through.

"What brings my favorite daughter all the way out here?" He got up and wrapped his big arm around her, then brought her back to the table. "I want you to know I'm really liking that daughter word a lot."

"Me, too, and I came out here because . . . well . . . it was better than going home and being miserable."

He closed his computer and shoved it under the arrangement. Ray broke the silence. "You know, I've ruined three of these things with spilled coffee, Beau's forbidden me to drink anyplace near it. Sometimes I sneak down to the boat-house where he can't see me. Don't you go ratting me out now, you hear." He chuckled like dads do, and she felt more at ease.

"No ratting out." She crossed her heart, liking that they shared a confidence.

"Well now, it's late and Donovan isn't with you, so I'm assuming this misery you're feeling has to do with the man himself."

"He's leaving tomorrow."

"Ouch. I'm sorry, sweet pea, I truly am. He's a good man. Didn't think so at first, but my thinking's changed." Ray got her a cup of coffee from a service tray. "Any chance of him coming back?"

"What would he do here? He's a Yankee. His whole family is in Boston and he's a cop and he won't even try grits, this from a guy who eats rye bread and potato chips on bologna sandwiches. Is that gross or what?" She took a sip of coffee and sat back in the chair. "It's beautiful here at night, not just the restaurant, but the whole place. You must love it here."

"Move on out with me and Beau. We've got plenty of room for you in the house." He took her hand. "It's just an offer; you think it over. I'll teach you how to drive a boat and fish and they say I'm a right good cook."

"I'll keep it in mind." She stood. "I better go. I have to work tomorrow and wade through a mountain of paper-work and you should know I'm really liking the *dad* word a lot, too." She kissed his cheek.

"See you tomorrow, Daughter?"

"See you tomorrow, Dad." Heading back to the Cruiser, she felt a little better, a bit stronger. It was good to have someone to talk to. Not necessarily to get answers, but just talk. That's one of the things she'd miss most about Donovan leaving. They talked about everything. And there were other things she'd miss, especially this time of night, because the man sure was hung. She made the sign of the cross. Prissy wasn't the only one never getting into heaven.

Bebe took the causeway, turned down Broughton, and stopped for a red light. A red light when there was no traffic was irritating, and she could run it easily enough and not get caught. Some of her best friends were cops. Except she was stopped in front of Magnolia House and there was a light on at the third floor, second window from the left.

Without thinking, because she'd done entirely too much of that today, she jumped out of the PT, ran though the double doors of the hotel, past the night clerk, and up the stairs, taking them two at a time, so she wouldn't chicken out. Huffing, she knocked on Donovan's door. He answered in jeans, no shirt, no shoes, and she flung her arms around him and kissed him while undoing her slacks and closing the door. Backing him toward the bed, she kicked off one shoe, then the other, and unbuttoned her blouse. Not breaking the kiss, her clothes fell to the floor along with his jeans and a condom wrapper.

Together they dropped onto the bed and then he was inside her, hard and hot . . . the hung part just as she remembered . . . but she needed to remember the rest of him as well. The feel of his coarse chest hair rubbing against her hardening nipples, his muscles flexing under her fingertips as he braced himself over her, her legs at his hips as he took her, his heavy breathing mixed with hers when they climaxed. Making love would never be like this with anyone else, she knew that with every part of her being.

And then she left the room as quickly as she came in. No words spoken and no more kisses, no backward glances.

Holding her blouse together in front and carrying her shoes, she darted back down the stairs and out the double doors to her car still running at the light. A young officer with his cruiser lights flashing stood by her car with a what-the-hell's-this look on his face.

"Booty call," she said as she climbed in. She started to cry, but the big smile on the young guy's face made her laugh through her tears. The cop would have this story all over the station by morning, heck it would be all over Savannah. And that was good. Much better to get ribbed about needing sex in the middle of the night than *you poor pitiful thing, you went and lost your man.* "Dammit, Donovan, why did I have to go and fall for you?"

The next morning Bebe made her way to the station and found her desk, a step in the right direction for getting on with life. She would do the same thing she did every morning. It was business as usual, except today instead of tracking down a killer and looking forward to seeing Donovan, there was a car theft over on Abercorn, someone broke into the Foxy Snoot, and Mr. Garson was peeping in Mrs. Allison's window again.

Joe Earl parked himself on the corner of her desk. "Heard that Donovan's leaving and Magnolia House had a late-night guest run through their lobby. So, how are you doing?"

"Prissy said they have openings at the nunnery. I look pretty good in black, we share the same fashion sense, and I can even keep the Hush Puppies. I might give it try."

"Don't know if you heard, but we got ourselves a visitor a few hours ago."

"Tall, dark, handsome? Wait, we just had one of those and it didn't end well, least for me it didn't. Can I have a blond this time?"

Joe Earl ran his fingers through his crew cut. "If you thought yesterday was a crazy day, just wait. We're in for a repeat performance. I'm considering dumping a fifth of gin in the water cooler. We're going to need it. Your daddy's here and you're not going to like what he has to say."

## Chapter Thirteen

Donovan closed the door of the hotel room behind him. He stopped for a second, picturing Bebe jumping into his arms when he'd opened it the night before. Some people brought home memories of the beach and meeting Paula Deen back from Savannah, he had memories of ugly suits, a rusted car, and the most beautiful, exciting woman he'd ever laid eyes on. He straightened the picture of Robert E. Lee in the hallway just as he'd done every day since he'd checked into Magnolia House, then added a little salute. "Take care of the place now, you hear."

Bypassing the elevator he opted for the stairway with white-spindled rails and brass sconces to the main floor. He put down his duffel by the reception desk, Charlotte offering him a good-morning smile. "You know there's been nothing but trouble since you walked in our door two weeks ago, Yank. Thanks for that. Don't know if we would have ever found that necklace without you around to stir things up and you sure stirred things plenty."

"It's been a heck of a ride." He signed the check-out papers. "Take care of Bebe, okay?"

"Always have, and you watch out for Oglethorpe Square. I just sent a bunch of tourists that way, they'll be clogging the streets up real good about now, and I know how you love that. And, there's something else you might be interested in. Ray Cleveland turned himself in at the police station this morning. I've had three calls in the last fifteen minutes."

Donovan felt as if his eyes would pop from their sockets. "Why? Did Bebe call?" He flipped open his cell. "She hasn't tried to call me. Why the heck didn't she call me?"

"Bebe loves you, Yank, there's no doubt about that, but she's survived on her own all these years without you and will continue on when you're not around. You really think she'd come running to you with a problem like some needy female?"

"Yes, dammit, I do . . . except for the needy part." He took the white rock from his pocket and thumped it on the desk. "It wasn't just a mindless ritual and an excuse to eat Skittles at midnight. When I say I'm in, dammit, I'm in."

"Well now I do declare, Mr. McCabe, you are some kind of hero. I didn't know. No wonder Bebe loves you likes she does." Charlotte kissed him on the lips. "You're a good man. I bet you got a little Dixie blood in you somewhere even more than what we were passing around last night."

"Could be. I'm sure picking up the lingo fast enough. Kind of scary, if you're asking me." He grinned and grabbed his duffel. "I'll let you know what's going on with Ray." Donovan tipped the valet and headed the Jeep toward the police station. "Well it's about damn time you got your act together," Sly said from the passenger seat. "You are one hardheaded man."

"I was wondering if you'd show up. Next time I go over a bridge I'm considering pushing you out of my car and getting on with my life. I hope ghosts can swim."

"You'd be surprised what we can do. So, what's it going to be, Bebe or Boston?"

"Does it look like this car is heading to Boston right now?"

"Until you heard about Ray you were in dumbass mode and heading in the wrong direction. So what about now? Cop or cupcake? You can't keep them both, you know. You're going to have to make decisions and wind up on one side or the other."

"Go haunt something. It's Savannah, you won't have a problem, no one will think anything of it. Hell, you'll blend right in, maybe even get your picture on one of those Haunted America shows."

"Are you always this cranky when you're not getting any?"

"Are you always going to be this much of a pest, and how do you know I'm not getting any? There's a bridge up ahead. Hope you packed your swim trunks." Donovan pulled in front of the station, then went inside, rushing up the steps to the second floor. Down the hall he could see Ray Cleveland sitting at Joe Earl's desk, drinking coffee and bullshitting with the other cops.

"What are you doing here?" Came Bebe's voice from behind him.

"What's *he* doing here?" Donovan pointed to Ray. "And what the hell are you wearing?"

"Pants? Blouse?"

"They . . . fit." Damn, he'd missed her and he hadn't even left Savannah.

"Ray's here and it's all your fault, and maybe some of my fault, and I don't know what we're going to do, but we have to do something because everything's falling apart. You're leaving, he's leaving. I don't do well with leaving, and Daisy dunked her cast in the water bowl and I had to dry it with the hairdryer, and that really freaked her out. Think of something."

"You're making no sense. It must be the clothes. Were you just waiting for me to get out of town to dress like this? You're looking for guys, aren't you? Going for a new boyfriend and I haven't even crossed the bridge."

"What are you talking about?"

"Every man here drooling over you. Two ran into the wall when they saw you, another dropped his coffee. The dispatch guy's staring and not answering the phones and you're all gussied up and—"

"Gussied? They're never going to let you back in Boston with 'gussied' and right now we need to be focusing on him and not my wardrobe." She pointed to Ray.

He took off his jacket and put it around her shoulders. "There. It's your old self back. I'm ready."

"Watch that old stuff." Bebe took his hand and led him to Joe Earl's desk. The cops chuckled and asked Donovan about room service and laying down the law and being an undercover cop. "Nice to see that the Savannah gossips were alive and well."

Bebe said to Ray, "All right, go ahead and tell him your great plan." She had the perturbed-daughter expression on her face and if she tapped her foot and shook her finger, Donovan wouldn't have been surprised. "You have no idea what you're doing. This isn't some game, this is serious, daddy."

"She called me daddy." Ray grinned like a proud papa, then said to Donovan, "So, how you doing this morning, son?" He reached around Bebe to shake Donovan's hand. "I see you found a place to hang your jacket. Can't say as I blame you one bit, thought about doing it myself." He gave Donovan a manly grin mixed with a hands-off-my-daughter glint in his eye.

"It's not really all that much of a plan, just something that needs doing," Ray continued. "And it should work well enough. You see, I just gave myself up to these fine police officers here." He saluted them with his coffee cup, which undoubtedly had more in it than just plain coffee.

"Give up what?" Donovan asked, glad his jacket hung down over Bebe's ass. What an ass . . . and he meant that in the very best way possible.

"I haven't been there for Bebe like a daddy should all these years while she was growing up and all. I was never around to fix her bike when it broke or her dolly if it lost an arm or build her a tree house or any of those things, but I am in the picture now."

Donovan shrugged. "So you're going to build Bebe a tree house? That's cool. But what she could really use is a new car. Have you seen her car?"

"I love my car, but this is not about cars or tree houses. Just wait till you hear the punch line."

Ray studied the box of doughnuts sitting on the desk. "It doesn't take rocket science to figure out that I'm right in the middle of this little dilemma with you and Bebe. You left Savannah, or have plans on leaving, because you didn't want to be part of me going to jail. I appreciate that, son, I truly do. Mighty considerate of you. But Bebe here has a big crush on you; fact is, I'd say it's considerable more than a crush and if you go back to Boston, she's going to be miserable . . . those were her exact words, I believe. So I'm here to confess to illegal gambling. I'm guilty as hell. I did it, I did it all. The roulette wheels, the twenty-one tables, the poker tables, the crap table, even got a nice little row of slots I picked up and they pay off pretty good, too—just ask around. Anyway, I came here and gave it all up and now I'm just waiting to get my confession typed up proper so I can add my John Hancock to it and then we'll be done and you and Bebe here can get hitched."

"Are you out of your ever-loving fucking mind? This is serious shit, Ray."

"You don't want to marry Bebe? I took you for being

smarter than that. She's perfect for you. Bright and pretty and enough gumption to keep you in line when you're needing it."

"We're not talking a parking ticket here or jaywalking, Ray. This is jail time and a lot of it. You can recant," Donovan said. "That's it. Hell, tell everyone you were . . . drunk. Are drunk. Right now it wouldn't be a hard sell, the place smells like a distillery. We'll say you came in here, fell and hit your head, and didn't know what you were saying. You don't want to do this, Ray. Why would you want to do this? I think you really are smashed."

"Not by a long shot," Ray chuckled, then added a dollop more to his cup from the silver flask on Joe Earl's desk.

"See, I told you this was big," Bebe said, looking completely frazzled. "I wanted to deck him, too, and he's my own father. It's like we're making up for thirty years of parent/child combat all at one time." She faced Ray. "You got to see that I can't build my happiness on your unhappiness. This isn't going to work."

"Now, baby girl, I ask you. Do I look like a man who's unhappy?" Ray puffed his cigar, sending smoke rings into the air. He took another drink of coffee. "After you left last night, I started thinking what a damn fine life I've had and now I can finally do something and make things right for you. This morning I was driving into town to get a haircut and decided to drive myself on over here instead."

"Oh Lordy, I should never have gone to the Cove last night. What was I thinking?" Bebe sat in a chair and put her head between her legs in hyperventilation mode. "What are we going to do? This is nuts."

Donovan poured himself coffee minus the silver flask addition and sat down beside Bebe, Ray still yukking it up with his friends.

"He doesn't get it," Bebe said, her head still down.

"He gets it, he just gets you more, and he's not going to

change his confession. He is one stubborn man and the apple doesn't fall far from the tree."

"I think I've just been insulted. Joe Earl was right, today is crazier than yesterday and that's going some. If you told somebody what was going on here they'd say you were . . . nuts."

Donovan stood. "Nuts. That might work." Donovan pulled up a chair across from Ray. He poured Ray more coffee. "These last few days have been unsettling for everyone."

"You can say that again." Ray drank the coffee and lit another cigar and Donovan added, "You found you have a daughter, you got held at gunpoint, you were a suspect in two murders, and your son got engaged. Sounds exhausting."

"I'm holding up."

"All that's enough to make anyone delusional, especially someone in their advanced years."

Ray put down his coffee cup with a solid thunk. "Advanced years? I'll give you advanced years. I can damn well take you any day of the week with one hand tied behind my back."

"See," Donovan continued. "That's my point exactly. He's picking fights with the police and thinking he can win. Delusional. Ray's confession is null and void; it'll never stand up in court. We all heard him. He's crackers . . . though we do have to come up with a more legal term to make it stick."

Ray grabbed Donovan by the shirtfront, surprising the hell out of him. "I'm sixty, not a hundred-and-sixty, and in full possession of my faculties, and there is no delusion about the gambling going on out at the Cove. It's for real, every single piece of it, and as soon as we get that warrant you'll get your proof."

"Warrant?" Donovan looked at Joe Earl. "What warrant? For two weeks I've waited for one and now that I don't want one it materializes? What the hell."

Joe Earl rolled his shoulders. "You know that a confession gives us probable cause, demands it, actually, and we have to go for the warrant, we don't have any choice. Looks bad for the department."

"And you couldn't have stalled?"

"When something's that cut and dried, it's hard to stall, Donovan."

Looking smug, Ray let go of Donovan and sat back. He tapped his cigar ash in the garbage can. "And Judge Montgomery is only too happy to oblige, since I decked him the other night. I have to say it was worth it, him threatening Beau like that. Should have hit him twice."

Donovan mentally banged his head against the wall. He was busting his butt to keep someone out of the slammer who was hell-bent on getting himself in. Not his usual cop role. "This isn't over, Cleveland. You are *not* going to jail no matter how hard you try."

Ray propped his feet on Joe Earl's desk. "I beg to differ with you, son. It is over." He nodded to Judge Montgomery marching toward them. He had on a black suit and white shirt and was looking way too much like an executioner.

Ray gave him a wave. "Howdy, Judge. You're looking mighty good today." He said to Donovan, "This is my final ace and the man had to deliver it personally. You got to admire a man who takes his job serious. You've been expected, sir."

"I suppose I am." The judge stood tall. "I'm here to deliver a search warrant and I figured I best do it in person to get it right and make sure there were no loopholes."

Bebe felt worse than the time she mistook the can of cat food for that pâté she got in a Christmas basket. Always read labels. The judge reached into his breast pocket, a surprised expression falling across his stern face. "Well now, I do believe I had that search warrant with me when I left the courthouse."

He reached into his other breast pocket and then his pants pockets. "Strange, I must have left it in my chambers, provided my secretary has typed it up. But now that I think about it, I'm not all that sure she has typed it up. Slow as molasses in January, that one. Then again, I don't rightly remember my clerk giving it to her this morning to get typed. That boy's spending too much time at Starbucks again, I need to be warning him about that."

Ray took his feet from the desk. "Say what?"

The judge felt his pockets again. "No warrant . . . least not yet."

"Impossible." Ray jumped up. "This just isn't right at all. It's just a simple search warrant. It's the law. You have to obey the law."

The judge sighed. "Nothing's simple with the courts these days, Cleveland. Reams and reams of paperwork, you wouldn't believe how much. Being a judge has its share of problems and rewards."

He said to Bebe, "Just to be perfectly clear, I've got work to keep me busy for a while, a few hours is probably the best I can do without there being talk of the search warrant not being properly handled. And you do understand that when the police go out there to search the boathouse they will have to find evidence there, the tables, the wheels, the cards, and chips. No proof, no conviction, you keep that in mind now, you hear."

Bebe stood on her tiptoes and kissed the judge on the cheek. "BrieAnn will be proud of you."

"You just tell her little Monty will be, too, and I'm starting a trust fund." Before Bebe could ask who this Monty person was and how'd he get a trust fund, the judge took a doughnut from the box on Joe Earl's desk and said, "Aldeen would pitch a fit if she saw me eating this." He held up the doughnut in a salute and gazed at Ray. "To daughters the apple of their daddy's eye." Then the judge turned and walked back down the hall, leaving a trail of powdered sugar in his wake.

Ray sat back down. "Well, if that don't beat all."

Bebe continued to watch the judge. "Just when you think you have all the answers, Daddy, somebody comes into your life and eats a doughnut." She started for the hall, then stopped and came back into the room. "I forgot something."

Donovan held out his hand. "My jacket? Me?"

She took her badge and gun and handed them over. "I'll keep the jacket, but you're not coming with me."

Confusion then understanding registered in his eyes. "But—"

"No buts, Yank. Not this time. You're a cop, a good one. I already said that and I meant it just as I meant where I stand with Ray and my job. I think I always knew it would come to this."

She gave him a quick kiss on the lips, then ran down the hall with Ray yelling after her, "Bebe, what's going on? What do you think you're doing? You get yourself back in this room right this minute, now you hear. I'm your daddy, you do as I tell you, and you are not to interfere with my being guilty and going to jail."

She got in the PT, headed for Magnolia House, then double-parked there, getting evil looks from the valet that changed to a toothy grin. "Hey," he said following her into the hotel. "Weren't you the lady who double-parked here last night and made that—"

"Yes."

"And you're back again for—"

"No!"

Taking this in from behind the registration desk, Charlotte laughed. "I do believe you have a fan club"

"Hold that thought, sister dear." Bebe waved her pinky with the fresh little cut. "It's my turn."

"No way, you just had a turn. I nearly got myself killed on your turn. You don't get any more pinky turns, and what the heck are you wearing?"

"Donovan's jacket and I do, too, get turns, lots of them. You and Prissy and BrieAnn have played the pinky card so many times I can't keep count. 'Oh, Bebe, I've run out of gas, I need twenty bucks, I need to borrow your car, I need to paint my room, I need you to take my chemistry test, pass my driving test, fix a ticket.'"

"You never fixed a ticket."

"But Lord knows you tried, and we really have to hurry."

"All right, all right, I get the picture, but you have to admit your last pinky card was a real doozy." Charlotte came around the desk and pulled off Bebe's jacket. "Holy cow, you have a body. Who would have thought?"

Donovan did. He was the one responsible for getting her to believe in herself, getting her to believe that she wasn't ugly, that she could wear what she was wearing now. He'd changed her in so many ways, made her see things differently. How was this all going to play out? Would Donovan go back to Boston and she'd have to go through the good-bye thing all over again? Or maybe . . . she would go to Boston. Could she really do that? Good grief, she's have to buy scarves and mittens! "We have to go right now. Get Griff and call Prissy and Sam and tell them to meet me at the Cove."

"Is Ray back home now? What's going on with him being at the station? Donovan never called and I can't believe you have such a really great bod and kept it under wraps—literally—all these years. Why?"

"Until a certain Yank came along, I never had the urge. Now I got the urge and the Yank's not going to be around." Then again, maybe she wouldn't, either. "Ray will show up sooner or later."

"So, what's out at the Cove? Lunch?"

"Well . . . I can promise lots of chips."

## Chapter Fourteen

B eau turned the key and Bebe pushed open the door to
the boathouse, except there weren't any boats, not
even close unless you considered the interior of some lux-
ury liner. "Mercy me," BrieAnn said. "Vegas, eat your
heart out. This place is excellent." She turned to Beau.
"Which tables do you work? Blackjack? Craps? Poker?"

"None. I was never part of this, except for convincing
Ray to put everything in Excel. He started the boathouse
when he needed money to defend himself against those
murder charges and then it just became part of the Savannah landscape and spread by word of mouth."

Griff picked a chip from a table. "Secret knock to get in
like in the speakeasy days?"

Beau rapped out a sequence on the poker table and all
their mouths gaped. Griff said, "I was kidding. You're not
kidding. This is for real?"

"No knock, no entrance. Simple and safe. No security
tapes to get stolen, no phones to tap, a thriving restaurant
to launder the money and Ray could pump it back into the
city, no questions asked and more than made up for any
lost taxes. It has the classy atmosphere and strictly fair
gaming. Everybody was happy, until Donovan showed up."

Beau ruffled Bebe's hair. "Of course I also got a sister out of that deal, so the guy's not all that bad."

A cloud of dust trailed in from the highway and Bebe looked close. "Only one car, it's not the cops yet."

"Cops?" Charlotte repeated. "What's going on with the police?"

Prissy and Sam climbed out of their SUV and Prissy said, "Okay, why are we here? Gamble?" Her eyes twinkled. "I wonder if my psychic abilities will work at blackjack?"

Bebe flipped on the light switch by the door. "Here's the plan; we have to move out everything gambling and do it quick. The dining tables and bar stuff can stay. The judge can only hold off with the search warrant for a couple of hours. And," she said to BrieAnn, "before you blow a gasket, the judge—your daddy—is a first-rate hero. Something about Monty and making a trust fund. I don't get it, but he said you would. He's the only reason Ray isn't in the slammer already."

"Time out," Griff said. "Ray in the slammer? You lost me back at dismantle."

"Donovan's leaving Savannah, so he won't have to be a part of arresting Ray. Ray turned himself in so Donovan doesn't have to leave. He's trying to make up for not being a dad all these years and he knows I like the Yank."

"*Like* is a little understated. So where is Donovan?" Charlotte asked, looking around. "I know he's still in town."

"He's also still a cop and wants to keep it that way. Getting rid of evidence isn't on the police to-do list. I have a different to-do list." She took in the room. "And I don't think we can get all this in cars. If we had a chain saw we could cut the tables in pieces." Bebe ran her hand over her face in frustration. "It's not going to work. I should have thought this through."

"It is the boathouse," Beau said then pointed across the cove to the other docks. "We have boats. We bring them here, load them up, and run everything out to this great little inlet BrieAnn happened to come across where no one's around. A real quiet place."

Brie said, "And I can drive. I'm good driver. I took lessons."

Beau moaned, BrieAnn poked him in the ribs, and Bebe said, "Joe Earl's going to call when the police leave the station. That doesn't give us much time."

Beau took Brie's hand. "Let's go get us some boats."

Prissy helped Bebe lug boxes and Griff and Sam dismantled. Charlotte tied the boats when Beau and BrieAnn pulled up. "I feel like I'm in a scene from *Ocean's Eleven*."

Beau said, "We'll make a bucket brigade and load the boats that way." He picked up a case of chips and passed it to Brie and they all kept passing till there were no more boxes or bags or cartons or containers or any sort of gambling stuff left, down to the very last deck of cards.

Bebe studied the tables. "Now for the hard part. Do they have to be so big?"

Prissy pulled the handle of an antique slot machine, watching the fruit and numbers and bells spin around. "We can't ditch this one; it's a beauty. Can I have it? Please? Can I, can I?"

Bebe's cell rang, she checked the caller ID. "Oh my, they're coming and we have the tables to load! Do any of you know a Grafton? Joe Earl texted Grafton's coming. Another pain-in-the-butt task force guy no doubt. Gee, the last one was so easy to get along with."

"But he is cute," Prissy added. All together they heaved the crap table, then the roulette, into the Donzi. The smaller tables like blackjack and poker went into Beau's boat.

"I see cars coming," Brie said, pointing to a line of dust coming off the highway.

"Go! Go!" Bebe yelled, the others piling into the boats. She untied the lines, then watched Beau, Charlotte, and Griff in Ray's Donzi, and Brie, Prissy, and Sam in the other boat motor out into the channel.

Afternoon sunlight spilled a million diamonds across the cove as the boats piled with boxes and upended tables and garbage bags made their way. *They're not going to make it. They're going too slow!* she thought till a roaring sound filled the air and the boats rocketed across the water. Thank God for boys and their big powerful toys . . . including the ones below their belts.

Car doors slammed, police hustled toward the boathouse. She opened the front door to Joe Earl holding a paper. "We have a warrant to search the premises, and I have Congressman Grafton with me from Atlanta. He has a special interest in busting illegal gambling establishments and has Detective McCabe with him to make sure things are done right." Joe Earl gave her a sorry-about-this look, then walked in.

Donovan was all business, like that night when they were in the attic and he yanked her behind him with his I-am-Moses attitude. Well, it looked like Moses was back.

"Hi, boys," she said stepping aside. "Welcome to the . . . Inlet. We're going to open this up as an extension to the Cove. It's going to be great. More casual, family oriented, serve fish sticks and tomato soup." She was nervous; fish sticks and soup was the best she could come up with.

Being a cop, she knew the search warrant drill . . . ransack the place. Donovan came to her, looking like the Waving Girl Statue down on River Street . . . stone cold. "I need my jacket."

"Sure. Hope you don't mind my cooties." She handed it over, then sat at one of the little dining tables, everyone bustling around her looking under and over and in between. What if she missed something, something important . . .

something like the laptop under the flower arrangement at the next table?

No! Her blood turned to ice. Good thing she was already sitting. This couldn't be. They busted their butts to get all the heavy stuff moved and now a three-pound chunk of metal and plastic would bring down her dad. It was more visible from where she was sitting than standing, but sooner or later someone would come along and—

"Is that a chip?" Donovan pointed to the far corner of the boathouse, drawing everyone's attention.

"It's a green chip with a white gull," Grafton said bending over it. "Not much to base a case on. There's got to be more here if there's this."

It was Donovan the master chip-finder all over again, just like at Dara's when . . . just like at Dara's when . . . Bebe looked back at the laptop, except it was gone. She watched Donovan walk out onto the deck where the boats had been tied. Jacket partially zipped up the front, he bent down as if to tie his shoe.

"You know," Bebe said in a loud voice, drawing everyone's attention to her. She stood on a chair. "We have Cokes and pop and chips—the eating kind—if you all are hungry. Would you all like some food? We don't have any of those fish sticks yet, but we could order in pizza."

Grafton gave her another nasty look . . . he was full of those. Who voted for this jerk? The cops knew better than to take her up on her pizza offer with the congressman around. If he wasn't around and she was springing for food they'd be all over it.

She looked back to the deck. Donovan was gone, gentle ripples floating out across the cove as if the water had been recently disturbed. He'd saved Ray and her but lost what meant the world to him . . . being a good police officer, a darn good detective. How could she ever make that up to him, the man that meant the world to her? She couldn't.

It was nearly dark when Bebe watched the Donzi followed by Beau's boat glide back into the cove. She waved from the boathouse deck. Prissy was the first one to jump off, nearly falling into the water. "What happened? What happened? You're still here and not locked up so they didn't find anything and all's well, right?"

"They found Ray's computer, but—"

"No," Beau said looking weak. They all sat on the deck. "Where was it? I didn't realize it was down here. Ray keeps it with him up at the restaurant."

"Unless he's sneaking coffee. And actually he's up at the restaurant right now covering the dinner crowd and probably answering a million questions. Donovan was the one who found the computer and he tossed it in the water."

"He did what? No! I never would have guessed he'd do such a thing," Prissy said.

Charlotte smiled. "I did. Doesn't surprise me for one minute."

Bebe pointed off the end of the deck. "The only other thing the police found was one of the gull chips, hardly enough to corroborate Ray's confession." She raked back her hair in frustration. "I was so intent on getting rid of the big stuff . . ."

"What does this mean for Donovan?" Beau said.

Bebe felt sick to her soul. "Nothing good, that's for sure. The police have been gone for over two hours and I haven't heard from him. Ray . . . Dad . . . has some good food waiting for you all up at the restaurant. Made it special himself. Said you all can eat free at the Cove anytime you got a mind to. He's grateful and overwhelmed." Bebe pinched Beau's cheeks together, his lips like a fish under water. "And don't you go giving him a lot of grief, okay." She grinned. "Leave that to me."

"Aren't you coming with us?" Brie asked.

"I'm going to try and find Donovan, but I'm thinking

he's on his way back to Boston by now. There's no good memories for him here."

"Depends what you mean by good memories," Donovan said from inside the boathouse, which was now shrouded in darkness.

He hadn't left! Oh my Lord, he hadn't left! That one fact made her happy beyond her wildest dreams. She had no idea what to say to him, but at least she had the chance to say something if it was just a plain old "thanks."

"You know," Beau said. "I think I'm famished, I think we're all good and famished. So we're going to leave you two alone and maybe we'll see you later or not. But I hope so, Donovan. I mean that. You're a hell of man."

Beau started for the road that led to the restaurant, the others ambling behind him. Lights from the Cove burned bright and inviting as they made their way along the water, laughter and chatter carrying back to the boathouse. "You have good friends."

"We have good friends." All she could make out was his silhouette in the dark room. Tall, proud, strong.

She went inside, the darkness surrounding them both now as if they were the only people on earth. She couldn't see his face, but that was okay. She knew it like she knew her own. "I was afraid you'd left before I had a chance to thank you. And now that you are here I don't know what to say. Thanks doesn't begin to cover it. You're going to resign from the police force, aren't you?" It was a statement not a question, because she knew the answer. "I hate this, Donovan. I'd do anything to make it not so."

She needed to get this out before she cried. She didn't want him to feel sorry for her, she just wanted him to know how much what he did meant to her. "I put you in an impossible position and there was no way you could win. You like Ray, I know you do. and you and I—"

"What about you and I?"

"I love you. I have since we landed in that sandpile and I love you now more than ever. No one's ever gone to the mat for me the way you have. No one. And the bitch of it is, you have to hate me for letting it happen. You're a cop, the best one I've ever known, and because of me you wound up in the middle of something that had nothing to do with you but cost you everything. You've got to hate me for that. If I were you, I'd hate me. You saved me, Donovan. So many times, you've saved me. Because of you I got Dad back twice. I have a family. But I don't have you and I can't fix that either."

"Did it ever occur to you that you might have saved me, too?"

"I got you shot, I've called you names, and I've tampered with evidence right in front of you driving you nuts. None of those things fit the role of a savior."

"You made me care. After Sly was killed, I swear I didn't think I'd ever care about anything ever again. For good or bad. Oh, there was the law and doing what the law says, but there's no choice there, you just do it. And then I met Bebe Fitzgerald Cleveland, who cares about everything and everyone. From a cat with a broken paw to an emotionally screwed-up cop from Boston who didn't know what the hell he was doing with his life."

"You always have it together, Donovan. You know who you are and what you're about. You're perfect."

"I met you, then everything was perfect. I loved again. I love you. Coming here made me slow down, look around, change. I like Savannah. I like the people. They stand by each other. Ray turned himself in because he loves you. Beau wanted to knock my head off because he loves Ray. The judge stalled on the warrant because he loves BrieAnn. Not necessarily good decisions but the most caring ones. No one was out for himself . . . or herself."

"You're going to stay?"

"If you marry me. I couldn't be here without you. Everything in this city reminds me of you. I talked to Ray about your idea of making this place the Inlet without fish sticks and tomato soup. McCabe's Inlet. I've got four generations of pub aptitude in my genes."

"No. You can't do this. You solve problems, protect people. You get the job done. It's who you are."

"Ray and I had a chat. Actually he had the chat with me. You said he went place where the cops can't go. Lot of islands out there. Citizens do get involved."

"You're throwing in with Daddy?"

"I'm throwing in with you. Life's no fun without you in it. You made me into a different Southie. Marry me. I'll write, I'll call, I'll send flowers. You have to admit I'm good at flowers."

She threw her arms around him. "You're good at everything, Donovan McCabe, especially making me happy. Welcome home, Yank."

Every girl could use A GREAT KISSER,
so pick up Donna Kauffman's latest today!

The man holding her elbow tugged her in out of the rain.

"Thank you," she gasped. "I'm so sorry—my umbrella—"

"Marco picked it up," came a very deep voice with a bit of a rough edge to it, like maybe he'd just woken up.

She was still blinking water out of her eyes and he still had a hold on her elbow. Her other hand was clutching her purse and laptop bag to her side in a death grip. Everything was just a blur. "Marco?"

"Ground crew. Here, let me take those."

Her elbow was abruptly released, which sent her a bit off balance, then her bags were suddenly lifted from her shoulder and slipped out of her death grip as if her hands were made from putty, sending her staggering a step in the other direction. Both her feet slipped a little as the smooth soles of her shoes were not made for . . . well, any of this. And then his hands were on her again, both elbows this time, and, and . . . well, the entire last sixty seconds had been so discombobulating, for a person who was never discombobulated, that she didn't know quite what to do. She blinked at him through wet ropes of hair and fogged glasses, arms still akimbo as he wrestled her to a balanced position.

"Bad day?"

It was the dry amusement lacing his tone that gave her the focus she so mercifully needed. She tugged her elbows from his grip, as if all this was suddenly very much his fault, but instead of being the liberating, independence-returning move she was so desperately seeking, the action only served to send her wheeling backward. Which resulted in being caught, once again, even more humiliatingly than before, by his very big, very strong, and very steadying hands.

"Thank you," she managed through gritted teeth. She carefully removed one elbow from his grip, not chancing leaving his steadying powers all at once, and scraped her hair from her forehead and removed her fogged glasses from her face. Finally able to see, she looked up . . . only to be thrown completely off balance all over again. But, this time, her feet were totally flat and stable, on hard, steady ground. "You can let me go now," she managed in a choked whisper.

He was just above average height, probably not even six feet, but given she topped the height chart at five-foot-six, and that was in three-inch heels, he was very tall to her. But it wasn't the height part that commanded the attention. Nor was it really the square jaw, the thick neck, broad shoulders, very nicely muscled arms and chest that were obvious even through the old sweatshirt and T-shirt he wore. The thick, sun-bleached brown hair might have been a teensy part of it, but mostly it was the piercing blue eyes—truly, they pierced—staring at her from his weathered, deeply tanned face.

Crinkles fanned from the corners of those eyes, and there were grooves bracketing either side of his mouth, but she didn't know if that was from squinting into the sun or smiling a lot. He wasn't smiling now, so it was hard to tell. But he was still holding on to her, and it was that, plus those look-right-through-you eyes, that were keeping her from reclaiming the rest of her much-needed balance.

"I'm—fine. Really. Thank you. Again."

He held her gaze for another seemingly endless moment, then gently let her go. "No worries."

"I, uh, need to rent a car." She was normally calm and cool under fire. It was why Todd had been so impressed and promoted her up the ranks of his campaign staff so quickly. It was also why she'd been one of the first ones the senator had hired to his permanent staff when he'd won his bid for office. If he could see her now, he wouldn't even recognize her. She didn't recognize her. Of course, the fact that she probably looked like a drowned cat didn't help matters. "If you could just point me in the right direction—" *I will slink off and pretend we never met.*

"You don't need a car."

She looked up at him again, and though she'd never particularly thought of herself as vain, she'd have given large sums for the use of a comb, a tissue, and a handheld mirror. Okay, so a full salon makeover probably wouldn't have hurt at that moment, but her pride wouldn't have minded at least a brief attempt at restoration. "Where I'm headed is about two and a half hours from here, and though it's probably not all that far-fetched to think they probably rent horses here, I'm thinking the locals, not to mention the horse, will be a lot safer if I get a nice SUV instead."

His lips quirked a little then, and her pulse actually did this zippy jumpy thing. And it felt kind of good—in a somewhat startling, disconcerting kind of way. However—reality check—she hadn't forgotten that her appearance was highly unlikely to provoke the same reaction in him. Besides, she was not here on vacation. She was here on a very serious mission that had absolutely nothing to do with having a vacation fling of any kind. Not that she was the fling type. Or that men ever flung themselves at her, vacation or otherwise, for her to know. But, still.

"Given the weather, it would probably be as uncomfortable for the horse, but that's not why I said you don't need a ride. You don't need one, because I'm your ride."

God help her, she looked him up and down before she could stop herself. *He* was her ride?

And don't miss Terri Brisbin's first book for Brava,
A STORM OF PASSION,
coming next month!

Whatever the Seer wanted, the Seer got, be it for his comfort or his whim or his pleasure.

She stood staring at the chair on the raised dais at one end of the chamber, the chair where he sat when the visions came. From the expression that filled her green eyes, she knew it as well.

Had she witnessed his power? Had she watched as the magic within him exploded into a vision of what was or what would yet be? As he influenced the high and the mighty of the surrounding lands and clans with the truth of his gift? Walking over to stand behind her, he placed his hands on her shoulders and drew her back to his body.

"I have not seen you before, sweetling," he whispered into her ear. Leaning down, he smoothed the hair from the side of her face with his own and then touched his tongue to the edge of her ear. "What is your name?"

He felt the shivers travel through her as his mouth tickled her ear. Smiling, he bent down and kissed her neck, tracing the muscle there down to her shoulder with the tip of his tongue. Connor bit the spot gently, teasing it with his teeth and soothing it with his tongue. "Your name?" he asked again.

She arched then, clearly enjoying his touch and ready

for more. Her head fell back against his shoulder and he moved his mouth to the soft skin there, kissing and licking his way down and back to her ear. Still she had not spoken.

"When I call out my pleasure, sweetling, what name will I speak?"

He released her shoulders and slid his hands down her arms and then over her stomach to hold her in complete contact with him. Covering her stomach and pressing her to him, he rubbed against her back, letting her feel the extent of his erection—hard and large and ready to pleasure her. Connor moved his hands up to take her breasts in his grasp. Rubbing his thumbs over their tips and teasing them to tightness, he no longer asked, he demanded.

"Tell me your name."

He felt her breasts swell in his hands and he tugged now on the distended nipples, enjoying the feel and imagining them in his mouth, as he suckled hard on them and as she screamed out her pleasure. But nothing could have pleased him more in that moment than the way she gasped at each stroke he made, over and over until she moaned out her name to him.

"Moira."

"Moira," he repeated slowly, drawing her name out until it was a wish in the air around them. "Moira," he said again as he untied the laces on her bodice and slid it down her shoulders until he could touch her skin. "Moira," he now moaned as the heat and the scent of her enticed him as much as his own scent was pulling her under his control.

Connor paused for a moment, releasing her long enough to drag his tunic over his head and then turning her into his embrace. He inhaled sharply as her skin touched his, the heat of it seared into his soul as the tightened peaks of her breasts pressed against his chest. Her added height brought her hips level almost to his and he rubbed his hardened cock against her stomach, letting her feel the extent of his arousal.

As he pushed her hair back off her shoulders, he realized that in addition to the raging lust in his blood, there was something else there, teasing him with its presence.

Anticipation.

For the first time in years, this felt like more than the mindless rutting that happened between him and the countless, nameless women there for his needs. For the first time in too long, this was not simply scratching an itch, for the hint of something more seemed to stand off in the distance, something tantalizing and unknown and something somehow tied to this woman.

He lifted her chin with his finger, forcing her gaze off the blasted chair and onto his face. Instead of the compliant gaze that usually met him, the clarity of her gold-flecked green eyes startled him. Connor did something he'd not done before, something he never needed to do—he asked her permission.

"I want you, Moira," he whispered, dipping to touch and taste her lips for the first time. Connor slid his hand down to gather up her skirts, baring her legs and the treasure between them to his touch and his sight. "Let me?"

Be on the lookout for
THE MANE SQUEEZE from Shelly Laurenston,
coming next month from Brava . . .

The salmon were everywhere, leaping from the water and right into the open maws of bears. But he ruled this piece of territory and those salmon were for him and him alone. He opened his mouth and a ten-pound one leaped right into it. Closing his jaws, he sighed in pleasure. Honey-covered. He loved honey-covered salmon!

This was his perfect world. A cold river, happy-to-die-for-his-survival salmon, and honey. Lots and lots of honey . . .

What could ever be better? What could ever live up to this? Nothing. Absolutely nothing.

A salmon swam up to him. He had no interest, he was still working on the honey-covered one. The salmon stared at him intently . . . almost glaring.

"Hey!" it called out. "Hey! Can you hear me?"

Why was this salmon ruining his meal? He should kill it and save it for later. Or toss it to one of the females with cubs. Anything to get this obviously Philadelphia salmon to shut the hell up!

"Answer me!" the salmon ordered loudly. "Open your eyes and answer me! *Now!*"

His eyes were open, weren't they?

Apparently not because someone pried his lids apart and stared into his face. And wow, was she gorgeous!

"Can you hear me?" He didn't answer, he was too busy staring at her. So pretty!

"Come on, Paddington. Answer me."

He instinctively snarled at the nickname and she smiled in relief. "What's the matter?" she teased. "You don't like Paddington? Such a cute, cuddily, widdle bear."

"Nothing's wrong with cute pet names . . . Mr. Mittens."

She straightened, her hands on her hips and those long, expertly manicured nails drumming restlessly against those narrow hips.

"Mister?" she snapped.

"Paddington?" he shot back.

She gave a little snort. "Okay. Fair enough. But call me Gwen. I never did get a chance to tell you my name at the wedding."

Oh! He remembered her now. The feline he'd found himself day dreaming about on more than one occasion in the two months since Jess's wedding. And . . . wow. She was naked. She looked really good naked . . .

He blinked, knowing that he was staring at that beautiful, strong body. *Focus on something else! Anything else! You're going to creep her out!*

"You have tattoos," he blurted. Bracelet tatts surrounded both her biceps. A combination of black shamrocks and a dark-green Chinese symbol he didn't know the meaning of. And on her right hip she had a black Chinese dragon holding a Celtic cross in its mouth. It was beautiful work. Intricate. "Are they new?"

"Nah. I just covered up the ones on my arms with makeup, for the wedding. With my mother, I'd be noticed enough. Didn't want to add to that." She gestured at him

with her hand. "Now we know I'm Gwen and I have tattoos . . . so do you have a name?"

"Yeah, sure. I'm . . ." He glanced off, racking his brain.

"You don't remember your name?" she asked, her eyes
wide.

"I know it has something to do with security." He stared
at her thoughtfully, then snapped his fingers. "Lock."

"Lock? Your name is Lock?"

"I think. Lock. Lock . . . Lachlan! MacRyrie!" He glanced
off again. "I think."

"Christ."

"No need to get snippy. It's *my* name I can't remember."
He nodded. "I'm pretty positive it's Lock . . . something."

"MacRyrie."

"Okay."

She gave a small, frustrated growl and placed the palms
of her hands against her eyes. He stared at her painted nails.
"Are those the team colors of the Philadelphia Flyers?"

"Don't start," she snapped.

"Again with the snippy? I was only asking."

Lock slowly pushed himself up a bit, noticing for the
first time that they'd traveled to a much more shallow part
of the river. The water barely came to his waist. She started
to say something, but shook her head and looked away. He
didn't mind. He didn't need conversation at the moment,
he needed to figure out where he was.

A river, that's where he was. Unfortunately, not his dream
river. The one with the honey-covered salmon that willingly
leaped into his mouth. A disappointing realization—it always felt so real until he woke up—but he was still happy
that he'd survived the fall.

Lock used his arms to push himself up all the way so he
could sit.

"Be careful," she finally said. "We fell from up there."

He looked at where she pointed, ignoring how much pain the slight move caused, and flinched when he saw how far down they were.

"Although we were farther up river, I think."

"Damn," he muttered, rubbing the back of his neck. "How bad is it?"

"It'll be fine." Closing his eyes, Lock bent his head to one side, then the other. The sound of cracking bones echoed and when he opened his eyes, he saw that pretty face cringing.

"See?" he said. "Better already."

"If you say so."

She took several awkward steps back so she could sit down on a large boulder.

"You're hurt," he informed her.

"Yeah. I am." She extended her leg, resting it on a small boulder in front of her and let out a breath, her eyes shutting. "I know it's healing, but, fuck, it hurts."

"Let me see." Lock got to his feet, ignoring the aches and pains he felt throughout his body. By the time he made it over to her, she opened her eyes and blinked wide, leaning back.

"Hey, hey! Get that thing out of my face!"

His cock was right *there*, now wasn't it? He knelt down on one knee in front of her and said, "This is the best I can manage at the moment. I don't exactly have the time to run off and kill an animal for its hide."

"Fine," she muttered. "Just watch where you're swinging that thing. You're liable to break my nose."

Focusing on her leg to keep from appearing way too proud at that statement, he grasped her foot and lifted, keeping his movements slow and his fingers gentle. He didn't allow himself to wince when he saw the damage. It was bad, and she was losing blood. Probably more blood than she realized. "I didn't do this, did I?"

"No. I got this from that She-bitch." She leaned over, trying to get a better look. "Do I have any calf muscle left?"

He wasn't going to answer that. At least not honestly. Instead he gave her his best "reassuring" expression and calmly said, "Let's get you to a hospital."

Her body jerked straight and those pretty eyes blinked rapidly. "No."

That wasn't the response he expected. Panic, perhaps. Or, "My God. Is it that bad?" But instead she said "no." And she said it with some serious finality. In the same way he'd imagine she would respond to the suggestion of cutting off her leg with a steak knife.

"It's not a big deal. But you don't want an infection. I'll take you up the embankment, get us some clothes—" if she didn't pass out from blood loss first "—and then get you to the Macon River Health Center. It's equipped for us."

"No."

"I've had to go there a couple of times. It's really clean, the staff is great, and the doctors are always the best."

"No."

She wasn't being difficult to simply be difficult, was she?

Resting his forearm on his knee, Lock stared at her. "You're not kidding, are you?"

"No."

"Is there a reason you don't want to go to the hospital?" And he really hoped it wasn't something ridiculous like she used to date one of the doctors and didn't want to see him, or something equally as lame.

"Of course there is. People go there to die."

Oh, boy. Ridiculous but hardly lame. "Or . . . people go there to get better."

"No."

"Look, Mr. Mittens—"

"Don't call me that."

"—I'm trying to help you here. So you can do this the easy way, or you can do this the hard way. Your choice."

She shrugged and brought her good foot down right on his nuts.